Praise for Corrina Lawson's
Phoenix Institute series

"[A]n energizing and thrilling ride into the world of covert ops."
~ *RT Book Reviews*

"A touch of the X-Men with a smattering of coming-of-age legend, *Phoenix Rising* certainly keeps the reader's attention. Lawson effortlessly switches points-of-view, from Alec to Beth and back again. [...] The edge-of-your-seat plot keeps the story rolling along."
~ *Library Journal*

"Readers looking for an adventure into a paranormally complex and political world with a quite literally hot hero will want to check this out."
~ *Long and Short Reviews*

"*Phoenix Legacy* is a wonderfully entertaining rollercoaster read that conjures up the fantastical worlds explored in comic books yet provides a romance between unconventional characters."
~ *Night Owl Reviews*

Look for these titles by
Corrina Lawson

Now Available:

Freya's Gift

The Phoenix Institute
Phoenix Rising
Luminous: A Phoenix Institute Novella
Phoenix Legacy

Phoenix Legacy

Corrina Lawson

SAMHAIN
PUBLISHING

Samhain Publishing, Ltd.
11821 Mason Montgomery Road, 4B
Cincinnati, OH 45249
www.samhainpublishing.com

Phoenix Legacy
Copyright © 2013 by Corrina Lawson
Print ISBN: 978-1-61921-520-7
Digital ISBN: 978-1-61921-424-8

Editing by Jennifer Miller
Cover by Kanaxa

First Samhain Publishing, Ltd. electronic publication: November 2012
First Samhain Publishing, Ltd. print publication: December 2013

Dedication

For Toni, Liv and Kate, who insist on the very best. They bash me over the computer when the writing isn't right and celebrate with me when it is.

Chapter One

I have the right to do this.

So why did she feel so rotten about it?

Delilah Sefton hit the brakes at the entrance to the Ledgewood traffic circle and put her hand over her stomach. She didn't feel that much different. Except the test had told her that something was *very* different.

Maybe she'd have made another decision if she remembered the act that led to this damned conception. She clenched the steering wheel tight. One minute she'd been closing up her bar, the next minute it was morning and she was waking up on the floor.

She knew she'd been drugged, but that was it. The lack of memory was worse than knowing exactly how she'd been violated. Her imagination supplied all kinds of horrible details. For all she knew, it'd been more than one man too.

Bastard. She had no intentions of having any reminders of that night. Certainly not one that would last nine months and then the rest of her life.

It wasn't wrong to want that.

Soon, she'd be back to normal. It was no use going to the police. Even if she trusted the cops—which she hadn't since she was a small child—she had nothing to give them to investigate. At best, they'd take her statement. At worst, she'd get a lecture about closing the bar alone at night or told she must have drunk too much. As if she'd drink on-shift.

Del nudged her car into the traffic circle, cursing as someone cut her off to the left. Stupid New Jersey. The circle should have been replaced years ago, but no, it remained a crash magnet. And it was delaying her. She needed to be on time and get this over with.

She saw a flash out of the corner of her eye. A dark blue van crashed into the minivan just ahead of her. Tires screeched. Metal crunched. Del slammed on her brakes, praying to avoid the car that had slammed on its brakes in front of her.

The dark blue van pushed the minivan over the curb. Unbalanced, the minivan tipped and fell on its side with a great thud combined with the crunch of crushed metal and broken glass. The blue van with blacked-out windows that was responsible for the accident backed out, tires squealing.

Assholes!

Del swerved her car onto the grass in the middle of the traffic circle, near the overturned minivan. With her window down, she could already hear crying coming from inside it. She sniffed and smelled gas. Shit.

She grabbed the hammer she always kept in her glove box and rushed to the minivan. She used the exposed front tire to clamber up on the van and closed her hand around the handle of the side door, which was now facing up at the sky.

The crying had stopped. The screaming had started. Del pulled at the door handle but it was locked tight. Jammed. Del looked at the ground. A small flame licked at the vehicle, down near the front driver's side tire that was wedged into the muck. The smell of gas was much stronger. Not much time.

She glanced around. No police or first responders yet. The van that had caused the accident sped away, down Route 10 east.

The world was full of people who didn't give a crap about the mess they'd left behind.

She slapped the window of the overturned minivan. There were two kids inside and one guy, all pushed to the far side by the force of the crash. She'd no idea how hurt they might be.

"Cover your eyes!" she yelled at them.

The man—probably the dad—repeated her words at a yell. The screaming stopped. She raised her hammer and brought it down on the window. The hammer bounced back without any damage to the glass. *Shit.* She braced herself better atop the minivan to get maximum leverage and swung again. A crack appeared. On the ground, the flames started to grow.

Crack, crack, crack. When she had a fist-sized hole, Del stuck the head of the hammer inside the opening and bashed at the edges, enlarging the hole.

She glanced down again. The whole bottom front of the minivan was on fire. Black, acrid smoke filled the air.

"Give me your hand!" She stuck her arm inside. Her jean jacket snagged the edge of a glass shard and ripped. A small, sweaty hand closed around her wrist. She pulled and the kid's head and chest appeared in the opening. A young girl, about ten.

Del grabbed the girl and pulled her free. "Jump down!" she told the girl. She was old enough. She could make it.

"My brother and dad are inside!" she wailed.

"Get out of my way so I can get them."

The girl jumped down, close to the flames. Someone (another motorist?) hustled her away.

Her little brother was lighter and easier to pull up. But he held tight to Del and wouldn't jump down. She needed to get him out of the way to make room for his dad. But the poor kid was scared to death. She didn't blame him.

"I've got you, son!" The offer was from an older man wearing a Yankees hat. Something about him must have pleased the little kid because he jumped into the man's arms.

Del could feel the heat from the fire already. The metal of the minivan was growing hot.

"Out! Now!" she yelled to the dad. She helped him scramble out of the hole she'd made in the window. He cursed, and she guessed he'd been cut by the glass. Better that than being burned up in the fire.

Between her pulling and his pushing, they managed to get him out, though he was cut in several places. Blood was streaming down his arms. He took one look at the smoke and flames, and his eyes went wide. He froze.

"We have to get down!" she yelled to get through to him.

They jumped together. She hit the ground shoulder-first and rolled several feet on the grass before stopping.

As she struggled to her knees, she saw the entire minivan engulfed in flames. She flexed her hand. Damn. She'd dropped her hammer. It must be inside the car. She'd never get it back.

She *liked* that hammer.

A cop put an arm around her waist and led her farther away from the flames. The traffic circle was full of emergency vehicles now. She almost snapped that they'd taken their time getting here, but she realized they must have arrived in mere minutes. It had only seemed like a long time.

The dad was sitting on the back bumper of the ambulance. His kids had their arms wrapped around him.

Okay, she would trade the hammer for that scene.

"You hurt, ma'am?" the officer asked as he pulled her closer to the ambulance.

She shook her head. "Just ripped my jacket. I'm okay."

The father caught sight of her. He was about forty, she guessed, balding with a little paunch. But she liked him. He'd made sure his kids got out first.

He stared at her, still holding onto the kids. "Thank you," he whispered and then coughed.

"Um, sure," she said.

"If I'd only seen the damn blue van before—"

"He cut you off," she said. "He came out of nowhere, and it looked like he deliberately slammed into you. It wasn't your fault. Ask anyone."

The father nodded and then turned away when the little girl asked him something.

"Ma'am," the cop said, "sorry to bother you but I need to see your license and take your statement about what happened." He cleared his throat. "You did a heroic thing, ma'am."

"Stop calling me ma'am." Of course, the cop was young, in his early twenties. She wasn't much over thirty but, hell, anyone over thirty was probably old to him. She likely didn't look her best either, with a ripped jacket and her long brown hair frizzed out from rolling on the grass.

She led the cop over to her car. She opened the door and noticed not only was her purse missing but so were the medical forms and papers she needed to bring with her to the appointment.

Son of a bitch. She slammed the car door shut and resisted an impulse to kick the tire. This wasn't her car's fault. "Got a little problem here, officer." She gritted her teeth and explained the missing purse.

Her opinion of the officer rose, as he not only sympathized with her loss but appeared as angry as she was about the theft. He left her for a few minutes while he walked the crowd that had gathered, asking for witnesses.

Her plans in flames like the minivan, she put her head down against the side of the car. Jesus tap-dancing Christ. Now she had to reschedule the appointment.

Del turned around and watched the firefighters douse the car fire. At least her car was in one piece. A missing purse was nothing compared to what that family had gone through. In seconds, their lives could have been over. Replacing the paperwork and her driver's license would be a pain in the ass but it could be done. But, damn, she wanted to stop feeling so low and move forward, not be stuck in this limbo. She wanted this alien out of her.

Why had the driver of that other van caused a crash? She'd swear it was deliberate. Who'd want to hurt that family? She shook her head. There were just too many lousy people in the world. Like the bastard who'd drugged her and left her pregnant.

The officer returned.

"Any news?" she asked.

"Some." He grimaced. "Seems someone jumped out of that blue van that caused the accident, went right for your car, grabbed the purse and some papers on the front seat, then got right back in the van."

"The guys in the van that *caused the accident* ripped off my purse?"

"According to the eyewitnesses, yes."

"Did you guys find the van yet?"

"No, ma'am, most of the responders came straight to the accident scene. The involved vehicle disappeared in that time."

"Why the hell would they cause the accident and take my stuff?"

"Most likely drugs, ma'am," the officer answered. "Probably they intended to work the crowd after the accident but were mostly scared off after the minivan flipped over."

She sighed and let the anger flow away. The officer's explanation didn't sound right, but she had no better theory. Now if the cop would just stop calling her "ma'am".

"If you'll come with me to the office, ma'am, we can write up the theft and I can take your statement about the accident."

"It's just Del," she said. "Okay?"

He nodded. "I'll pull out with the patrol car and you can follow."

She had no better place to go. She couldn't keep her appointment, not without her identification and the insurance card. If she called and pleaded, the doctor should let her reschedule before it was too late. She was working against a time limit to get this done.

She followed the officer back to the police department, filled out several forms for her stolen purse and gave a statement about the accident. Several cops walked by as she and her young officer sat at a conference table and told her "thank you" for what she'd done at the accident scene.

It was far too weird, cops thanking her. She wished she could shrivel down into her chair or somehow vanish. She couldn't do that, so she instead insisted to the officer that he keep her name private.

"I just happened to be closest to them. It was no big deal."

He tried to talk her out of it and said there were awards for citizen heroes. She wanted none of that. She'd had a hammer, she'd been close by, and she'd used it. That was it.

Del sat on the edge of her dock watching the sun set over the mountains surrounding Lake Hopatcong. Her toes dangled in the green water of the lake. Biggest lake in New Jersey, she mused, and not many people really knew it was here. Probably because it had such an odd shape, its little branches reaching every which way. And the lake itself was ugly, the relic of a lost canal system.

But she liked it.

The bar and grill she owned on its wooded shore was home now. Once, it had had a name. But by the time she had bought it five years ago, everyone just called it Bar & Grill. So that was the name she'd put on the deed and the sign.

She hugged her knees to her chin. She had called the doctor to reschedule, explaining what had happened. The receptionist had promised to call her back tomorrow with a new time. Life would soon be back to normal.

Behind her, she heard someone walking down the dock. She turned and saw it was her assistant manager, Tammy, carrying a tray with some baked goods. Del took a deep breath and smelled cake. Trust Tammy to show up with cake.

The older woman sat down carefully and offered her the tray.

Not cake. Cupcakes. Del grabbed one and started gobbling it up. She knew one thing. She was hungry.

"Heard you were a hero today, Del," Tammy said.

"Not really."

Del licked the frosting off the cupcake. Always better to eat the frosting first. Tammy had come in on her day off. But then, she'd known about Del's doctor's appointment. Tammy had not been judgmental but it'd been clear she hated the idea of Del getting an abortion.

"I'm just someone with a hammer. And to think, you teased me about keeping it in my car."

"It always seemed odd to me."

Del shrugged. To explain the hammer would mean explaining her whole messed-up childhood, complete with paranoid, radical parents convinced the government was out to kill them. Turned out, they had finally attracted the attention of the government because of that paranoia.

"I heard you got your purse stolen for your trouble," Tammy said.

"Yeah. It's going to be a pain to replace the license."

If Del were paranoid like her parents, she might think the guys in the blue van had deliberately targeted her. Or her purse. But that was ridiculous. There was nothing of real value in the purse, and she certainly wasn't of value to anyone.

She would not go over the edge to insanity like her parents by giving in to the slightest paranoia. She would *not*.

Del looked over at Tammy. If you looked up sane and stable, Tammy would be at the top of the list. Del's chief cook/bartender had lived on or near the lake her whole life. Her skin was weathered from years of being outdoors, and her gray-streaked hair was pulled back by a bandana. She had a good life. A long marriage, good kids and work she liked.

Del bet Tammy never had parents who taught her to always have a hammer in the glove box and a shotgun in the trunk.

"Where'd you hear about what I did, anyway?" Del asked.

"My brother-in-law's brother is with the fire department." Tammy bit into her own cupcake. She didn't lick the frosting off first.

Philistine, Del thought.

"I lost the hammer," Del said. "I'll have to get a new one."

"I'm thinking of getting one for my car now too."

Del grinned. "See, I told you it was useful. My dad was always worried about ending up in the water with no way out." Among other things.

She didn't tell Tammy that besides the hammer, she also had rope, a shovel and a shotgun in her trunk. You never knew when those would come in handy, her father had said. Stupid that she still listened to him, even though he was long dead.

Tammy offered another cupcake, this one with chocolate frosting. Del took it. It lasted about as long as the first.

"Did you make your appointment?" Tammy asked in a low voice.

"No."

"Did you reschedule?"

"I called. They said they would fit me back in before it's too late."

"You could cancel altogether," Tammy said. "It's a lousy way to get pregnant, I know, but motherhood might work for you."

"I seriously doubt it." Del had no expectations that she could do any better than her crazy parents. And this kid's father was a rapist and who knew what else.

That was a lot stacked against anyone before birth.

"Just because the father's bad doesn't mean the kid will be," Tammy said.

"Tammy, I know you mean well, but I was *raped*. I want this over with. Why are you arguing with me about it?"

Del would never have told anyone about the missing night, but Tammy had found her that morning on the floor of Bar & Grill, still groggy. Del had blurted out what happened before she was fully herself. Tammy had urged her to go to the police, but Del had refused. She wished she'd listened. The hospital probably would have run a rape kit, found out she was pregnant and given her a morning-after pill.

Instead, it had taken over a month for Del to realize what was wrong with her. Too late for anything but an abortion.

"Children are a blessing," Tammy said.

"Maybe that's true for some people. It's been my experience that lousy dads produce lousy sons." Exhibit A on that was Hawk, her childhood companion, the son of the other crazy

17

couple who had been on the run with her parents after they'd blown up a federal building.

There had been seven years between them but Hawk had been her best friend.

At least, she'd thought he was her best friend. Until he had killed her parents.

She looked out over the lake again.

"The kid's got one good parent. You," Tammy said.

"I don't want that. Not this way."

Hawk had seemed sane too, despite the repeated pummelings he endured at the hand of his stepfather. Then came the day the government assault team had cornered them all, and Hawk had gone over the edge and turned his rifle on her parents. He'd killed his stepfather too, just for good measure. Her mom and dad had been screwed up, but they'd been nice to her, in their way. They hadn't abused her like Hawk's stepfather did to him.

She loved them, and Hawk had killed them. So much for overcoming nature.

"Del, think," Tammy said. "You were a hero today. You'd be a good mom."

Del shrugged. "Again, why are you so opposed to the abortion?" Tammy had never been particularly religious.

"I was adopted."

Oh. "I didn't know."

"Adoptions were kept mostly quiet in those days," Tammy said. "Not many people know. And it doesn't really matter because the family that raised me is my family. I mention it because if my biological mother had had an abortion, I wouldn't be here." She cleared her throat. "My oldest son is adopted too. I thank God every day that his mother carried him to term."

Del didn't know what to say to that. It sure explained Tammy's opposition to abortion, though. "Thank you for telling me."

She looked back at Bar & Grill, looming behind the dock. It wasn't much, it wasn't pretty, but it was a good watering hole for the locals. And it was hers. She had finally settled down and was happy. She didn't want change. She liked things this way.

"You think I should give up the kid for adoption?"

"That's better than cutting off any chance the baby has for a life," Tammy said. "What the father did has nothing to do with the baby. The first time that child smiles at you, you won't give a damn how conception happened. You'll just love him back."

"You sound sure about that." *I'm not.*

"You care. Look at today."

She wanted this over. But Tammy was her friend, and she was making sense. There could be people out there just waiting for a kid to be part of their lives. Del could make that happen. Take something lousy and make it something good.

Maybe the kid that she never wanted, hadn't asked for and wished didn't exist should have a chance, if not with her, with somebody. She touched her stomach. If someone had held her responsible for her father's sins, she'd be dead. This baby had nothing to do with the man who'd raped her.

Though if she ever found the rapist, she would use her hammer to bash his head in.

She hoped the kid would be okay with that.

Chapter Two

Philip Drake pulled into the entrance of the bland suburban New Jersey condominium development just as many of his neighbors were leaving on their morning commute. Feeling perverse, he gunned the '67 Charger, making more noise than necessary. He might live here but he'd never be one of them.

He smiled as the Charger took the corner on a dime. Old, but not feeble. Like him. Though the car looked its age, standing out, not in style anymore.

Unlike him.

He had wanted to experiment with the limits of his newfound conscious healing ability. Instead, he'd de-aged his body to at least a decade younger. Days of trying to reverse the process had convinced him he was cursed to look like this for a long time. Maybe until he died, whenever that was.

He was too damn old and cynical to look under thirty.

He'd never get his gray hair back. He would never grow old, either, at least not naturally. Still, given what he was, it was always possible someone might kill him in the meantime. That was a comforting thought.

He spotted the car parked outside his condo from the top of the street. Beth's Honda. He was definitely too damn old to be visited by his adult daughter this early in the morning, especially after the debauched way he'd spent the night. He wanted a shower. And sleep.

And then...well, he hadn't figured that out in months. So maybe Beth's visit was a good thing. He'd worn so many identities over the years, even as a child, and now his current alias of Philip Drake. He had no clue which of him was his real self or even if he had one.

Being Beth Nakamora's foster father—that was solid ground.

He parked next to Beth's vehicle and entered through his garage. He nearly tripped over a beer can. He tossed it back in the overflowing recycling bin. Hmm...he hadn't realized there were so many cans. At least Beth hadn't come this way. She worried too much about him as it was.

He opened the condo to the smell of coffee and the blinding brilliance of early-morning sunshine. He blinked and squinted to shut out the light. She'd opened all the curtains in his kitchen.

"Hey, Drake."

Philip nearly growled. This wasn't his daughter at all. It was her boyfriend.

"What do you want?" he snapped.

Alec Farley leaned casually against the kitchen counter. Drake didn't trust the man, but he did understand his daughter. There was no denying Farley was handsome and well built, and his telekinetic and firestarting abilities produced a palpable aura of charisma that surrounded him whether he was using his power or not.

Philip grudgingly granted that Farley was also good to Beth. In fact, he seemed to adore her unreservedly. As well he should.

"Uh, maybe you want some coffee? I made some."

Philip grumbled under his breath. Alec filled a mug with coffee and used his telekinesis to send the mug floating in midair toward him. Philip snatched it and held it up to his nose, hoping the smell would restore his alertness. He should have known Alec was in the house. He was usually more careful.

"You could have just handed the mug to me," Philip said.

"I was worried you'd slug me if I got closer."

"Not now. I'm tired. Come back in a few hours."

"You don't look tired. Hell, you look younger than the last time I was here."

"So?"

"How'd it happen? Side effect of your healing ability?"

Philip shrugged, took a large gulp and studied Farley again. The firestarter seemed taller than he remembered. Or maybe Philip had shrunk himself accidentally. Could he do that with the healing power? No idea. He drank more coffee. "Why did you open my curtains?"

"It seemed like a tomb in here with them closed, Dad." Beth walked in from the hallway. "That's a new look. I think I'm going to miss your gray hair."

"Me too." Philip smiled.

His daughter smiled back, and all was better with his world.

"I like it dark inside. It's more secure that way. What brings you here so early?"

Alec and his daughter exchanged glances. Their eyes grew distant and unfocused. They were probably speaking telepathically, so he couldn't overhear.

Damned nuisance.

He couldn't read minds, like Beth, but Philip didn't think they were here for something personal. For that, Beth would have come alone. "I assume you're here for something to do with the Resource?"

"Not me. Alec needs your help," Beth said. "And I have to run. I have a plane to catch."

"You're going out of town without Alec?" The firestarter had one valuable quality: he was a fierce protector. Beth was safe from harm with him.

"Yes, without Alec," Beth said. "I think I can manage this one. I have a possible new client in Charlton City. Someone who needs my specialized help as soon as possible."

"Someone who needs your telepathy," Philip said. "Are you absolutely certain it's safe?"

"I sent Daz out there for recon first. He'll be her back-up," Alec said.

Daz, the head of Alec's special-ops combat team. Philip's opinion of Alec's intelligence went up a notch. "Good."

"I'll be fine. Dad, do you think you can help Alec without too much grumbling?"

Philip shrugged again.

Beth walked over, kissed Alec goodbye and went out the front door. Alec sighed and watched the Honda pull out of the driveway. His eyes lost focus again.

The pair was sharing a telepathic goodbye. Philip turned his back and poured another cup of coffee. "So what's this problem?"

"It's a leftover I inherited as part of the Resource. Like you warned me, Lansing hid a lot of his holdings. I wish we'd found this one sooner. It's another of his genetics labs." Alec grimaced. "From what we pulled from the records, they made some advances in genetic manipulation."

"Lansing was trying to grow an army of supermen, like you. That's no shock."

"Yeah, but this lab's research is advanced. We think they might have gotten as far as genetically altering DNA to create or improve on certain psychic powers. It's also possible they're enhancing Lansing's sperm to ensure passing on his immortality too."

"If Lansing provided sperm samples, he wouldn't have told them it was his sperm. He was too secretive for that. What else?"

Alec looked away. "The lab probably was working with my sperm too. Lansing could have had some lab techs take it from me when I was unconscious. It'd have been just like him."

Philip threw the empty coffee mug against the wall. It shattered with a satisfying sound. Once again, he wished he'd killed Richard Lansing a very long time ago.

"Send F-Team to surround the lab and shut it down, by force if needed. I'll help."

Alec looked at the shattered remains of the mug and shook his head. "I won't do that. It's a legitimate lab on the outside. The people working there could be innocent."

"Innocent to a degree, but none of them have their hands clean. If you don't want to shut it down by force, why did you come to me?" If Alec didn't eliminate the lab, Philip would. Explosives were easy to come by if you knew who to ask.

"Yeah, well, even if all the workers knew about the DNA being taken without consent and they're all scum, I still want to evaluate the place first. I'll learn more that way."

"You came to me because you need a spy."

Alec nodded. "You can blend in and not look scary. I'm not sure how you do it, but every time I see you in public, you look nondescript. Normal. Nobody will mistake me or any member of F-Team for normal. We all look like soldiers."

"People sense your power," Philip said.

"And not yours. How do you do that?"

"It's easy to learn to blend in when standing out can cost you your life." Philip had learned that lesson as a child. The years with the CIA had only honed that skill. "But I'm not familiar with genetic laboratories. I would need a full briefing before being able to advise you on it." How big was this lab? How much explosive would he need to destroy it?

"How about a visit to the lab today? It'll give you a chance to look it over."

"I won't necessarily know what I'm looking at."

"You notice everything about people. You'll know if they're trying to hide something."

He nodded. "True enough. But your visit could spook them anyway. Once you show up, you have to assume they'll know who you are. They might rabbit."

"Yeah, I thought of that. I'm going to have F-Team put it under surveillance the minute we leave. I thought maybe you could plant a few bugs while we're inside to keep tabs on them too."

"You know, Farley, sometimes you don't act as young or naive as you are."

Alec smiled. "You know, Drake, somewhere in all that I think there was a compliment."

"Why not watch them first for a while?" Philip asked. "I can plant bugs without making them aware they're being watched."

"Because we need to act quickly."

"Why?"

Alec looked away again. Philip felt the temperature in the room rise. That happened when the firestarter became angry.

"The report I read said that the experiment had gotten as far as a pregnancy. They either implanted an experimental embryo in a woman or they used altered sperm to artificially inseminate her."

"They've done *what*?"

Philip stood and drove a shard of the shattered mug into his palm. The pain triggered a pleasant surge of adrenaline, dissipating the anger. Pain felt very good lately. He feared he might be becoming addicted to it. "Women have been used as lab rats? Without their consent?"

Alec nodded slowly. "The records we uncovered talk about at least one test subject. We know there's a woman out there pregnant with the results of their first experiment. I just don't know the exact details." Alec balled his hand into a fist. "Someone out there could be carrying my kid, Drake. I've got to find her and protect them both."

Even from the grave, Lansing had hurt innocents again.

"I'll look at this lab. And then we'll sort out how to destroy it."

Chapter Three

"Tammy, you didn't have to come." Del whispered, trying to not let the words carry to the others in the waiting room. "It's just a simple ultrasound."

"Of course I had to come. I'm the one who talked you into it. I said I'd help, and I will. You're not alone in this, Delilah."

Well, that settled it. No use arguing with anyone when they used your full name. Del tried to settle in the uncomfortable chair. Drink lots of water, they'd told her. A full bladder was needed for a clear look at the fetus. And now she felt ready to burst.

Idiot. She should have never let Tammy talk her into carrying the baby to term that day three months ago at the dock. Nobody had given her a warning that pregnancy would be like this.

They'd better call for her soon or she'd have to go to the bathroom and then reschedule and have to do this all again.

"I don't know why I need to do this."

"They need to know how the baby is growing and when it was conceived."

"I know the exact date of that."

"But they just want to be sure. It's for the baby's health," Tammy said.

The baby's health. Del shook her head and looked at the other women in the waiting room. A couple were visibly pregnant, their faces tired. *Already?* One of them had a toddler with her. The mother tried to calm the fussy toddler, first with reading a book—thirty seconds of quiet—then with an electronic toy with noises and whistles—a whole two minutes of toddler quiet but electronic noise—and, finally, with a discreet snack of crackers the mother carried in her pocket. That produced a lengthy quiet.

Adoption was definitely the way to go. Del could never have that kind of patience.

Several other women didn't look pregnant at all, and one of those was accompanied by a man Del assumed was the father of the child. Of course, maybe their ultrasound wasn't for a pregnancy. They did all kinds of ultrasounds here.

"It will be fine, Del," Tammy said again. "This is the fun part. This technology was barely around when I had my last one."

"I don't want there to be a fun part," Del whispered.

She didn't want to like being pregnant. She didn't want to get excited about it. This kid was going to a good home. There was absolutely no reason to get attached. "Why do you act as if I should be excited?"

"You might change your mind about adoption." Tammy patted her hand. "My kids would all make great babysitters."

"They're not going to get up with me in the middle of the night."

"That part is over quickly," Tammy said.

Del snorted.

The toddler started crying. Her mom picked her up and soothed with a few more crackers. Seemed if you wanted to do motherhood right, you had to plan ahead and be on constant alert. *That leaves me right out.*

Del supposed it was possible the ultrasound would show a problem. Maybe the fetus wasn't growing normally. After all her agonizing about this, what if the decision was taken out of her hands?

Her name was called. Tammy came with her. They followed the nurse/technician/office worker/whatever she was down the narrow hallway.

Tammy clutched her hand while a humorless attendant applied the gel to her bare stomach. The attendant had her hair pulled back, wore no make-up and didn't even crack a smile. Some bedside manner.

The gel felt cold, then warm as the tech moved the device over her now slightly swollen abdomen. There was definitely a baby bump. Small but growing.

Del looked over at Tammy. Tammy smiled at her, encouraging. Stop being so happy, Del thought.

The tech kept her eyes glued on the monitor. Del had no idea what she was looking for since she certainly couldn't make out anything in all that black and white static.

Finally, the attendant smiled.

Careful, your face might crack. "So, how's it look?" Del asked.

"We have fingers," said the attendant, pointing. Del squinted and wished she could reach out and trace what was on the monitor. Tiny, tiny blobs. She'd have to believe they were fingers. Huh. The alien child had fingers.

"This is wonderful," Tammy said.

If you say so, Del thought.

"And here." The attendant played with a dial and moved the ultrasound to another area. "Listen."

A tiny, tiny heartbeat, sounding unbelievably loud, echoed around the room. Del swallowed, feeling as if her throat had closed. A heart.

Her baby's heartbeat.

Tammy grinned.

Del shook her head. A person was growing inside her. It happened every day. People got knocked up all the time, and all those babies had hearts.

Del still felt stupidly excited about it. She didn't want to be.

The attendant stopped the images, stilling the heartbeat for a second, panicking Del.

"She's just stopping it to capture the images, Del," Tammy said.

Del nodded. First, she didn't care about the kid, then she worried it might not be healthy, and now she'd nearly panicked at the idea it was dead or something.

Motherhood. Some rollercoaster. And this was what Tammy wanted her to sign up for?

In a few seconds, the images went live again. Del started breathing once more. Photos, they were taking still photos. *Relax.*

There was the little baby's head. First fingers, then a heartbeat and now a head.

"Do you want to know the sex?" the tech asked.

"No," Del said. The less she knew, the better.

"Yes," Tammy said. "I know you, Del. You hate surprises."

True. Plus, maybe knowing the gender might make the kid easier to adopt. Some people cared about that.

"Okay." Del looked at the tech. "So, boy or girl?"

"Boy," the tech said.

A boy. A boy with fingers, a heartbeat, a head and a penis.

A baby.

"Your son, Del," Tammy whispered.

Del couldn't speak. She watched the monitor instead. All those swirling images were distracting.

A son? She had a son?

The tech narrowed her eyes and looked at the clipboard containing Del's chart. "About five months along?"

"Four months," Del snapped. It wasn't like she could forget that morning she'd woken up on her bar floor. Before that, she hadn't had sex for two years. "Why do you ask?"

"I'm just making certain of the date."

"Okay."

Del tried to stay quiet as the gloop was wiped from her stomach, but her bladder was screaming at her. The tech smiled and told her to get dressed as they were finished.

The tech handed over a still photo of the fetus before she left. Del ignored it. "I have to use the bathroom. Meet you back in the waiting room," she said to Tammy.

When she got back to the waiting room, Tammy held the ultrasound photo up to Del.

"I don't want that."

"You might someday," Tammy said.

Del put it in her coat pocket without looking at it.

Later, in the middle of the night when she couldn't sleep, she slipped the photo out and held it under the bright lights in her bathroom.

It looked like a baby. Oh, sure, the legs looked like one big blob but the head, chest and one arm were there. She couldn't see the penis. The ultrasound tech must have seen something she did not.

A boy. Her son.

What the hell am I supposed to do with you, kid? Tell you what, I'll make sure someone takes good care of you. Promise you that, at least.

Chapter Four

Philip showered quickly before leaving with Alec. He had been up all night and didn't want to smell like it. As he dressed, he strapped on his ankle holster and slipped a knife into his jacket to go along with the Sig Sauer nestling in his waist holster. The lightweight jacket would conceal that well enough. He gathered up a small pocketful of tech toys, including several micro-bugs. Alec was right to want the place bugged.

He took a look at where he'd jammed the shard into his palm. The shower had washed off the blood, and the wound had fully healed already.

Pain and the rush of healing after it were all that had made him feel alive in the last few months. He'd always had a high tolerance for pain and had known that tolerance sometimes slid into pleasure.

But now it was as if he needed that rush. Even his careless one-night stands had been unsatisfying unless the sex had been rough.

Beth would have much to say about that, if she knew. He had no plans to tell her.

Philip drove the Charger with Alec providing directions, but he didn't need them. He knew that area. The lab was located next to a rundown area in Passaic, just over the town line in an industrial zone of warehouses, offices and laboratories. It was accessible via the highway but Philip planned a less obvious route. Just in case, again. He didn't know who could be watching, but that was the point. One never knew.

When he explained this to Alec, the boy shook his head. "Appreciate the security lesson, Drake, but that seems extreme."

"You need lessons in extreme." The firestarter was powerful, smart and he wanted to do the right thing. He'd changed the name of the Resource—which he'd inherited from his adoptive father Richard Lansing—to the Phoenix Institute to signal a new start for the place that had effectively held him captive all his life.

Alec intended to find and help children like him use their power responsibly. It was an excellent, noble goal. But Alec had been raised in a vacuum, essentially isolated from the rest of the world. It made him more than naive on a few subjects.

"Someone is using your DNA to create a race of superbabies, and you think taking an undocumented driving route is extreme? Not to mention the CIA might be monitoring me or you. Whoever kept this genetics lab running after Lansing's death could be doing the same. And there's still the matter of those watchers out there from an unknown source that you sensed on the container ship job. Aside from the one mention in Lansing's notes, there's no other information. Which tells me Lansing knew something but thought it was too volatile to write down. That's never good."

He paused to let the words sink in. Alec shifted in his seat, clearly uncomfortable.

"If you want to survive to do all this good you talk about, then you have to assume enemies are watching. *All the time.*"

Alec stared at the car's dashboard for a while instead of replying. Perhaps the young man was considering what he'd just been told. Or, given his sheltered upbringing, he was checking out the car. Alec loved cars.

"I hate having to think that way."

"If you want to live long enough to accomplish your aims, you're going to have to learn." *And you damn well better learn enough to keep my daughter safe.*

Alec nodded. "What if my kid is out there, Drake? Not a situation I've been trained to handle."

Philip realized that the boy was truly looking for advice this time. Like it or not, Alec was a permanent part of Beth's life. Which meant the question should be answered rather than ignored. No one had told him giving advice to a man sleeping with his daughter was part of fatherhood when he'd volunteered.

But here he was.

"We find the child and the mother and we help them. I can't imagine you'd walk away from the child."

"Never." Alec stared at him. "Glad you know that."

Philip nodded. "A child who's alive and needs caretaking is a problem that can be solved. It could be much worse. For instance, if you're too late to help someone and they wind up dead. Can't fix that."

Alec nodded.

"Are you worried about Beth's reaction? She'd take care of any lost child, whether it was yours or even Lansing's."

Alec smiled. "We already talked about that. Actually, I think she's more worried about your reaction than mine."

"My reaction?"

"It brings back the whole mess with Lansing for you."

"He's dead, it's over."

"He was your father. And you just smashed a coffee mug because you were so pissed at him."

"I have plenty of mugs." Philip shifted into low gear as he slowed down for a stoplight. "Lansing wasn't my father. He screwed my mother, then walked out. When I refused to join his unholy crusade as an adult, he hated me. My only reaction to his death is to be glad he's gone."

"Something changed when he died. You quit the CIA, you don't seem to be doing anything, and you might as well live in a cave the way your home is closed up. Not to mention all those empty beer cans all over the place."

"That speech must have come directly from Beth."

Alec shrugged. "She's worried about you."

"If she's worried about my apartment, tell her I like caves." The best year of his childhood had been spent living in a makeshift home in a cave. He and Lily had been able to wander away for hours. On their own, in the quiet of the woods, the two of them had had the best times. Once, they'd even laughed after they'd had to run up a tree to escape a bear. Lily had been the only good part of his childhood. Until he'd destroyed their friendship with two shotgun blasts. "And the beer was work."

"C'mon."

Philip shook his head as he turned left and headed the back way to the warehouse through Passaic, quite possibly the most misbegotten urban area in New Jersey. And that was saying a lot.

"Beer is a drug. I needed to know how my healing ability would work when I was drugged."

"Wouldn't it be better to avoid being drunk altogether?"

There it was. Alec's innocence again.

"I'm not worried about controlling myself with alcohol. I'm worried about others using drugs to control me. Beer seemed the least intrusive drug."

Alec clenched his jaw. "You mean like how Lansing drugged Beth when he took her prisoner?"

"Exactly." Perhaps Alec wasn't so innocent. Lansing had raised him, after all.

Alec wasn't interested in power as Lansing had been. Philip gave him points for that. But Alec had kept some of the Resource holdings intact for his new Phoenix Institute in case they might be useful. Philip would have dissolved the company altogether. Keeping control made Alec a target. Hence, it made Beth a target.

They didn't agree on that. They never would.

"So does getting drunk affect your healing abilities?" Alec asked.

"Once I was fully drunk, yes." He shrugged. "But it did help sober me up quickly. If you've never been drunk, you might want to do it under controlled conditions. See if it affects your firestarting or TK. Better that than finding out the hard way."

They turned onto the main drag of Passaic. Alec looked around for a few minutes and whistled. "This city looks like the war zones that some of the F-Team soldiers talk about."

"Sounds about right." Many of the storefronts in Passaic were either permanently closed or locked up tight with steel doors. The only place left open was a bar. The pub door was half open but the window was covered with a metal screen. The streets were absolutely deserted. "No one comes here unless they have to. And most people don't have to."

He drove past the empty lot and industrial-style building that had once been the city's newspaper.

"I thought Newark was bad," Alec said.

"Newark is a living city. This is a dead one." There were rarely police here or anyone in authority. No one to bother anyone save for the neighborhood gangs. Philip liked Passaic. It was an easy place to hide.

He pulled into a more residential area, with rundown two- and three-family houses almost on top of each other. "Tell me what this lab looks like inside. How large? How many employees does it have?"

"About fifty employees. It seems to have several different lab areas and a refrigerated storage area."

"Name and cover story."

"Orion Systems is working on creating a genetic magic bullet to combat cancer at the cellular level."

Good cover. An altruistic goal and yet one that would not yield results quickly. That meant money could be poured into this Orion Systems and no one would question why there were no immediate results.

He crossed out of Passaic into the neighboring town. The lawns instantly grew more green, the street less bumpy and the atmosphere lighter. He could see the highway overpass on the next street over. *Hate highways.* Especially now that they took photos at every exit and toll station.

"Drake, if you hate people watching you, why drive this car?" Alec asked.

Philip shrugged. "Because I'm retired, and I finally decided I wanted a car like this." He knew it was foolish to have a 1967 Charger. People noticed it, especially since it was a nice shade of midnight blue. On the other hand, having a very recognizable car as his primary mode of transportation gave him a lot of options for misdirection if he ever wanted to disappear. People would look for this car, not the two or three nondescript vehicles he kept stashed around New Jersey.

He supposed Alec would call that paranoid again. Likely because it was.

Office buildings dotted the landscape as they drove the last mile. Philip pulled into the parking lot of a slate-gray building with narrow windows. At five stories, it looked squat and ungainly among the larger and glassier office buildings. There were no signs identifying it as Orion Systems.

"Do they have any warning at all that you're coming?"

"I thought it best to simply show up. I have I.D. showing I'm an executive with the holding company that owns Orion Systems. Which I am. I inherited Lansing's role as CEO."

Philip spotted the cameras on the parking lot light as he pulled into a space. "They're watching the parking lot. They'll have warning before you step inside the building. Be ready."

Alec nodded. "I will."

The weight of the concealed handguns at his waist and ankle comforted Philip, along with the knife in the pocket of his overcoat. Alec probably wasn't armed. He didn't need to be. He *was* a weapon.

Alec started to get out of the Charger. Philip grabbed his elbow. He pointed to a well-dressed man leaving the building. "Wait. Watch him."

The man carried a briefcase and talked on his cell phone. Philip judged him to be well over six feet, perhaps six-foot-four. His blond hair was short but curly in the front. He was handsome with a classic face of well-defined cheekbones and a sharp chin. That face belonged on a movie screen.

Expensive suit, expensive tie, expensive cell phone. Likely someone important at Orion Systems. Someone who should be watched.

The blond man hit a button on his keys. The lights flashed on the BMW parked next to them.

Glad he had brought his little toys, Philip exited the car and used his body to block the view of the approaching driver. He pushed a little device in the edge of the passenger window of the BMW.

He and Alec walked away before the suit reached the car.

Alec drew close to him. "You did something."

Philip frowned and shrugged. "Yes, the modifications to the baffles did lower the engine noise."

Alec might have no idea what he was talking about but he had the presence of mind to nod as if he did. Message received. They might be overheard.

When they entered the office building, they were confronted by a security guard at the central desk. That in itself said a great deal. Why have a guard when one could easily hire a welcoming receptionist? Cameras were everywhere in the lobby.

Alec presented his credentials and those of his assistant. Philip almost snorted about being called Norman Parker. He didn't think he'd ever used the first name "Norman" before. Probably because it was too memorable.

Their credentials checked out. The guard opened a solid, metal door labeled "Orion Systems" with the push of a button. Philip cut in front of Alec and went first, alert. He hated going through doors blind, but he hated going *second* through doors blind even more.

What was on the other side was surprisingly ordinary. The laboratory looked exactly like he'd envisioned. There were rows of tables with small electronic microscopes and what he thought might be refrigerated centrifuges. Stored above the tables were labeled glass bottles of various sizes holding chemicals. Beyond the laboratory area he could see a large gray metal door that looked like an entrance to a freezer.

About twenty people were clustered around the tables. Some sat at nearby desks, typing at their computers and others looked busy with the various beakers and Petri dishes.

A man wearing a white lab coat came out from the offices located to the left.

"Mr. Farley?" The man extended his hand. "I'm Doctor Cheshire. Welcome to Orion Systems. This is an unexpected surprise."

An unpleasant surprise, judging by Cheshire's discomfort. The man said he was pleased to see them. Yet he was nervous. Sweat rolled down his neck and soaked the collar of his shirt.

"Norman" shook hands with Dr. Cheshire. The doctor paid little attention. He was focused on Alec.

He knew who Alec really was, Philip guessed.

"What brings you here, gentlemen?" Cheshire asked.

"I've come to check on our investment. I understand you're the assistant director here."

Cheshire nodded. "Yes. Mr. Genet is our director but he's just left. In his absence, I can give you the full tour."

Cheshire's eyes darted around the lab. Philip suddenly wished he could grab the doctor and interrogate him privately. This was a man hiding secrets. Badly.

"I would have preferred Mr. Genet. He's the author of the reports I've been reading. Is there any way you could call him back? This is important."

"No, he's absolutely unavailable." Cheshire fiddled with the pencil in his hand. "Besides, Mr. Genet may write the reports, but I'm fully qualified to discuss our progress with you, Mr. Farley. Likely, more so. Mr. Genet is a fine manager but he's not a scientist, as you know."

That finally sounded sincere.

"Of course. Mr. Parker and I would be honored to have you show us around."

"Good." Cheshire finally noticed he was fiddling with his pencil and put it in the pocket of his lab coat.

As Cheshire moved to lead them on a tour, Philip decided that if Genet was the suit who had just left, Cheshire definitely had cause to dislike working for him. That might be a good lever to use if they needed information on Genet later.

Alec listened intently and asked a number of intelligent questions on DNA, enzymes and their interaction. As they walked around the lab, the firestarter drew his share of stares and covert glances, mostly from the women but several men definitely checked out his backside.

Philip let his shoulders sag, trying to draw as little attention as possible. He suspected this was the "public" area of the laboratory. It would show them little. They needed the private area, where the real work was done.

"What are they working on?" Alec asked.

"They're conducting research on how the environment in the womb affects DNA and genetics. It's not just enough to map DNA. In layman's terms, we have to find out how its surroundings affect it."

Alec leaned closer to Cheshire. "Forgive my bluntness," he said in a near whisper, "but how many of these people know what they're really creating?"

Subtlety was definitely not Alec's strong suit. Philip would have just let Cheshire ramble. People said more that way. But this was the boy's show.

Cheshire stopped dead in his tracks. He started fiddling with the pencil again. "Well, you do come to the point."

"Mr. Farley runs a multinational corporation," Philip said. "He needs an update on your progress, and he needs it now."

"Of course," Cheshire snapped, now annoyed with them as much as he was annoyed with Genet. Philip perversely thought about baring his teeth at the scientist to see what kind of reaction it would provoke. Hostility, however, was not what was needed. At least not right now.

Instead, he merely nodded and dropped in behind Alec and Dr. Cheshire, playing his part once more.

"Mr. Genet's reports showed considerable progress in manipulating some of the unique sperm samples provided," Alec said.

Philip caught the edge to the firestarter's voice. He wondered if Cheshire did as well.

"Yes, one of our projects has moved beyond the laboratory stage." Cheshire cleared his voice. "But not here. We can speak more freely in the second lab. It's more secure."

"So long as we speak about it," Alec said.

Cheshire pointed to a *Restricted Area* sign to the far left, past the offices and cubicles. The private facility. Philip had guessed right. The real work was done behind closed doors.

As they passed the large, metal door that had been visible upon entering the lab, Philip tapped it with his knuckles. "What's this?"

"Our refrigeration area. The samples can be quite delicate," Cheshire said.

"Do you transport them for testing elsewhere?" Philip asked. *Where else are you keeping the samples, doctor?*

"We don't trust them to any outside facility. Our samples do not leave this lab."

Philip couldn't judge the truth of that. Cheshire was already too nervous from lying about something. He would need to be interrogated at length later.

"All the sperm samples are here?" Alec asked, voice bland again.

"And some embryos as well, though none have yet proved viable. That could be a problem from the eggs we obtained anonymously. If we do this again, we will have to have fully vetted eggs. We have to learn from our mistakes. And, sadly, the sperm samples from the three subjects are fewer than we would like."

Three sperm samples?

Philip frowned. Lansing and Alec. That was two. So who was the origin of the third sperm sample?

Motherfucking son of a bitch.

Philip turned away from Cheshire and Alec to keep them from seeing the anger that must be written all over his face. His own sperm must be the origin of the third sample.

He'd been in the hospital recovering from injuries often enough in his CIA career. Unconscious in those hospitals more than once as well. Lansing would've known that. It would have been easy enough to obtain his sperm, he supposed. He hadn't kept a particular eye out for people wanting to collect it.

He fought an overwhelming desire to slam Cheshire against the wall and demand answers to every single question that burned in his mind. Instead, he clamped down on his anger and smoothed his face back so he looked more like "Norman Parker" than "Philip Drake".

"We'll need an up-to-date accounting of the test sample's progress," Alec said as they reached the door to the restricted lab.

"Of course. It's very encouraging, you know. One implantation and it worked." Cheshire smiled. "We need to talk more about that. I want to monitor our subject more closely. Mr. Genet was of the opinion it was best to stay in the background until the child was born instead of bringing the mother into our facilities. Before he passed, Mr. Lansing thought that was the best way as well. But I don't. Perhaps you can make Mr. Genet understand how essential information during the pregnancy is to our research. We need to have her with us."

"Perhaps we can," Philip said. "Where are the facilities to hold her?"

"Oh, no, Mr. Parker, we wouldn't hurt her. We'd take very good care of her and the child. They're both incredibly important, don't you think?"

Philip pictured his hand wrapped around Cheshire's throat. The real culprit behind the stolen sperm, however, was Lansing, and he was dead already.

Cheshire punched a code into a keyboard to the left of the restricted access door and inserted a key simultaneously. The door buzzed, and Cheshire pushed it open.

Philip heard a very quiet but distinct click. *Fuck.*

"Bomb!" he yelled to warn Alec.

Philip tackled Cheshire, sending them both to the floor as an explosion roared around them.

Philip hit hard on his shoulder. He heard Cheshire's head bounce off the floor with a nasty *thunk*. Above them, Alec stood in the flames. The fire licked at his feet, his waist and his shoulders. He paid no mind and sent the flames upward to the ceiling.

Philip sucked in a breath. Beth dubbed this Alec's superhero mode but, to him, the young man looked like a god in motion. He had no doubt that despite his quick action, he and Cheshire would be dead if Alec hadn't taken control of the explosion.

Alec pushed the fire upward, mitigating the heat and the flames. Philip scrambled to his feet and yelled at the employees—some already running—to get out as fast as possible. Philip grabbed Cheshire off the floor and held him by the lapels of his lab coat. "What was in there that was so valuable, Doctor?"

Cheshire's face was white. Sweat rolled down his cheeks from the heat of the fire. "We have to get out of here!"

"What was in there?" Philip asked again.

"Our main lab. And the back-up storage for our records. And, my God—Demetrius, my assistant, is in there!"

Demetrius was likely collateral damage. The records had been what someone wanted destroyed. That someone likely equaled Genet.

Philip shoved Cheshire over to Alec. "Get him and get out of here."

"Where the hell are you going?" Alec yelled over the sounds of a glass bottle shattering behind them.

"Someone's in the lab."

"There are probably toxic fumes in there. Are you insane?" Alec shouted.

"Yes," Philip said and plunged through the doorway.

Chapter Five

The ob-gyn pushed Del's shirt back into place. Del was learning to tolerate these appointments. Four months down, five to go. She'd even talked Tammy into letting her come alone today. Tammy was being great about checking up on her, but Del didn't want her hovering. She especially didn't want Tammy knowing about the meeting with the adoption lawyers Del had scheduled immediately after finishing with the doctor.

Tammy still maintained Del should keep the baby. Del hadn't decided. Adoption seemed the more logical choice.

"Everything looks good, Ms. Sefton," the doctor said. "I did want to ask you about one thing in the ultrasound report we received."

Del sat up. She knew it. That odd hesitation by the ultrasound tech had meant something.

"What's wrong?"

Dr. Fine smiled. She'd come highly recommended by Del's regular gynecologist, and Del could see why. Dr. Fine looked like everyone's favorite grandmother, and she had a comforting, maternal manner. A little like Tammy, Del decided.

"Your baby's healthy," Dr. Fine said. "But I wanted to ask you about the due date. Are you sure that your date of conception is accurate?"

Damn straight, I'm sure. "Yes. Absolutely."

"Your baby showed development much more in line with a five-month-old fetus than four months."

"Is that bad?" Del asked.

"Only if we have the due date as incorrect and you go into labor a month early, before you're ready." Dr. Fine smiled reassuringly again.

"Ah, no worries then. I'm positive of when the baby was conceived." The date of conception was one of the few certain things about her pregnancy.

The doctor made a note on the chart. "No doubt future ultrasounds will pinpoint exactly when we can expect this child. The important thing is that your baby is healthy and growing."

"Right." Dr. Fine didn't believe her. Del tried not to take offense. After all, probably a lot of women shaded the truth about their pregnancies, even to their doctors. If her son was growing faster than normal, the doctor had a right to be concerned.

Maybe she should have reported the rape. Then no one would question whether she'd mixed up the timing. But reporting anything to the police didn't come easily to her. She'd grown up hiding from the authorities. Besides, she had nothing to give the police about her rapist. All she had was a hole in her memory. What could they possibly do with that?

She wondered what she should tell the adoption lawyers about the baby's father. They'd probably want to know because of parental rights and all that. Del had absorbed that language when she'd been in foster care. But would people turn away this kid because his father was a rapist? Maybe it was better to keep that part quiet.

Del was still debating the question in her head as she left the doctor's office, went down one floor of the office building and looked for the lawyer's office. It was definitely convenient that the adoption lawyers and the doctors were in the same building. Not a coincidence, Del guessed.

She took a deep breath, a cleansing breath, as she opened the door. She'd have to learn more about those deep, cleansing breaths. She probably should take prenatal classes. Tammy had volunteered to be her partner. But she'd be in a class with women who all were keeping their kids, all excited about having another family member. All excited, Del guessed, about being moms, with all sorts of plans for the future.

Del didn't know if she could take that much gushiness about becoming a parent.

She walked into the lawyer's office. No one was in the waiting room. The receptionist was behind a glass window, just like the one in the doctor's office. The young man smiled, got out of his chair and opened the door into the main hallway. "Ms. Sefton, welcome, the gentlemen are expecting you."

Del nodded and let the receptionist lead her into yet another office.

Two men were already there, both dressed in suits. Of course they were in suits. They were lawyers.

The older one sat in a chair opposite the oak desk, brown glasses low on his round, somewhat weathered face. The second lawyer was standing, staring out of the window slats into the parking lot. His suit was obviously tailored and so dark blue it almost seemed black, a stunning contrast to his blond hair, cut short with a few natural curls in the front.

He turned to her, no expression on his face, and she felt as if she was looking at a movie star. She was no shrimp at five-foot-ten, but this man was at least five inches taller than her. He was so good-looking that she finally understood the expression about "melting at someone's feet".

"Welcome, Ms. Sefton." The older one stood. "I'm Rudy Buchanan and this is my colleague, Mr. Edward Genet the fifth."

The fifth? Of course the movie star would have an important-sounding name. Genet smiled at her. *Whoa.* Del blinked and looked at Buchanan because to keep her gaze on Genet would be like staring at a shining star.

Buchanan shook her hand.

"Very nice to meet you."

Buchanan had a firm grip, but his hand was a little sweaty. "Nice to meet you too, Mr. Buchanan. Should we get started?"

"Please, take a seat," Buchanan said.

Del sat down, suddenly tired. The waves of fatigue were coming more frequently lately. It was supposed to be normal. If this was normal for motherhood, she'd take a rain check. That was why she was here, after all.

Genet sat down behind the desk, taking command of the room. Of course he would. Where else would a king sit?

"We're so pleased to meet you," Genet said.

"Thank you." She had a million questions about this whole process. She didn't ask them. She had found out from years of tending bar to wait while people talked. They said more that way.

Genet sat forward and put his hands flat on the desk. He smiled that dazzling smile again. She wondered if anyone ever went blind from it. She seriously doubted he was an ordinary attorney. She wished she'd kept this to phone or email. She didn't want to deal with Mr. Perfect in person.

"We're so pleased you are considering our offer to set up a private adoption," Genet said.

"You came highly recommended by the clinic," Del said. They'd been happy to provide the name of an attorney after Del had canceled the abortion. "So what does all this involve?"

"In short, an adoption means you will carry the child to term and sign away your parental rights after the baby is born. After the adoption is final, you will be reimbursed for any medical expenses not paid by your insurance plus any incidental expenses like travel to your doctor and lost wages."

"Where would the baby go? Would I meet the parents?"

"Our clients prefer a closed adoption," Buchanan said.

Damn. Still, a closed adoption might be better. Out of sight, out of mind, Del thought. "How would I know the baby's being taken care of if I have no contact at all with the parents?"

"We can provide you with information about the parents, general information about where the baby will live, and send you photos of the child once a year," Buchanan said.

Genet sat forward, intense. "You're doing an incredibly wonderful thing by allowing this child to be adopted, Ms. Sefton. Rest assured, we guarantee that this baby will have a loving home."

"And you'll put that in writing?"

"Of course." Genet leaned back in the chair and gestured to Buchanan.

Buchanan adjusted his tie. It was pale blue, nothing remarkable, just like the rest of him. She glanced back over at Genet. His tie was bright red, an unusual color. It was decorated with three yellow lions facing outward. Regal, she thought.

"I know this sounds overwhelming, but we've done this a number of times, and it's worked well for everyone," Buchanan said. "The baby has a good home, the parents who want a child are happy, and you will be able to move on with your life." He opened a file on his lap. "I do have to ask you about the baby's father, to make certain he will consent to the adoption. You mentioned he was out of the picture?"

Del took a deep breath. Moment of truth. "I was attacked and, I think, drugged. I don't remember what happened. I'd still be wondering what happened, I think, except that I took a pregnancy test a month later and it turned up positive."

"You have my profound condolences for your ordeal," Genet said.

"Thank you." Del stared at him. He seemed genuinely sorry. So why did she feel so nervous? "So, obviously, contacting the father isn't possible."

Genet made a note on his legal pad. "Sadly, this situation happens more than you think. We can work around it."

"So what else do I need to do to make this happen?" she asked.

"There are some legal forms you can sign now stating your intention about giving the baby up for adoption, but those are not binding until after the child is born."

"Take me through how it all works," Del said. Not binding. She liked the sound of that.

Genet turned his full attention on her, charm wattage on high voltage. He began by explaining that he was adopted himself, that was why he had specialized in this field. Like Tammy, he talked about what a good life he'd had and how he considered his adoptive family as his family. He'd never searched for his birth parents, he said.

She found herself warming to him because sincerity began to peek out from underneath the charm. His story was certainly a good reason why he was working in suburban New Jersey as an attorney when he should be out modeling or something.

"You naturally want to give your child the best chance to succeed in life, the best chance to be the most intelligent, healthiest, strongest child possible. You would do anything, I would imagine, to ensure that bright future for your child. Any parent would. Sometimes ensuring that means making a sacrifice that will benefit the child."

She could afford to have a child. Bar & Grill wasn't a huge moneymaker, but it was enough to support two people. More so because Del lived in the apartment on the second floor of the bar. That was big enough for two. Tammy had been serious about supplying babysitters.

I should not be unsure about this.

She should have thrown out the ultrasound photo. That was why she was having second thoughts now. She definitely shouldn't have put it up on her fridge where she could see the photo of her unborn son every time she wanted a glass of ice water. Which was a lot lately.

"Why do your clients want to adopt a baby, Mr. Genet?"

Genet leaned back in the chair again, damping down the charm. Buchanan leaned forward in the chair across from her. He was less charming but in some ways, more reassuring. He seemed much more normal.

"We have several couples who want to adopt the child you carry," Buchanan said. "Two of them have tried in-vitro fertilization and it hasn't worked. The other—" Buchanan cleared his throat, "—is a married gay couple who are desperate to start a family. This is the only way they can."

Del nodded. "Do you think the couples that tried to have their own kid will consider mine their second choice?"

"Never. Our clients undergo a psychological screening. They will not have issues like that. All they want is a child to love."

So the attorney said. Del sighed. "You said I had to sign a preliminary statement. What else? Do I pay you guys a fee?"

"No, our fees are paid by the adopting couple," Buchanan said.

"How much are your fees?" she asked.

"If you're asking if we benefit financially from this, we do," Genet said. "But we wouldn't practice this kind of law if we didn't believe in it. It's not about money for us."

Del nodded. He had her convinced on that.

"As for what's involved, once you sign your intention to proceed with an adoption, you'll have to sign over permission for us to view your medical records. Our clients will want to track the progress of the baby."

"My medical records?"

"Your child will become something of a joint venture," Buchanan said. "We have to verify what you tell us with your medical records. And the adoptive parents want to track the child's progress. It makes them feel a part of the process."

At least someone wanted to volunteer as part of the "process". "I guess I get that, but it seems intrusive."

Genet said, "It's information that is already in your medical file. Nothing intrusive about it."

She looked at Genet. He returned her gaze with a benign smile, yet she had sensed some hostility in his words.

"So I sign my intention to give the child up for adoption and sign permission for people to get my medical records. What else? Don't I get some say in something?"

"We will provide you with profiles of the couples interested in the baby," Buchanan said. "The choice of where the child goes is yours."

"I see." Something inside her wanted to walk out of here. She couldn't tell if it was uncertainty about the adoption or if it was Genet. For some reason, he was impatient. That didn't make a lot of sense for a go-between. At least, she thought it didn't.

He was too good to be true. It made her suspicious.

"I can understand your discomfort." Genet relaxed back in his nice, shiny leather chair. "But you will be doing your child a great service, giving him an advantage few others would have. And your records, of course, would be kept completely confidential. All that we want is the medical information, not anything personal."

She wanted her kid to start out right, but the old paranoia nagged at her. *"The government is out to get us, the corporations are out to get us. Lawyers are the worst of all."*

Shut up, she told the faded memory. Doctors were supposed to be safe. And these men had been recommended by the people at the clinic. They had no stake in steering her wrong.

Buchanan, sensing her hesitation, launched into what could only be the company spiel about the wonders of adoption. He cited a bunch of studies and testimonials from adopted kids, about what a godsend it would be and why she should be a part of it.

It all sounded wonderful. Buchanan was an engaging person, friendly without being too oily. She liked him.

But she didn't like this. She finally knew why. It felt too much like running away, abandoning a bad situation instead of sticking it out. She'd done so much of that as a kid as her parents wandered from town to town, afraid of being caught. She'd learned to hate it.

Sticking with this situation was different from moving, however. For one, she'd be stuck with the decision for eighteen years and beyond.

Genet smiled at her again. Most women probably swooned when he did that. She might have, another day. But she was tired, pregnant and mentally exhausted. She didn't feel in the least bit sexy. And she didn't feel up to signing the damn papers either.

Hell.

Genet and Buchanan would have to find another girl.

"Tell me, what is making you hesitate?" Genet asked, holding out his palm as if asking her to touch it.

She ignored the implied offer. "I'm just not comfortable with anyone overseeing my medical records. And I've never been pregnant before. What happens if I get attached to my baby at the last minute?"

"We understand," Genet said, still all charm. "And, yes, you can change your mind at the last minute. But I think what's bothering you are natural fears and concerns. Once you get past them, you'll have faith in your choice of adoption. What can I do to reassure you?"

"Give me time to think this over."

"I wish we had time." Genet sighed dramatically. "To put it bluntly, Ms. Sefton, we need a decision soon. Our couples are frustrated, frightened and feel like they are running out of their chance for parenthood. I wanted to at least provide them with some good news, that there may be a child available soon. All you need to do is take the profiles over to our conference center, look them over, and decide." He leaned forward, intent. "We would love an answer today. You'll be helping us out by doing so."

And wouldn't that be a fine thing, Genet seemed to be saying. Not many people turned down a chance to help this man, she guessed.

"I'm sorry, you've both been very persuasive and understanding, but I need more time to think it over. So if you need an answer today, I'd have to say I've changed my mind about adoption. I want to keep the baby."

That felt good, she decided. It felt better than the fear she felt when she looked at her son's ultrasound photos. It felt better than when she'd walked in the room. It made no sense but it felt good.

She was going to be a mom.

She stood up. She was tired, she was hungry and she finally realized why Genet made her nervous. He reminded her of Hawk's stepfather, who had been charismatic as hell. He'd also been the cruelest person she'd ever met. He'd ruined Hawk and indirectly caused her parents' murders.

Her instincts said not to deal with him. Even if, under other circumstances, she'd want to drag him off to bed.

"Thank you for the appointment, gentlemen, and I'll keep thinking about this. I'm very sorry I couldn't help your clients as yet."

"You can find my number on the top sheet of those documents." Buchanan handed her a folder with a brochure of more testimonials by adoptive parents on top. "Please think about it. Think of how beneficial this could be in the long run for you and your child."

"I understand." She took a deep breath. "When I walked in here, I fully intended to commit to an adoption. Now, I'm just not sure."

"What changed your mind?" Genet asked.

"I think it's as simple as thinking about doing something is not the same as doing it." She nodded. "I'm so sorry for wasting your time."

"But you can't..." Buchanan sputtered. Genet stood up and glared at her. Del walked out without saying another word.

What an odd thing for Buchanan to say. He shouldn't be so invested in whether she agreed or not. He was just a lawyer, a go-between. And Genet had looked pissed off. She bet he'd already considered this a done deal and she'd bruised his ego by walking out.

Good, she thought.

She felt them staring at her as she walked away, though she knew that wasn't possible. When she reached the main lobby of the office building, she even glanced back over her shoulder to make certain they were not following.

Now *that* was definitely paranoid.

Chapter Six

Philip plunged into the burning laboratory. Smoke billowed in the air, cutting his visibility down to less than two feet directly in front of him. He banged his hip into a table. He swore and pulled a mini-light out of his coat pocket. The small but powerful light cut through the thick air, but it only gave him a narrow field of vision.

He saw a figure in a white lab coat on the floor across the room. Heat seared his skin as he drew closer to the flames and the body. The toxic smoke burned his nostrils and blurred his eyes, causing him far more problems than obscuring his sight. He dropped to his knees beside the body. The scientist had a squishy spot at the base of his skull. His chest did not rise or fall. Dead, perhaps. His left hand was clenched tight, as if he was holding something. Philip pried the hand open and found a thumb drive. He pocketed it, grabbed the scientist underneath the arms and started dragging him to the exit.

Something popped, like a balloon bursting. He heard the tinkling of glass exploding and fell on the limp scientist, covering him as much as he could. He hid his eyes behind his forearm.

Molten glass and metal rained down on his sleeve, burning through the cloth and directly into his skin.

He grimaced at the sharp flash of pain and patted down his fiery sleeve with his other hand. More pain, more burned skin. Out, get out, he told himself. Staying low, he stumbled for the door, scientist in tow. Alec should be at the door and could protect him from the fire. All he had to do was get there.

Pain sliced through his forearm. One of the glass shards must have buried itself deep in his skin. His lungs felt like molten fire. Instead of denying or suppressing the agony, he rode with the pain, letting it roll through him. The strong tinge of pleasure, even arousal, overcame the pain.

He was more alive and more aroused even than during sex. The intense pleasure kept him moving, but it did nothing for his blurry vision. His mini-light was now useless. He focused on the blaring red of the exit sign, using it as a beacon as he tugged the scientist in his wake.

He was only one step through the ruined door when a fuzzy figure appeared. The firestarter.

Alec grabbed the inert body of the scientist from him and placed the man over his shoulder seemingly without effort. Philip tried to breathe. It felt like a thousand pinpricks of flames burned inside his chest.

"I'm losing the fire. Too much fuel in here." Alec coughed. "Run."

As they ran for the outer lobby, Philip heard a crash from behind. It sounded like a light fixture or a support beam. Bad, either way. He couldn't keep Alec's pace and suspected the boy was slowing down for him.

It was only when they reached the outer lobby and the relatively clear air there that Philip could take another breath. And that short breath was full of agony/pleasure. Spots appeared before his eyes. Not enough oxygen, he thought. He was losing consciousness.

Alec took him by the elbow and led him outside to safety.

Philip put his hands on his knees to steady himself. Pleasure pulsed through every nerve ending. His breathing began to steady as the fresh air and his healing ability began soothing his injured lungs.

He looked up. The lab employees gathered outside, shocked and frightened, and milled around in a loose group. Fire engines, sirens blaring, pulled into the parking lot. A patrol car, lights flashing, joined them.

Alec set the inert scientist on the ground. Now that he could see clearly, Philip could tell the man was dead. He'd seen that glassy look in corpses' eyes all too often.

Alec shook his head and left the dead man to the first responders.

Philip walked behind the crowd of employees and leaned against a car. His breathing was still ragged. Likely his lungs had been seared badly by the smoke. If he'd been in the fire longer, he might have truly died. If he were a normal man, he'd never have made it out alive, even with Alec's help. He concentrated, imagining healthy, pink and functioning lungs. The healing flooded his body again, mingling with the pleasure he derived from the pain until it was all one.

He had never been addicted to drugs or alcohol. He could do without his job at the CIA. He liked sex, but he could be celibate for long periods. But if he ever wanted proof that he not only liked pain but craved the feeling, this was it.

Beth's telepathic talent had been the catalyst for upgrading his healing from an unconscious and sometimes unreliable power to its current level that allowed him to repair seared lungs.

If Beth knew that she had also mixed up his pleasure and pain circuits, she'd be appalled. He never intended to tell her.

"Drake?" Alec asked.

"I'm fine." Philip opened his eyes.

"Your sleeve is burned and there's blood all over it. And if I'm coughing from the smoke, you have to be much worse."

"I'm better now." Philip shrugged. He'd barely paid attention to the arm injury. "Can you handle the questions from the police?"

Alec nodded. "Why? Are you going somewhere?"

"Genet just took out his lab. That means he's about to go underground, which means he's going to make a move on the woman carrying the experimental baby. Today, maybe even right now." If he was Genet, he'd move that fast.

"How do we find her?"

"You don't, I do," Philip said. "Bring Cheshire to me. He'll give me her name and address."

Alec's eyes narrowed. "Don't kill him."

"I won't. Not today, at least. We need the information in his head." Philip squinted at the bright light of the sun. "Once I get the name and address from Cheshire, I'm leaving. Make damned sure you never let Cheshire out of your sight. Bring him back to the Institute any way possible. He's our key. We can't afford to lose track of him."

Alec nodded. "Right."

Philip put his hand in his pocket and pulled out the USB drive. "The dead man was clutching this. Get your tech expert on it, but be careful. It could be coded or, worse, rigged to delete the data without proper authorization."

"I could go get the woman and you could deal with Cheshire and the police," Alec said. "This could be my kid, Drake."

It also could be my child. Or brother, if this was Lansing's baby. "This is my type of work, not yours. You wanted to be in charge of the Phoenix Institute, then be in charge and leave the field work to me."

Alec frowned but did as he was asked. Relieved, Philip watched as Alec went over to Dr. Cheshire. Whatever the firestarter said, it worked, because Cheshire headed over to him.

Alec began talking to the police.

Cheshire, face white, stared at Philip. "No one should have survived going into that room."

Philip shrugged. "And no one should be dead because of your experiment, Doctor, but they are. Give me the name and address of this woman carrying your 'successful experiment', and give it to me now."

"But that's confidential."

"Not to Genet. He destroyed your lab and murdered your assistant. She's next."

"He won't hurt her. She's too important to the work."

Philip stepped closer and lowered his voice to a whisper. "He won't kill her, Cheshire. But he will take her and hide her from everyone, including you. All that effort, all those hours in your lab and you'll never know how it turns out."

Cheshire's eyes widened, proving to Philip that he'd picked the right button to push. "Where will you take her?"

"The same place where you're going with Mr. Farley. Now, name and address. For all we know, Genet could be moving on your experiment as we speak. He has a head start."

Cheshire blurted out the name and address.

"What does she look like?" Philip asked.

Cheshire pulled up a photo on his smart phone. Philip grabbed the phone and stared at the photo, committing the woman to memory.

Thick, wavy brown hair and dark eyes set in a smiling face. Yet her expression held something beneath the surface, as if she was amused by a private secret. Add that to beautifully sculptured cheekbones and a small mouth that seemed intensely kissable, and he was intrigued.

Lansing had picked a woman with some substance, if he read her face properly. Not an innocent, this woman had seen some of life. And there was something about her that felt familiar.

No, if he'd seen this woman before, he'd never have forgotten her.

Alec walked over to them, and Philip, ignoring Cheshire's protests, handed the phone to the firestarter. He left the doctor in Alec's capable hands.

Philip headed to his car, musing on how quickly Cheshire had given away Delilah Sefton's name and identity. People seemed to believe torture was the way to get information from people. That hardly ever worked. The way to get information was to get into the subject's head. Empathy worked too, but there was no time for that with the doctor. So he'd lied to make Cheshire think he could continue his experiment.

Though there were times Philip wished he had resorted to torture. Like with Cheshire, who didn't give a damn for the Sefton woman, only his work.

Philip pulled out of the parking lot without revving the engine. But he gunned it when he reached the highway. Right now, speed was more important than security.

Chapter Seven

Del spotted the classic blue Dodge Charger in the Bar & Grill parking lot through her bedroom window as she dressed for her midafternoon shift.

That was an awesome car.

Her regulars agreed. They'd gathered around the car instead of hunkering down in the bar.

She finished dressing quickly and walked to the living room window. Residing on the second floor of Bar & Grill allowed her to see who was coming or going, and she'd learned to recognize the cars that belonged to her regulars. This was definitely the first time the Charger had been here. Unless one of her regulars had just bought a new car, the driver was new to Bar & Grill as well.

Like her regulars, she wanted a closer look too.

Gathered around the Charger were Tammy's oldest son, Mike, their sometimes bartender/dishwasher; Jake, who had lived on the lake all his life and ran a local bait store in season; Jessica, the single mom who dropped by at night to relax in a familiar crowd; and several of the weekday barflies.

There was one unfamiliar face, though it was hard to get a look at him from this far away. All she could tell was that he had a thick shock of dark hair and that he was nicely built. She judged him to be about six feet tall. He wore jeans, boots and a short blue coat that showed off strong shoulders. From the possessive way he gestured at the Charger, he must be the driver.

Tall, dark and handsome man walks into a bar. She smiled. Sometimes clichés did come true. She could use a night of staring at someone like that. The distraction would be welcome, after today, just so long as he wasn't arrogant, like Genet.

She hoped the stranger had restored the car himself rather than buying it as a toy. That would mean he was a real mechanic, not somebody out for a joyride in his new toy.

She wondered how he'd happened onto Bar & Grill. People had to know her place was here to find it. Only locals came here, and he wasn't a local.

Del opened the window and leaned out. The fall breeze blew her hair in her face and she had to push it aside to see. "Are you going to all spend the night in the parking lot drooling over that car?"

Jessica laughed. "It's not just the car I'm drooling over!"

"Well, bring him inside and buy him a drink instead of staring at him in the parking lot! I need paying customers!"

The car's owner looked up at her. Del couldn't see his features clearly, but there was something familiar about the way he focused his attention on her. At first, she thought, "cop", but that wasn't it. Intense, she thought, despite the fact he was standing there calmly. She took a deep breath as her face grew warm. Oh, my. No wonder Jessica was drooling over him. He had presence, much like his car.

Yet even as he held her gaze, his stance gave away the fact he was wary. He was on alert for some reason. Perhaps a former soldier who'd not lost his battle-readiness yet?

Maybe he needed a night of drinking and some feminine comfort to relax. Well, if so, he'd come to the right place. If Jessica gave up on flirting with him, Del would take over.

"You heard her!" The stranger turned to the crowd. "Inside, everyone. Drinks on me!"

Jessica, laughing, led everyone inside. Del closed the window, glad of something new tonight. It would get the encounter with Genet out of her head. She thought once she arrived home, she'd be less paranoid. Instead, thinking back on what happened, she was more concerned. Those two men had been genuinely ticked off that she'd changed her mind.

It wasn't paranoia. She knew that now. Her instincts were usually good, and she needed to listen to them. Genet was all wrong. Tomorrow, she was calling the clinic to let them know she didn't approve of their recommendation.

She pulled her hair back into a ponytail, thought about fiddling with her clothing or make-up to wow the stranger and shook her head. It wasn't like she expected to catch him, and it would probably be good if she didn't. Her life was complicated enough right now.

Del walked down the narrow steps to the bar, holding tight to the handrail. Pregnancy, she found, affected her balance. These rickety stairs had to be repaired before the baby was born. She should put that item at the top of a new to-do list.

Tammy would probably love to throw a baby shower. Maybe she should let the older woman do it. She could use all the help anyone would give her.

Loud voices and laughter from the bar were audible before she even entered the room. The car's owner had lived up to his promise of buying a round.

She turned the corner into the bar and stopped to take in the scene. Tammy was at the bar, pouring Irish whiskey for the barflies. That would cost the stranger. Jessica nursed a margarita, and a pint of the local microbrew they had on tap sat in front of Jake.

A tough night on the stranger's wallet, but a good night for the bar.

The stranger sat at the corner of the bar, away from Jessica. Perhaps he wasn't in a flirting mood. He'd chosen Del's favorite seat. From that corner, you could see the entire front room plus the open windows that led to the bar's deck. During the hot summer months, she opened up the deck for service, but she'd closed it down to customers early last week, before she became too pregnant and tired for such a big project.

It wasn't lost on Del that the stranger had picked the one seat in the bar where he could watch all the entrances and exits. That was also one of the reasons she liked it.

He had to be a soldier of some sort.

The stranger watched the room. No beer or alcohol for him. He was sipping a Coke.

She slipped behind the bar, drew a draft and set it in front of him. "Drink all you like. If you get drunk, I'll be happy to drive the Charger home for you."

He smiled and saluted her with his Coke. "I'll keep that in mind."

Oh, nice eyes, she decided. Nice smile too. She put her hand out. "Del Sefton."

He shook it, quickly and firmly. No flirting there. Too bad. "Philip Drake."

He drew his hand back, exposing rips in his jacket sleeve. "Those stains look like dried blood," she said. "What happened to you?"

"The car happened." He grimaced. "Radiator overheated and I was too eager to fix it."

"No permanent damage, I hope?"

He smiled. "Never. But I decided I needed a drink to wash away the stink of the close call."

Now that she was close, Del decided Drake's face matched the excellent body. His face was solid and distinctive, with high cheekbones that hinted at Native American ancestry. His deep, dark eyes confirmed that impression. He looked like he was in his mid-twenties but he spoke and moved with more self-assurance than that. She bet he was older than he looked.

And damned if he somehow didn't look familiar too. Something about his face nagged at her.

Tammy called for help.

"Be right back."

"I hope so," Drake said.

Del had to serve several drinks while Tammy went back to the kitchen to whip up some sandwiches. Jessica scowled at her and glanced in Drake's direction, obviously put out by being shunted aside.

"Whoa, Del, should you be behind the bar in your condition?" Jake asked.

"I'm pregnant, not injured." Jake had noticed the baby bump a few days ago. She didn't have the heart to lie to him and besides, others had guessed. She thought his worry was sweet but wished he'd kept it to himself. By mentioning it tonight, he'd opened up yet another round of speculation about the kid's father.

She supposed it didn't matter anymore, now that she planned to keep the kid. Tammy would be thrilled.

"Going to give us a hint as to the dad tonight?" Jessica asked.

"George Clooney showed up at my door one night and I treated him to a fabulous time."

"That's dumb," Mike said. "Everyone knows Clooney's gay. He keeps picking up these young, unknown women as beards and then dumps them after a while."

That drew indignation from Jessica and sent them off on movie stars who might or might not be gay. Mike moved over to be closer to Jessica. Mike was just barely eighteen. He had a crush on Jessica, who was too old for him at twenty-six, but that didn't seem to bother Mike.

At least they wouldn't be talking about her baby's father anymore.

Del walked back to Drake.

He'd drunk the beer.

Offering accepted, she thought. "I'm getting closer to driving that Charger."

"I need more than one beer to get drunk."

She poured another and set it in front of him. He drank down a few swallows and set the glass down very deliberately.

"Could you handle the stick shift?" he asked.

"I can handle whatever stick shift you have." It was stupid that the flirting made her feel good, but it did. And Drake seemed willing to go along with a little harmless teasing. She gave him points for not mentioning her pregnancy.

She did wonder if she was playing with fire. She was sure Drake wasn't harmless in the least.

He drank more beer. "I see."

"I grew up driving stick shifts. I miss them." She put her elbow on the bar and braced her chin on her hand, putting them at eye level. "And you?"

"The same. I prefer them."

She'd no idea how to parse the hidden meaning in that. Was he gay? Maybe he meant it exactly as he'd said. He liked cars with a manual clutch. Besides, it didn't matter if he was gay. She didn't intend to go beyond flirting.

She straightened. "So no one to go out driving with, Mr. Drake?"

"Call me Philip. And I usually go on drives by myself. I could be talked into making an exception, however."

"I'll keep that in mind." He wasn't quite staring at her, but she got the feeling he had memorized every single laugh line and freckle on her face. Don't blush, she ordered herself. *You're not a teenager.*

"I understand congratulations are in order," he said.

"Thanks." Damn, he'd brought up the baby. And this had been going so well. "What made you pull in our driveway, Philip? Plenty of bars in this area and we're not exactly on the beaten path."

He paused, as if deciding what to say. The feeling that he was familiar, that she'd met him before nagged at her again.

"I was out this way and, as I said, once I tested the repairs to the car, I needed a drink. I like trying new things." He leaned forward. "Your bar turned out to be a pleasant surprise. Great beer and equally great company."

"We aim to please here at Bar & Grill."

Jessica slid into the bar stool next to them. "So, Philip, do you like to dance?"

Without missing a beat, he said, "Not without music."

Jessica slapped a dollar bill on the bar. "Del, got change for the jukebox?"

Del sighed. She wasn't quite jealous but... "Sure, I'll get change but I thought you didn't like the songs on the jukebox. You were insulting them last week for being way out of date."

"There are a few good ones on there."

Del slipped the bill into the cash register and drew out four quarters. "Nothing too loud, all right? Last time you had Jake's ears bleeding."

"It'll liven this place up." Jessica glanced at Drake before sauntering over to the jukebox.

"I should've said that I don't dance, shouldn't I?" Drake asked.

Del shrugged and leaned on the bar. "She's not a bad dancer."

"She's not the partner I was hoping for." To emphasize his words, he closed his hand over hers.

"Somebody's gotta serve the drinks." She cleared her throat and straightened. Flirting was one thing, but there was something intense about Drake that made her uneasy.

Jon Bon Jovi's *Living on a Prayer* began to reverberate through the bar. Del went to refill Jake's drink. Jessica had made a decent choice this time. And her mood seemed infectious. Despite Drake's protests, he seemed to be enjoying himself on the dance floor. Possibly not as much as Del was enjoying watching him shake his booty in those jeans, however, even with Jessica draping herself around him. No business of hers, really. Drake was probably closer to Jessica's age than hers. Men in their twenties were not big on women over thirty. Let them have their fun.

She wasn't the only one staring at the pair. Mike's gaze was fixed on Jessica. He certainly was jealous. Tammy should talk to her son about this. That powerful a crush could not be healthy. When the song was done, Mike put in more quarters for another song, claiming Jessica for this dance.

Del wondered if Drake would protest, but he seemed happy enough to fade back. She turned to ring up the sandwich

Tammy had made for Jake. When she turned back, Drake was across the bar from her.

He said something, but the new song—something by the Ramones—made it too loud inside to hear very well. Drake shook his head, annoyed, and pointed at the deck. He took her hand.

She snatched it back. "Got a bar to run."

"It's important. Please." He grinned. "C'mon. I'll let you drive the Charger after."

"Okay." The car was excellent incentive and the grin almost as much. Dammit all, she knew that expression. She knew Drake or had known someone who looked a lot like him. She wished she could place him. If she heard him talk more, it might just click.

She unlocked the door to the deck and stepped outside. Drake shut the door behind them. She walked over to the railing and closed her eyes. Water lapped against the wood. Birds chirped overhead. Home, she thought.

She loved that old jukebox but it wasn't what she needed tonight.

Drake stood next to her. "You dance well," she told him.

"It's not that hard to learn. Do you dance?"

"Not much lately," she admitted. "So what did you want to talk to me about?"

Before she could protest, he had an arm around her waist and his hand closed over hers. "Dance with me, Del."

He led her in an old-fashioned box step. His moves were fluid and easy. And his body was rock solid.

Her dancing wasn't quite as fluid. Too much on her mind. "What do you really want?"

"To keep you safe."

"That's not the answer I was expecting." Such a strange comment. She'd expected something sexual, the way they had been flirting.

He hummed bars to a song. Del recognized *It Had To Be You.* Her parents hadn't liked any modern music, but they had allowed her to listen to some of the classics. Why a young guy like Drake knew the tune, she had no idea.

"Are you going to tell me what's so important that you lured me out here to talk?"

"As you may have noticed from the car, I like classic things."

"I'm older than you."

"Are you sure?"

He hummed the melody again. This time, she joined him, hearing the rest of the words in her head. They fell into step together.

It felt good, moving with him, an unexpected moment of fun in the midst of all her upheaval. Joy and arousal, being so close to this man. Her face grew warm, and she wondered if the old adage that pregnant women get horny could be true.

She could almost imagine she was having a romantic moment with an attractive man and at the beginnings of a relationship. A dream, a perfect dream.

But she had a bar to run, she was pregnant, he was a stranger, and enough was enough. Magic moments didn't happen. At least, they didn't happen to her.

"You're stalling," she said. "What's so important?"

"I'm not stalling. I'm enjoying myself. And it's important that this seem normal to everyone."

"Just for your information, it's not normal for me to dance with a customer while working."

"Then I'm honored. I don't usually dance while working either but..." He sighed and stopped, holding her at arm's length. "Your pregnancy has put you in serious danger. I'm here to help."

"What? Who are you?"

"I'm investigating some circumstances that affect you."

Cop, she thought. Her first guess had been right. "That's a mealy-mouthed sentence if I ever heard one. Get to the point."

He held out his hand. "Come with me if you want to live?"

With his head tilted to the side and his half-smile, she was tempted to laugh, despite her annoyance. "My life is odd at times but not weird enough to include robots from the future after my unborn baby."

"Sarah Conner was also a waitress."

"In a family restaurant. This is a bar and I'm a cynical bartender fast losing patience. Just what is going on?"

Drake stepped closer again. He glanced through the glass doors to the bar. Jessica and Mike had now gotten all the regulars up on their feet. They were all dancing or doing some approximation of it. Del recognized the song as Prince's *1999*.

"The situation is complicated. It'll take time explain, and I'd rather do it somewhere else. Somewhere less in the open. We need to leave here."

"You say it's complicated, that you came looking for me, want me to leave and won't tell me why. Fat chance that I'm going anywhere."

"You don't trust me. I don't blame you." Drake paused again as if he was going to say something else and then stopped. "I'm here to help. And to tell you why you're pregnant."

"If you're here for that, you know I'm pregnant because some asshole raped me. Are you FBI? A cop?"

"No, though I used to work for the CIA."

"That makes me feel *so* much better." She took several steps back toward the glass doors. She didn't want to be trapped out here with him. "So was the Charger some ploy to get everyone, including me, to like you, so you could come in here and ask questions?" The flirting too? Dammit, she had liked him. A lot. It had felt good to be in his arms. She had a good radar for liars. She usually didn't make mistakes like this.

"No, I'm usually much more subtle and effective when I'm working. I didn't want deception with you. You've been deceived enough." He sighed. "I'm doing this badly. The car's mine. I rebuilt it, I like driving it and that's all there is to that. It's not a ruse."

"And the flirting?"

"I wasn't flirting. I meant everything."

"And the dance?"

He looked out at the lake. "I wanted to dance with you. I couldn't resist."

"I have to admit, as lines go, that's a good one."

He put himself between her and the glass doors. "Ideally, I need to get you somewhere safe right now. I'll settle for going somewhere we can talk privately but public enough so that *you* feel safe."

"I'm in one of those places right now. So talk."

"There are more listeners here than you know. How about meeting me at the Victoria Diner on Route 10 instead?"

More listeners than she knew? Cryptic didn't begin to describe this guy. "When did you have in mind?"

"Now."

"I'm working."

"Del, it's very important."

"Using my first name won't work to convince me." That was an old con's trick, gaining familiarity by using the name of the mark.

He ran his hand through his hair. Around them, she heard the chatter inside the bar. They were probably talking about why she was out on the deck with Drake. He moved out of her way, as if showing he meant her no harm.

"I admit, I'm lousy at being this direct. But you must want to know more about how your child was conceived. And I *know* you want to keep the child safe."

"I can't change the past. The kid's mine now, end of story. I don't need your help to protect what's mine."

"Yes, you do." He held up his burned sleeve. "I didn't get this from the car, I got it from an incident in which someone died. The people who caused this will be here soon and after you. The sooner you know the full story, the safer you are. All I want is one hour at the diner. Hear me out."

The path was clear to the door. She walked back inside, Drake on her heels.

She turned around. "Let me think about it, okay?"

"Do you have any experience with someone named Edward Genet?"

She froze. *"Who the hell are you?"*

"I'm here to help. And if you tell me that you trust Genet more than you trust me, I'll walk out of here right now."

"You're a hell of a gambler, Philip Drake." She went behind the bar and wiped it down, thinking. He said nothing more. Tammy called her over for help and Del fixed a cocktail for Jessica, who now had her arm around Mike. While she was shaking up the White Russian, Del glanced over at Drake. He couldn't have sat more still if he were a statue.

In less than thirty minutes, he'd gone from charm to flirting to soldier mode. Yet he'd bet right. She trusted him more than she trusted Genet.

Del set the drink in front of Jessica.

"He asking you out?" Jessica said.

"Something like that."

"Maybe I never had a chance?" Jessica lowered her voice and leaned over the bar. Her blonde bangs fell in her face. "Oooh...you know him, right? Is he the kid's father?"

Del shook her head and smiled. "You people need to get a life."

"We have one. It's in this bar." Jessica smiled back.

Del walked back over to Drake, still indecisive. She didn't believe him, not fully. But he knew about Genet and that meant he knew something. She wanted to hear it.

"Did you decide?" Drake asked.

"Do you plan to drive me over in your car?"

"Only if you want me to. I thought you'd rather follow me." He spread his hands apart. "It's urgent that you hear what I have to say."

"For all I know, you caused my problems a few months back. You could be my attacker."

"No." He frowned. "But it's possible you're in this mess because of me."

"You're not doing a good job of making me trust you."

"I know, but someone's already died today. I'm in a hurry," Drake said, voice low. He'd changed from merely annoying to dangerous in a heartbeat.

"Someone died today because of *my* pregnancy?"

"Exactly."

She took a step away from him and almost backed into the fridge behind her.

"Wrong thing to say," he muttered. "I'm still screwing this up. Sorry. Think, Del. Besides Genet, who you've obviously met, have you had anything else unusual happen since you became pregnant? Anything that was out of the ordinary, weird, or alarmed you?"

"You showing up in my bar."

But that wasn't completely true. Before Drake had arrived, there had been the accident with the minivan when her purse had been stolen. Hell, start with the way she'd gotten pregnant. She didn't remember who'd grabbed her or drugged her or if she'd spent the night in the bar on the floor or somewhere else.

"If you tell me nothing strange or odd has happened, that there's no real mystery behind the child's conception besides that you want to keep it private, I will leave right now and not bother you again," Drake said.

She couldn't. She wasn't that good a liar. That was two bets he'd won. "You must win a lot at poker, Drake."

"I can tell something has scared you. Besides me, I mean."

"I could be paranoid."

"It's not paranoia if someone really is out to get you."

She smiled. "You said you're investigating the circumstances of my pregnancy."

He nodded. "Those responsible for what happened to you want to come back and finish the work. I'm here to prevent that from happening."

She frowned. "And you really can't tell me about all this here?"

He shook his head. "Too many listeners, as I said. I'm only asking for an hour, in a public place. What's the worst that could happen?"

"I can imagine all sorts of things."

He could have an ambush set up. He could try to drug her food or her drink. He could—

Damn, she *was* paranoid.

She also wanted answers. She just hadn't had a way to find them until now. Maybe Philip Drake was her rapist. If so, if he was toying with her to make her feel vulnerable, he had another thing coming.

There was always the shotgun in her trunk.

"All right. You leave, and I'll follow you in fifteen minutes."

"No, follow me right away. You shouldn't be driving around unprotected."

She rolled her eyes. That sounded like something her father would have said when he was alive. She had a feeling she had just stepped into a mess like the ones he used to create.

"Okay," she said.

Chapter Eight

Del let Tammy know she was going out for an early dinner. Tammy flat-out snickered.

"I saw you out on the deck with Dodge Charger man," Tammy said. "You're having dinner with him, right?"

Del shrugged. "He said he might let me drive the car. And what's the worst that can happen? I get pregnant?"

"You don't know him," Tammy said.

"Which is why I'm driving over to the diner myself."

"Smart. Well, go have fun. I'll cover. It's not like you'll be able to do this after the baby is born."

Del stuck out her tongue at Tammy and headed to the parking lot. Drake was leaning against his car, arms crossed over his chest, wearing his sunglasses, waiting for her.

Yum. He matched the car perfectly. If only this was a real date. It had felt good, natural, to dance with him. He'd even picked one of her favorite songs. Stupid illusion. She could have dismissed his whole crazy story if he hadn't known about Genet and hadn't hit a nerve by asking her if she even knew how the kid had been conceived.

His story might be bullshit, but he knew *something.* Too many odd things had happened in the last few months for her to believe they were coincidences.

She started her car and pulled out of the lot. Drake followed close behind. She climbed the packed dirt driveway up to the intersection with Lake Road, darting glances at her rearview mirror. Drake stayed about two car lengths behind.

As she turned right onto Lake Road, a van cut in front of her. She slammed on the brakes, her tires squealed, and she barely missed T-boning it.

Fucking idiot! Her heart was beating so fast she could hear pounding in her ears. If not for her seatbelt, she'd have been thrown against the steering wheel.

She took a deep breath and looked closer at the van. Wait, it was the same style as the one that had caused the accident at the Ledgewood Circle. Though this van was white and the other one had been blue.

She opened up her glove box, groping for her hammer, then remembered she hadn't replaced it yet.

A man wearing a watch cap and dark clothes slipped out of the passenger door and pointed a gun at her. "Get out of the car! Now!"

She practically fell out of the car, her keys clutched in her hand. She could press the panic button. That might draw attention.

"Don't make a noise, don't say a fucking word," the gunman said.

Scratch that.

A hand snaked around from behind her and a dirty, smelly palm covered her mouth. Another guy must have circled around while she was staring at the gunman. She tried to scream, but it was muffled by the hand. She kicked for the man's instep but didn't connect. The gunman ran forward, grabbed her keys from her fingers and tossed them aside. The one who had her captive from behind started to drag her to the van. She tried to dig in her heels, but all they did on the blacktop was slide.

"Inside, fast," the first attacker said, lowering the gun.

Screw you.

She reached up, grabbed the thumb of the hand around her neck and yanked it backward, hard. Her captor yelped and loosened his grip enough for her to sidestep out of his hold. She screamed, long and loud, hoping to attract attention.

The first man aimed his gun at her again.

She heard a popping sound, saw a red mark appear on the gunman's chest, and the gunman crumpled to the road.

She turned and saw Drake tackling the second man, knocking her would-be kidnapper onto the ground. Drake bashed the man's head into the pavement.

"Run!" Drake yelled. "Keys are still in my car! Get the hell out of here."

Two more men were scrambling out from the van.

Del did what Drake asked. She turned around and ran like hell for the Charger. She saw the front bumper poking out at the entrance from the driveway to Lake Road.

The engine was idling. Drake had left it running.

She slid inside, released the emergency brake, pushed down on the clutch and the brake and shifted into first gear. Dad had had a lot of faults but he'd made sure she could drive a stick.

She let off on the brake and pushed down on the accelerator while letting go of the clutch. The Charger nearly flew onto the road.

She caught a glimpse of Drake, locked in a fight with two men. His face was covered with blood. She turned and hit reverse, tires squealing, back to him. The edge of the back bumper caught one attacker.

"Get in!"

Drake kicked the knees of the man holding him, breaking them apart. He sprinted to the passenger side of the Charger and tumbled into passenger seat. She hit the gas again.

In the rearview mirror, she saw her attackers scramble into the van. They were going to chase her. Oh, yeah? *Let's see what you got.*

She shifted up to fourth gear, praying no one was trying to pull onto Lake Road or walking their dog or jogging or doing *anything* in the road. The engine roared. The speedometer quickly climbed to eighty.

"What the hell kind of engine is this?"

"A 426 Hemi," Drake answered, buckling in.

The way was clear, no traffic. She pressed down harder on the gas. She could still see the van behind her. They had a big engine too, but that van couldn't be as good as the Charger around these turns. And she knew the roads around here a hell of a lot better than they did. She hoped.

Her hands dripped with sweat. She reminded herself to keep them on the wheel and not wipe them off on her pants. Her luck held as the light at the bottom of the hill was green and she didn't have to slow down.

The Charger's speedometer hit ninety. She downshifted as they roared up a hill. There was a wicked curve coming up. She knew it was there. She hoped to hell the van driver didn't.

Drake mumbled something that sounded like a prayer. She could use one of those. She could use some cops too. Where the hell were the authorities when you really needed them?

The Charger flew faster up the road, despite being in lower gear. *I love you, car.* The van became a smaller speck in the rearview mirror.

Hah. No way would they catch her, not in this.

"Excellent driving."

With that dry tone, she couldn't tell if Drake was insulting or complimenting her. "Screw you. Who are those guys?"

"At a guess, they work for Genet."

She hit the top of the hill. The van was still behind them. Persistent bastards. She started to turn right before she even saw the curve. The Charger fishtailed. The tires burned rubber. But they negotiated the turn.

"Nice handling."

"Screw you," she said again.

She gunned the Charger, only to be confronted with a sharp curve to the left. She turned the steering wheel with one hand, shifted with the left, and the Charger turned neatly this time.

Drake gripped the dashboard tight, but he seemed to be grinning. Or grimacing. Hard to tell given the blood streaming down his face.

The Charger straightened, and she sped up again. "I love this car."

Drake grunted. She glanced behind, just in time to see the van spin out into the dirt and hit a stump on the side of the road. She grinned.

The road twisted, and she lost sight of them, which meant they couldn't see her either. She turned right at the third fork in the road, drove up another hill, past a new housing development onto a dirt road, and navigated a narrow bridge that took her to one of the many fingers of Lake Hopatcong.

She slowed, downshifting, and pulled into a space off the side of the road, hiding the car completely behind a grove of trees. She turned the engine off and let her head rest on the steering wheel.

She couldn't tell if she was excited or terrified. She thought of the blood that spurted from the chest of the man Drake had shot. Dead. She'd just seen somebody die.

Like she had when she was a child.

Her fingers started shaking.

Drake got out of the car, gun drawn, looking behind them.

"We're hidden here." She raised her head from the steering wheel.

"Maybe." He holstered the gun at his waist and walked to the back. "Open the trunk."

You'd never know he just killed somebody. He acted as if this stuff happened every day. She fumbled around with her hand until she found the trunk release and pulled. The trunk popped open. Her legs felt like jelly. Her arms weren't much better.

But she wiped the sweat off her hands and got out of the car.

Drake was leaning over the trunk.

"Who the hell were those guys?" she asked.

"At a guess, Genet's goons, as I said."

Drake removed a sawed-off shotgun from the trunk.

So she wasn't the only one who carried weapons in her trunk. But she hadn't killed anyone with hers.

He cocked his head to the side. Listening.

"I think you're right. You lost them," he said.

"So why did you pull out the shotgun?"

"Just in case." He lowered the trunk lid but didn't close it. "The Charger left tracks in the dirt. They could find us. And there could be more of them. Are you armed?"

"No." He has to have been a soldier, she thought. He also had to be someone who'd killed before or he wouldn't be this calm after doing so. The sexiest man to walk into her bar in a long time, and he was certifiable too. Fuck.

He reached down to his ankle, pushed up his jeans and pulled a handgun from a hidden holster. "Take this."

"Am I going to have to kill someone too?"

His face lost all expression. "I don't know. But they will be after you again."

"Why didn't they just shoot me?"

"They want you alive and well. More specifically, they want your baby alive and well. They're the same thing right now. If you want to protect yourself, take the gun."

She held out her palm flat. The gun fit perfectly in there. The last thing she wanted.

"Don't you feel anything about killing that man?" she asked.

"Relief that he didn't kill me or hurt you."

Ducks quacked on the lake. Such a normal sound. The ducks didn't know it was an abnormal day where people were shot and killed in front of her.

Drake opened his coat, revealing the handgun he'd used earlier.

"Just how many guns do you have, Drake?"

"Enough." He focused on her. "Are you all right?"

"I should ask you that. That's blood on your face."

He shrugged and wiped most of it off with his sleeve. "It's nothing."

"Nothing?"

That struck her as the strangest thing he'd said so far.

Here she was, standing on a hidden fishing spot on Lake Hopatcong with a handsome stranger who carried guns in his trunk, killed a man and didn't seem concerned about it and didn't care about blood all over his face. And they were on the run from guys who wanted to kidnap her. Or something.

"Fuck nothing," she said. "Who the hell are you and what the hell is going on?"

"I told you, you're in danger because of your baby. My apologies for that ambush back there. I should've scouted ahead." He wiped the remainder of the blood off his face. Oddly, she couldn't see the cut responsible for all that blood. Maybe it was covered by his hair.

"You saved my life," she said.

"You returned the favor, coming back for me. I didn't expect that. And you lost the van. When you said you could drive a stick, you meant it."

Drake had such an odd expression on his face. Almost amused. Definitely admiring. The same expression as when he'd taken her into his arms for their dance. The man switched from dangerous to charming to infuriating without any effort.

"Do you think something is funny about all this?"

He shook his head. "No. But I imagine those who want your baby realize now they underestimated you. That's a comforting thought."

"To you, maybe." She blinked, then kept her eyes closed for a few seconds. When she opened them, Drake was still there. Nope, she wasn't dreaming. "Stop avoiding the subject and start telling me what's going on."

"You won't believe me if I give you the truth flat-out. Let's just say someone's badly used you and they want to keep doing that."

"Let's not say that. Let's talk about what's really going on. You said they wanted my baby." She stuffed the car keys in her pocket. Likely, he could take them from her. He was a killer.

Though he had given her a weapon too. She felt the weight of it in her palm. She set it down on the hood of the car and absently rubbed her neck where the driver had grabbed her. Okay, she trusted Drake a little more than those guys. He'd been willing to take a beating or worse to cover her escape.

He'd also trusted her to drive his car.

"We need to get going," he said.

"Like hell we do." She flung the keys into the water below. "Looks like we're here for a while. So talk."

He stared at the circles made in the water by the keys for a few seconds. "Huh. Remind me not to underestimate you."

"Are you crazy?"

"Yes." He leaned against the hood, staring through the woods, watching the approach to their parking spot. He held the shotgun loosely in his hand. "I'm not the only one hiding secrets. You still haven't told me how you became pregnant."

"You seemed to have worked that out all by yourself."

He shrugged. "I'd rather hear it from you, Ms. Sefton. For all I know, you're somehow in on this."

"That's me, a criminal mastermind. And, hey, call me Del. We just got shot at together. Ms. Sefton seems stupidly formal."

He snorted. "You have the smarts and the physical courage for a criminal mastermind, you know that?" He sighed. "You're right, you deserve the full story."

"Which is?"

"That you were picked to be the mother of a genetically engineered baby. The scientists who developed the gene-gineered sperm that resulted in your pregnancy kidnapped you with the help of hired thugs, artificially inseminated you and then let you go."

She laughed. "Funny guy. Okay what's the real story? The rapist who left me pregnant is a mobster or something and now he wants the kid?"

"I wish I'd thought of that as a cover story, but no."

"Genetic engineering? Altered sperm? Artificial insemination? That cannot be what's going on."

"Afraid so. It's your fault. You wanted the truth. But give me a few minutes. I can come up with a good, logical lie instead."

She shook her head. "Not only is your story crazy, but it makes no sense. Why pick me as the mother? And, say if these crazy people exist and want the baby, why pick me and then *let me go*?"

"I don't know."

"Bullshit."

"I've only been on the job since this morning. Give me time to find definitive answers."

That almost pulled a smile from her. What a screwed-up sense of humor Drake had.

"But how could these mystery scientists know I wanted to be pregnant? For all they knew, I could want an abortion. I almost had one, you know. I was raped. I had every right to have an abortion."

"I agree. What happened to change your mind?"

She leaned back against the Charger's hood, the bottom dropping out of her stomach. "The van. A van like the one chasing us caused an accident, then someone from that van jumped out and stole my purse and my medical claim info. I had to reschedule the abortion."

"Then you canceled it."

"Obviously."

"Was it the same van as today?" Drake asked quietly.

"Different color, same model," she whispered.

"And when did you meet Genet?"

"Earlier today. I went to a law firm specializing in adoptions. He's supposedly representing several couples who want to adopt my baby."

"Did you agree to go forward with the adoption?"

"I told them I'd think about it. I didn't like Genet."

"You have excellent instincts. That must have made him angry."

"It did. I've no idea why, since they're supposedly go-betweens. They didn't have a personal investment."

"The adoption lawyer identity was a front. They have a personal interest in your baby. They want it for themselves."

"Fuck that."

"I agree," he said again.

She stared out over the lake. How did one absorb or comprehend this kind of surreal thing? She'd just wrapped her mind around being raped and having a baby. She didn't need mad scientists with thugs. Or to be talking to someone who killed a man and shrugged it off.

"You still sound crazy."

"But you believe me."

"I don't know about that part. But I'm not afraid of you."

"That's encouraging. Why not?"

She stared at him. "You saved my life." She smiled. "And you have a cool car."

"You trust me because of the *car*?"

"And you dance well."

"You like me because of the dancing and the car?"

"What can I say, I'm shallow."

He smiled at her. Not like earlier, when he was darkly amused. This was genuine approval. And, again, familiar. Very familiar. Maybe he was someone she'd met as a kid? They had moved a lot while she was growing up.

"I'll play along. So assuming I've been implanted with some sort of super sperm, why? What's so special about my baby?"

"It'll be far easier to show you. I want to take you to a safe place. It's only about thirty-five minutes from here."

"What's there that will convince me?"

"Not something. Someone. He can show you why the DNA of the sperm that helped create your baby was genetically altered and how your child could be special, but in a good way. But you have to see it to believe it."

She looked down at the gun she'd put on the hood. "It's loaded?"

"Yes. You can keep it for as long as you want."

He'd saved her life or, at least, from a kidnapping. She owed him hearing him out. Maybe.

She sighed. "You were right in the bar when you confronted me about the father of the baby. I don't remember the night I became pregnant. I remember closing Bar & Grill by myself and then waking up groggy on the floor the next morning. Tammy found me. She told me I needed to go to the ER. I didn't. I should have. If they'd run a rape kit, they would have found out I was pregnant and I'd have taken a morning-after pill. Instead, I took a home test about a month later when I missed my period."

"I'm sorry. That's a horrible way to become a parent."

"It didn't sink in at first."

His gaze kept darting toward the road, still on alert for their pursuers. "Why didn't you report your assault to the police?"

"The whole night's a complete blank. Bar owner passes out in her place, wakes up pregnant. Sounds like someone got drunk and did something they shouldn't have. Not much of a story for the cops."

"You weren't drunk."

"Thanks for the vote of confidence. No, I wasn't drunk. I rarely drink."

"What made you decide to keep the child?"

"That wasn't the plan, like I said."

"What changed your mind?" He asked in the same polite tone that she'd used.

"Circumstance, though maybe it wasn't circumstance after all." She gave the full details of the accident at the Ledgewood Circle, including rescuing the family in the minivan, how her purse had been stolen and how the van had driven off and disappeared.

"Nothing since then?"

"Not until I met with Genet and turned him down."

"And less than half a day later, he tries to grab you." Philip shook his head. "Right after he'd blown up Orion Systems too."

"What? Blown up *what?*"

"Sorry, I forgot you didn't know."

He explained about the lab he said had gene-gineered the sperm that had been used in her artificial insemination, how he'd seen Genet leaving as he arrived, and how a bomb had destroyed the facility just this morning.

"That part of the story seems made up too."

"You can Google it. You'll find something on the fire this morning."

"It doesn't mean it happened the way you said it did."

He shrugged. "Feel free to check."

She didn't like the sound of that. It meant he thought she'd find exactly what he said.

"In my bar, you told me someone had already died today. You meant the lab assistant."

Drake nodded. "It seems like Genet is getting rid of all the evidence of this experiment. But I convinced the doctor who'd performed your procedure to give me your name and address and came straight here. I thought Genet might make a move today."

He stared at her, as if the attack proved his whole story.

"How did Genet know I was considering abortion or adoption? How did he manage to set up our meeting?"

"They were watching you from the beginning. You said they dropped you back at the bar that first night. It's certain they also left behind surveillance devices."

"My home is bugged?" She stomped her feet. "Fuck. That's why you didn't want to talk at Bar & Grill?"

"Yes."

"But someone at the clinic recommended Genet as an attorney for adoptions. That was legit."

"He probably paid them off."

"Shit." She frowned. "This doesn't get any less crazy."

"I know I'm bad at telling the truth, Del. And because this particular truth is more unbelievable than a good lie, I'm even worse at it. I thought about creating a cover story to get you to safety. But you've been used and hurt enough."

"You believe this."

"Don't you?"

"I believe that guy's gun was real. I believe the blood on your face was real. I believe the dead man is real. I believe my baby is real. And I believe my rape happened. The rest? I'm reserving judgment."

Only if what Drake was saying was true, she hadn't been traditionally raped. In a way, this was worse. She put her hand over her stomach.

The sunlight was suddenly too bright. She squinted, losing focus, and braced her hands on her knees for balance.

"Is this my baby at all, or some experiment? What the hell did these scientists do to the sperm?"

"I don't—" He looked away. "I don't have an answer for you."

"I...I'm carrying...a...?" She turned around and leaned on the car's hood, trying to breathe normally.

"You are carrying a child." He patted her back, as if lost as to what else to do. "*Your* child. And I'm going to make certain no one ever takes it from you."

"Not 'it'. Him."

"Your baby is a boy?"

She nodded. "I saw his fingers and toes," she whispered. "I saw his head. I heard my son's heartbeat." He was her son now, however he had gotten inside her.

She slid to the ground and put her hands to her knees. The scent of burnt rubber from the tires still lingered. Drake sat down next to her.

"This is sick. The whole story is sick, sick."

He nodded.

"I don't care how I ended up with this kid. He's mine."

It had taken her a while to come around to this decision, but she had, and she'd be damned if she'd let go of her son. "I will destroy whoever wants to take my son from me."

"That's my job," Drake said.

She stood and studied the midnight-blue paint on the Charger. Smooth, no drips that she could see. A beautiful job. It also handled perfectly. She wondered if Drake's competence extended to protecting. He'd done all right so far.

"So who was the sperm donor? Does he know about this? And why was his DNA so valuable?" she asked. "What's the point of the genetic engineering thingee?"

"I don't know yet. But if you come with me as I asked, you will get answers." He stood. "It's time to get moving. They'll eventually narrow the search down to this area."

He reached under the front passenger wheel well and pulled out a small box. He flicked it open to reveal a key.

"You had a spare key all this time."

"I like to be prepared."

And he'd answered her questions instead of overpowering her. Drake had a lot of patience for a crazy person.

She had carved out a nice, quiet life. She had friends, she had a routine, she had peace. Until the morning she'd woken up on her barroom floor, pregnant. She had sensed that morning that her life was irrevocably changed.

Now she knew it was.

Above her, the tree fluttered in the wind. Somewhere far away, a hawk flew overhead, screaming. Dragonflies buzzed in the swampy wetland under the bridge. Numb, she stared at her hands, opening and closing them into fists, over and over. Her son could do that already, open and close his hands.

Drake looked up in the sky, at the hawk. "You have to come with me now."

"You mean go with you to hide."

"Genet and his people are crazier than I am, which puts them in a class by themselves and makes them unpredictable. The only solution is to make sure you're protected while I go take them out."

"You sound like a complete loon, Drake."

"If I'm going to be a bird, make it a hawk." Above, the hawk cried again. He looked up, shading the light out with his hand. "Beautiful, isn't he?"

"Could be a 'she'. Protecting her own. Hunting for those who would bother her nest."

"Making her very dangerous." He nodded. "Point made. Let's go."

The phone in her coat pocket rang. She'd forgotten it was there.

She pulled it out. "It's Tammy," she said to Drake.

She answered the call and found herself talking to a nearly hysterical woman. Tammy had sent her son home soon after Del left. Mike had found her Ford Focus on the road, the driver's side door open. He'd freaked and run back down the road to tell his mother.

"I'm okay, Tammy. Yes, I'll be right there. Yeah, it was bad but I'm okay, the baby's okay. Hey, you didn't happen to see anyone or anything around my car? No? Never mind. I. Will. Be. Right. There."

After she hung up, she glared at Drake. "What happened to the dead man?"

"They probably scooped up his body before chasing you. No sense leaving evidence in the middle of the road."

"There's got to be blood on the road."

"No one will notice. The surface is dark."

She sighed. "I guess you're right."

"You shouldn't go back to the bar. They'll pick up your trail there again."

"I'm not just going to run off." Disappear without a trace, then start over. She'd done that five or six times before her parents were murdered. "I'm going home and talking to Tammy."

He nodded. "Okay."

"You're not going to argue any longer?"

"They tried to grab you when they thought you were alone. I doubt they'll come after you at the Bar & Grill. Your visit might give them time to regroup and come after you again when we leave, since they'll know where you're starting from, but I'm not going to force you to come with me." He grinned. "I don't do that anymore."

"Drake, you're about as reassuring as a drunk driving home after closing."

He grinned again. She shook her head.

He opened the passenger door for her. "We should take a different route back to avoid crossing the van's path. You'll have to give me directions."

"What the hell will I tell Tammy when I get there? They'll never believe this insane story. *I* don't believe this insane story."

"You'll think of something." He started the Charger. "While you're deciding whether to trust me or not, please remember I let you drive my car."

She smiled.

Chapter Nine

Philip followed Del's directions but otherwise said nothing. Why speak when he kept putting his foot in his mouth? He should've made up a believable story instead of telling her the truth. The mobster idea she had thrown at him was a good one. Too bad he hadn't thought of it.

He even had a fake but authentic-looking FBI badge in the trunk. He could have showed her that. He could have claimed Genet was a front for a mob business or something.

He should have adopted a role. He could have sold that better. At least he hadn't completely fumbled it. She had agreed to go with him. The sooner he could get Del to Alec, the better. Alec's gift was impossible to deny. But he had to get her to the Institute first, and there was no guarantee she'd keep her word.

He could insist Alec come out here. But he didn't like the idea of Alec exposing himself to a situation where armed gunmen were already involved. Alec could take on an army, but Philip had no idea how big this conspiracy went or how many people Genet had at his command. He hated fighting unknowns. Right now, he and Del were the only ones in danger. That was enough.

Hell, he had no idea who Genet was, except he knew enough to take over Orion after Lansing's death, and he'd fooled Dr. Cheshire. That meant Genet had influence, information and money. If he found out from where, Philip could track him.

Dr. Cheshire was a good place to start. The man knew more than he was telling.

Philip glanced over at his newly acquired charge. Del's eyes were closed.

Corrina Lawson

He should have checked her for bruises or injuries. Sometimes you got hit during a fight, didn't feel it, and it turned out worse than expected. He doubted Del would strip and let him look, however. She'd think he had ulterior motives.

Which, he admitted, he did.

He would love to see her naked. Not, not just see her. Touch her. Tumble her into the nearest bed. Or on top of a table in her bar. Or right here in the car. He was sure it wouldn't be the first time someone had sex in this car. If it happened now, with his body still jazzed from the pain, it would be perfect.

Good thing his pants were loose-fitting and his jacket went past his waist, or Del would realize exactly what he wanted. His erection could be simply a result of adrenaline from the chase. Or it could have been the charge he got from healing the gash in his head that had spilled blood down his face.

Del might not have much to do with his lust.

Like hell she didn't.

Any woman who stayed calm during a kidnapping, came back to rescue him and handled his car so it turned on a dime, that was someone worth lusting after. To say nothing of how pretty she was, with her long brown hair, dark eyes and a lithe body made just a little bit soft by the pregnancy.

The photo hadn't done her justice. Though he wondered if he'd have reacted to her the same if he'd not been in pain. He'd still have wanted her. But would he still be as rock hard as he was now? Unlikely. He needed that extra boost.

All the more reason to banish his lust for her.

"Do you feel all right?" he asked.

She nodded. "Turn right at the next road and that will take us over to Bar & Grill."

He did as she ordered.

He wanted to trust her. But one gigantic loose end bothered him.

Why would Lansing choose her for his "experiment"? It was, Philip decided, possible that Del was one of Lansing's descendants. It would be just like the old bastard to have kept track of his descendants from the family he'd had over one hundred and fifty years ago. Lansing might even have believed they still belonged to him. That was the attitude his blood father had displayed toward Philip, despite having absolutely nothing to do with him save at the moment of conception.

If Lansing would use his bastard son, why wouldn't he use someone who was less closely related? It was either that or believe Del was involved in this twisted plot and not telling him the truth If so, she was a good actress, which meant she was damn dangerous.

Philip sighed inwardly. He would have to investigate Del Sefton's past. She wouldn't like that at all. So he wouldn't tell her that he was doing it. "The Charger shifted perfectly. You're a good mechanic."

He didn't know why she'd broken her silence—he was just glad she had. "Thanks."

Her compliment only increased his desire to pull the car off the road and kiss her. She's pregnant, he thought. She's been raped, he thought. And, for all he knew, the child she carried was created from his sperm.

The unknowing mother of his son.

Not an ideal situation in which to give in to lust.

"I know you must be worried about your bar being short-handed while you're with me," Philip said. "I could send someone to cover your shifts."

"And just how long will I be with you at this safe place?"

He winced. "You wouldn't be with me, exactly. You'd be at Phoenix Institute, a facility in north Jersey that specializes in military training and education. They have the best security I know. Once you're safe, I can investigate Genet."

"And how long will that take?"

"A few months, maybe. I hope to have the mess cleaned up before your son is born. Then you can go back to your life."

"Just like that?"

He nodded. "The Institute could send someone not only to cover your shifts but someone qualified to sweep your home and bar free of all those bugs. They'll put it all back to normal."

"Right now, all I'm committed to is going with you and meeting this guy who you think will convince me of this crazy story. So let's leave the rest for later."

He nodded. Dammit, he did keep putting his foot in his mouth.

"You don't care if I tell my friends where I'm going?"

"Genet's people already know the Phoenix Institute is involved. He will guess that's where you are, so there's no point keeping it secret. But at least there, you'll be protected twenty-four/seven. And, as I said, it won't be for long."

"Because you'll get to Genet first."

"Yes." Philip grinned.

Del closed her eyes. "You should scare me, Drake. I don't know why you don't."

Shit. He didn't want to scare her. Ever. "You have a soft spot for oddballs, I think, if I'm guessing right from the bar clientele."

"Odd, yes. Crazy, no." She snorted. "Who's this amazing person who's going to convince me the story is true?"

"His name is Alec Farley. And he's a lot less scary than I am." *In some ways.*

Philip supposed it depended on how Del reacted to Alec's fire. Beth had been entranced in so many ways by Alec's power. Another person might see its destructive ability or panic at the sight of the fire. Del seemed calm enough to handle it. He bet she would take it in stride, as much as possible.

They arrived at the entrance to Bar & Grill from the opposite direction of where they'd left. Del had had him circle the lake. There was no sign of the van and no sign of the man Philip was sure he'd killed.

Del stared at the spot in the road that was stained with a dark liquid.

"You were right. They grabbed him and ran off."

Philip nodded. "They don't want police involvement."

"Neither do I," Del muttered. "If what you said is true, I want these guys dead."

She clenched her hands into fists as the Charger descended over the dirt road into the bar's parking lot. She was so calm, so collected, even when people were pointing guns at her.

But she wasn't calm about her rape.

"I'll do what I can to make these guys dead for you," he said.

She snorted again. "I think that was supposed to comfort me."

"Yes."

"I'm not sure what's worse. That you offered or that it made me feel better that you offered."

Clearly, he needed to stop talking.

Tammy was waiting in the parking lot next to Del's Focus. He parked, closed his jacket to hide the Sig Sauer and helped Del out of the car.

"Where did you put the gun I gave you?" he whispered.

"Glove box."

He nodded.

"Del!"

Tammy rushed forward and hugged her friend. The two women stood locked in an embrace for several seconds.

No wonder Del wanted to return. She was cared for here.

Tammy broke the hug and stepped back. "Are you all right? What happened?"

Philip looked around, finally registering something. Del's car was parked in the lot. That wasn't where it had been left. He pointed at it. "How did that get back down here?"

"Mike found the keys in the middle of the road, near the open driver's side door. He moved it back here before I could tell him to leave it for the police."

"Did you call the police?" Philip asked.

"Not yet." She glared at him. "And who the hell are you to ask the questions, anyway?"

"He saved me, Tammy."

Philip stayed on guard while Del told Tammy the full story. Around him, the parking lot grew darker as the sun began to set. Night would offer more cover to Genet's men. He wanted out of here as soon as possible.

"And you don't know why the men in the van wanted you?" Tammy asked after Del was finished. "You really should let me call the cops."

"I am the cops," Philip lied. "Well, of a sort." He popped his trunk and pulled out his fake FBI badge from a duffel bag. He presented the badge to Tammy.

"I see. Why are you involved?" She didn't seem impressed by the badge.

Del took a deep breath. "He thinks the man responsible for my..." Her voice wavered. She cleared her throat and started again. "He thinks the man who raped me came back for the child."

"We've been tracking this suspect," Philip said. "He's a very dangerous man with a lot of resources."

"Oh," Tammy said.

"Agent Drake wants me to go with him to a safe house for a few days, until he can arrest them," Del said.

She caught his eye. Philip nodded, relieved she was going along with the story.

"I can send someone out to cover her shifts," he said.

Tammy asked to see his badge again. Philip let her hold it. It would fool an expert. It should, given that identity had been one of his best covers. "We should go as soon as possible," he said to Del.

"I just need one thing from upstairs. Be right back."

And she was gone before he could object. What if someone was waiting for her up there?

"Is there any way someone could have gotten into her apartment without being seen?" he asked Tammy.

Her eyes widened. "This guy wants her that bad?"

"Yes," Philip snapped. "Now, tell me if anyone got past you to the upstairs."

"No way. And that's the only entrance too."

Except for the roof. Philip watched the second floor. The lights went on as Del presumably went into her home. Women and clothes. He sighed. He hoped she didn't plan on spending forever packing.

"So, tell me, Agent Drake, is this car standard FBI issue?" Tammy asked.

She was still suspicious. Philip forced himself to pay attention to the woman. She was close to Del. Always possible she was in it with Genet. Not likely, but possible. He judged Tammy to be about fifty, with that look and air of confidence he often noted in mothers who had grown children.

Too bad his own mother never had it.

"I'm the kind of agent who is used to working anonymously," Philip answered.

"The Charger's not anonymous," Tammy said.

"But, as you said, it's also not usually connected with the FBI."

Del's figure was silhouetted in her window, then the light went out.

If she wasn't down in twenty seconds, he was going up.

"You're taking her to a safe house?" Tammy asked.

"Yes. She'll be able to call and check in, if that's what worries you." He looked up and saw a hawk caught in the rays of the setting sun. It could be the same hawk that he'd seen with Del. He considered that a good sign. Hawk had always been his favorite name. Well, until...

Del came out the door with just one small bag, but she was followed by several of the regulars. She reached Philip before the crowd caught up.

"Mike's been talking to them about finding my car," Del said. "Tammy, I am *not* telling them about the rape."

Before Del could say anything more, the older barfly reached them. Jake, Philip remembered. From what he'd observed, the man had developed a fatherly attitude to Del. He was going to ask a lot of questions.

"Just what's going on?" Jake demanded, pointing at him with a bony finger.

Careful, old man. You stick me with that finger again, I'll break it.

"Jake, it's not your business."

"Guy shows up, buys everyone a round, you leave right after him, your car's abandoned, then you come back looking freaked out, and now you're leaving with him again?" Jake shook his head. "I ain't buying that. What's wrong?"

"Not your business." Philip said the words low and with emphasis. He wanted to scare this one into silence.

Jake backed off a step, to the safety of the others who'd come out with him. Philip recognized Tammy's son, Mike, Mike's crush, Jessica, and two of the younger barflies.

"What's she to you?" Jake asked.

Philip glanced over and saw Del grit her teeth. She'd told Tammy a version of the truth, but he saw that she never, ever wanted to reveal the rape to anyone else.

If that was what she wanted, he would give it to her.

He put an arm around Del's shoulder. "She's the mother of my child."

Jake gaped. Tammy, who knew part of the truth, glared at them. Del rested her head on Philip's shoulder. Grateful, he hoped, though he'd created another mess.

"You ain't been around," Jessica said.

What a unique bunch of defenders Del had. "No, I haven't been, and that's my own damn fault. I'm trying to fix it now."

Del put an arm around his waist. His pulse jacked up, even more than during the chase. He was used to people trying to kill him. He was less used to feeling this way. He'd tamped down on the lust while dealing with Tammy. Not anymore. He was sensitive to Del's every movement. He supposed it would be too much to cup his hand around her neck and kiss her in front of everyone to prove the lie. He'd love it. She'd hate it. She had made it clear she considered him little above a maniac.

"We need to spend time together to sort it out." Del glared at them. "Without a freakin' audience, okay?"

Jake threw up his hands in defeat and headed back inside. The crowd followed him. Philip breathed a sigh of relief. He didn't let Del go. Neither, he noticed, did she let him go.

Tammy turned to them. Del slid away from Philip, and the moment was gone.

"What made you say that?" Del snapped.

"It seemed the quickest way to get rid of the crowd."

Del looked away. Obviously, lust wasn't a two-way street.

Tammy shook her head. "The minute I walk in there, they're going to ask me about you, Charger. What the hell am I supposed to tell them?"

He shrugged. "Make something up. I don't care."

"Just tell them it's personal, please?" Del asked.

Tammy nodded. "You call me," she told Del.

Del shoved her hands into her pockets and nodded. Tammy turned around and trudged into Bar & Grill.

Del stared at the big, painted "Bar & Grill" sign for almost a full minute.

"I wish I had a place where I felt so at home," he said.

She shrugged and then tossed her bag at him. He caught it against his chest.

"Let's go, *Dad*," she said.

He didn't respond to the jibe and started the car. As he turned off the emergency brake, he noticed that Del took a photo out of her coat pocket.

"What is it?"

"The reason I'm going with you."

She handed it over. It was a black-and-white photo. Most of it looked like gray blobs. But he could make out the head clearly enough. And the hand and fingers. The baby's ultrasound photo.

"He's sucking his thumb." *Huh.*

She nodded.

Philip pulled out of the parking lot, a curious lump in his throat. What if his lie had been the truth? There was a one in three chance that his sperm had been used to create the baby.

This boy could actually *be* his son.

"Don't get any ideas about anything. This kid is mine."

"Of course."

He turned and drove up the long, dirt driveway to the intersecting road where Del had been ambushed. As he turned, he spotted nothing. So far, so good.

"Your son wouldn't want me as a father anyway. Not my specialty."

She smiled. The light hit her eyes, and suddenly she seemed much younger and so very familiar.

He *knew* her. He just didn't know *where* he knew her from.

"Ah, you're okay for a crazy person, Drake."

"Nicest compliment I've had in a long time."

Chapter Ten

To Del's relief, the car ride was quiet save for Drake's phone call to this Alec Farley that mostly consisted of one-word answers on Drake's end. Her newly appointed protector did ask about someone named Dr. Cheshire. Del repeated the name a few times in her head, so she'd remember. If she believed this crazy story, maybe he was one of those involved in her rape. Medical rape, she thought, to be more accurate.

Medical rape that had resulted in some stranger's child inside her. She stared out the window into the dark.

The night descended around them, and she fought to keep her eyes open. She wanted to stay awake to know where she was going. But between Drake's route on back roads, the overcast sky and the lack of streetlights, she had no idea where they were headed.

They'd been driving for about thirty minutes when Drake drove past a gate that opened automatically for him and pulled into a parking lot at the place he called the Phoenix Institute. The building looked like a corporate conference center or even a hotel. There was a central tower of at least ten stories. Lights were on in the room at the top and in the circular entrance on the ground floor, but otherwise it was dark.

She blinked her eyes as she adjusted to the bright lights in the parking lot. Most of the lot was empty, with the exception of a Porsche, a Hummer and a Range Rover to her left. The Honda sedan on her right looked oddly out of place.

Drake walked around the car and opened the door for her. He offered her his hand. She hesitated a moment, then clasped it with relief. She'd never get out of the car without help.

Her back muscles were stiff, her feet swollen, and her energy had completely drained away. Given how she'd sweated during the car chase, she probably smelled like a locker room. Drake gave no sign that she reeked but he did notice her lack of balance. He held her by the elbow to steady her.

"Were you hurt earlier?" he asked.

She felt the warmth of his hand and the strength of his arm around her waist. He killed someone today, she thought. Yes, protecting me, she told herself. It wasn't like she was an innocent. She rode around with a shotgun in her trunk. She had little respect for the niceties of the law.

Still, someone who killed like that should make her uncomfortable. She shouldn't want to curl up against him. She shouldn't wish that their dance hadn't been interrupted by real life. She wanted to put them back on the deck, with him humming a classic. A perfect moment, spoiled now, like most of her perfect moments.

"I'm fine. All they did was grab me from behind. They didn't even hit me."

She couldn't shake the feeling she knew this man. Maybe tonight, as she closed her eyes, it would come to her. She must have liked him whenever they met, though. That might explain her ease with him.

Her head drooped. She let it rest on his shoulder. Around them was silence. He cleared his throat. "I could carry you, if you like," he whispered in her ear.

Oh, she would like. She smiled. "No, I think I can manage. I just needed a moment."

Taking her at her word, he let her go. Now she wished she'd answered yes. He grabbed her duffel bag from the backseat, giving her a nice view of his backside.

"How tired are you? Do you want answers now or after some rest?"

"Now."

"That's what I thought."

He tossed the duffel over his shoulder and offered her his arm again. She took it, curling her hand around his forearm. "Who the hell are you, Drake?"

"Good question." He tilted his head down toward her face.

"You're good at not answering questions." And now he was so close that she thought he was going to kiss her. She thought she'd let him.

"I know."

She would definitely let him. "Is Alec Farley going to be better at answering questions?"

He straightened and the opportunity for a kiss vanished. "Much better."

"See, you can give a straight answer when you want." She touched his cheek. "Thank you. I don't think I said that enough."

He cleared his throat, and when he said, "you're welcome", his voice seemed raw. He'd been deliberately charming earlier. A role to play. This, she thought, was no role.

"It's safer inside. We should get moving," he said.

She nodded. He led her inside the circular entrance at the bottom of the tower. She noticed the smell first. It was like a combination of cinnamon and another sweet spice. She closed her eyes and took a deep breath, feeling more relaxed by the second. She tightened her grip on Drake's arm.

When she opened her eyes, she took the circular lobby in. Unexpectedly, it was decorated in a Japanese style. There was a pond with a small, burbling fountain in the middle. The running water added to the atmosphere and made her think of an exotic health spa.

"This is a beautiful place." She stepped away from him and pointed at the windows. "I love the bonsai planters on either side of the glass." The three shelves of each planter held a miniature bonsai tree.

"My daughter decorated it."

His voice had gone flat, back to soldier mode, and he'd moved away from her when she'd taken a closer look at the bonsai trees. She frowned. What had shut him down?

"Your daughter did this? You just said parenthood wasn't your specialty. And you couldn't have a kid that old!"

He shrugged, refusing to meet her gaze. "She's my foster daughter."

"Somehow, I don't think that explains everything." *Talk to me, Drake.* Better yet, he should take her arm again.

"No."

He stood at attention, rigid as a stone. If she hadn't just seen him relax, she'd never have thought this man could be funny or charming or someone who could dance with abandon, like he had with Jessica. And this because she mentioned something to do with his daughter?

His foster daughter. Maybe there was pain associated with that. God knew there were subjects she'd never talk about.

She glanced around the lobby again. There seemed to be six...no, seven hallways leading away from the lobby.

"Which one?"

"None—you're going upstairs to the main penthouse."

He directed her to an elevator disguised as part of the central marble column, but again he kept his distance from her. The buttons and door were around the back. As the doors opened, Drake set her duffel inside. He pressed the button to hold the doors open.

She stepped inside. He didn't.

"You're not coming with me?"

He shook his head. "Work."

"Did I piss you off about something, Drake?"

For a second, his stance softened. "No." In a whisper, he added, "You never could."

He reached under his jacket and took out his handgun, the one he'd used to kill the man earlier. "You put the other gun in my glove box. Keep this." He held it out to her.

"Why? You said I was safe."

"You are. But if you have the gun, perhaps you'll believe me when I say no one will hurt you here." He paused, all business now. "You have your cell phone—you can call anyone you want."

She closed her hands around the gun. In his way, he was giving her power. She could sense that much about him. "Do you equate guns with safety, Drake?"

He frowned. "When people are shooting at me, yes."

She shook her head. "Real safety is living in a place where people don't shoot at each other."

"I'm very glad you found one of those places." Again, his voice was a raspy whisper.

"You could too."

"No."

"Safety comes from finding a home, not guns."

He opened his mouth to say something but closed it without speaking. He stepped back. "You'll like talking to Alec," he said as the doors closed.

Just when she thought she had a handle on the man, he shut down, as if he'd never held her, never offered to carry her and never leaned in close to kiss her.

She zipped the handgun into her duffel, careful of the trigger. She knew some handguns didn't have safeties, and she definitely knew Drake's gun was loaded.

She should have stayed home. Then she could sleep in her own bed without the weight of a gun in her belongings.

She leaned against the wall for balance. *Fine, desert me now, Drake.* She shook her head and wondered exactly how seriously he took his promise to kill the men after her. It was wrong to wish them dead. Let her wish for the wrong thing, then. She was fine with it as long as her son was safe.

There was barely time to notice that the walls of the elevator were a warm bronze and the controls a bright silver before the elevator stopped and the doors opened on the top floor.

She stepped out into a softly lit hallway of pastel walls. An open door to the right beckoned her. She clutched her duffel tighter. If one more strange thing happened today, she was going to scream.

A young man walked through the doorway.

He smiled and, for a brief second, Del was reminded of Genet. This man was just as attractive in his way, exuding a charisma that was palpable. A wisp of his jet-black hair hung in his eyes. The black T-shirt and jeans hugged his skin tightly enough that she could see his muscles ripple as he walked.

If nothing else, this place was full of gorgeous men.

He took the duffel from her. "Del Sefton, right?" He smiled.

There was no smugness, no arrogance in that smile. His resemblance to Genet faded. She nodded. "Yes, that's me."

"I'm Alec Farley. This way. I have some hot tea brewing," he said, leading her into the door. "Beth says tea always relaxes her. I thought it might help you." He frowned. "Where's Drake?"

"He said he had work to do and that you'd answer questions better than him."

"Hah." Alec set her duffel carefully on the kitchen counter. "He's right on that. Did you get more out of him than grunts?"

"He danced."

"You're kidding?"

"No. He's a good dancer. I think he was trying to charm me so I'd believe him."

Alec nodded. "Playing a role, then?"

"I guess." So grunt mode was Drake's normal way of dealing with people. Even after he'd told her the truth, he'd been more open than that. For a while.

"Sit down. You must be tired."

She settled in a warm brown leather chair and suppressed a smile. If the lobby had been ordered yet relaxing, this room reminded her of a teenager's game room. A huge television dominated one wall. Below it, a case held several different game systems, speakers and various other electronics she didn't recognize. Man toys.

"You picked the best chair in the place." Alec handed her a mug of tea. "Beth says this is a relaxing blend. I figure it's better for you than coffee."

"So long as it doesn't have caffeine." She examined the mug. It was decorated with Japanese symbols.

"Those are Japanese words that can be translated as 'restful'." Alec settled onto the long couch opposite her. "At least that's what Beth claims."

"That's the third time you've mentioned this Beth." Del sipped the tea. A hint of lemon, a hint of chamomile, and something sweet. Whoever Beth was, her tea was lovely.

"Beth is Drake's daughter. And my girlfriend."

His face lit up. Lucky Beth. So why had Drake shut down when talking about her? "So Beth is good to have around?"

"If Drake didn't tell you about Beth or brag about her, he was being even more tightlipped than usual."

"He mentioned his daughter. Just not her name."

"No more information than necessary. Now that sounds exactly like Drake."

At least someone else was as confused by Drake as she was. She drank down another swallow and felt herself sink deeper into the chair as her muscles relaxed. "Drake said I'd never believe the full truth about my baby but that you could convince me he wasn't crazy."

"Drake is crazy." Alec stood. "I doubt I'll change your mind about that. But I think he was talking about your baby and how it was conceived. He's right, that is a crazy story, but it's also true."

"He said I was impregnated with sperm that was genetically altered." She was surprised that came out so calmly. "He didn't have any explanation for why anyone would do that or what the hell kind of experiment it was. He didn't answer me about why my baby is so special."

"That's because you wouldn't believe him." Alec picked up a football sitting on the floor of a corner of the room.

"And I'll believe you?"

He tossed the football in the air and caught it. "Most people do."

Alec picked up one of the *Sports Illustrated* magazines that littered the coffee table. "So, let's do this."

"Do what?" Del said.

"Beth says I should explain to people about my fire before I use it. She says they'll get less freaked. If you've spent the day with Drake and you can sit there and drink tea calmly and without being hysterical, I think you can handle it. Besides, no matter how many words I use, they never do the fire justice."

A lunatic. Drake had bought her to the home of a rambling lunatic.

He held up the copy of *Sports Illustrated.* "Nothing up my sleeves, right?"

"You have no sleeves."

"Exactly. Look, it'll be better if you hold my hand while I do this. That way you don't have to worry that I'm doing something sneaky." He held out a hand and smiled. "Trust me, Del Sefton? I promise, it'll be worth the show."

Charm to spare, this one, and he wasn't playing a role, she sensed, as Drake had done. She wondered if Alec was a violent lunatic. She stood and took his hand. It was callused, warm and strong, but his grip was gentle enough.

"What kind of birds do you like?" he asked.

"What?"

"Just tell me."

She thought of the bird soaring in the sky at the lake. "Hawks."

"Great. Watch," he said.

In his other hand, the *Sports Illustrated* magazine began to smoke. She flinched. Alec gripped her hand tighter and grinned.

"Oh, God!" She was with a pyromaniac. She tried to pull away but Alec held her tight.

A flame shot up from the center of the magazine and then the whole thing went up in flames. Her mouth fell open. How the hell did he start that fire?

She looked at Alec. He didn't acknowledge her. He stared at the fire, his face frozen into a partial smile, his jaw clenched tight.

She coughed. *Run, there's fire!* her body screamed at her. Alec gripped her hand tighter, preventing her escape. A little squeaky noise came from deep in her throat. She looked at the flames. If the carpet or the curtains caught on fire...

As the magazine dissolved into ashes, the flames rose higher, taking shape. She nearly bit through her tongue. The fire looked like a sparkling ball at first, but it quickly grew wings and sprouted a birdlike head and clawed feet. The fiery bird spread its wings, sending heat blasting at her, warming her face.

The flame creature opened its mouth in a soundless cry.

A fire hawk.

The fire hawk rose and hovered a few inches from the ceiling. It spread its wings wider and flew around the living room several times, blasting heated air over her. The fire creature grew smaller and smaller with each circle around the room. After the fourth time, it landed on the rocking chair and vanished.

Alec let her hand go. "Cool, huh?"

"Warm, rather." She collapsed back into the chair. She swallowed, trying to moisten her dry mouth. "That was...that was... You..."

Alec let the ashes of the magazine fall onto the coffee table. "That's..."

"Astonishing? Cool? Awesome?" Alec had crossed his arms over his chest and was grinning like he'd just pulled an elaborate joke.

"How can you do that?" It couldn't have been a trick. She knew what she'd seen. She didn't believe it but she'd seen it all the same. She rubbed her wrist where Alec had held her.

"I'm a telekinetic and a firestarter." He pointed at the football he'd set down on the couch. It came to him, as if tossed to him by invisible hands. "Technically, telekinesis and firestarting are about the same thing, since what I'm doing with the fire is moving molecules with my brain, just like telekinesis. I'm just moving them much faster." He tossed the football back to the couch. "The fire is more fun, though."

"What you did is impossible."

"That's what makes it so cool. Want another demonstration?"

She shook her head, wishing she could disappear into the chair. "*Who are you?* What is the Phoenix Institute?"

"I'm Alec. Just Alec." He sat down on the couch. "The Phoenix Institute is a place to teach and help those with abilities like mine. I had to learn how to control my fire when I was a kid or else I could have burned down everything around me. I want the Institute to be a place where telekinetics and other psychics can come to be trained in safety." He put his elbows on his knees. "They need to know they're not freaks and that they can have normal lives."

"You're not normal."

"Nope." He leaned back. "Besides my fire, I never had a normal life. The man who used to run this place raised me from a child and trained me in my power. He wanted to turn me into a weapon under his command. He wanted a whole army of super soldiers like me eventually."

Alec began to explain his past. Del wasn't sure when she hit overload. It was either when Alec explained he was both head of the Phoenix Institute and part of an elite combat team that was often deployed against extraordinary threats or when he talked about his girlfriend, the telepath, Drake's daughter.

Her blank look must have registered something to Alec.

"You can look it up," Alec said. "F-Team stopped the bomb in New York Harbor last spring."

"The one where there was a huge explosion in the sky?"

"That's the one," Alec said. "The bomb detonated before I could stop it, so with Beth's help, I pushed the explosion up into the sky. Our psychic connection enhanced my power and I needed every bit of what she gave me. It was very close."

"Beth helped you? Is she a firestarter *and* a telepath?"

"No. Like I said, she's a telepath, but she's also a catalyst. Twice now, when she's come into contact with other psychics, she increased their abilities." He pointed to her empty mug. "Hey, do you want a refill on that tea?"

"How about a do-over on today. I go home, sleep, and when I wake up, none of this ever happened."

Alec laughed. "I think I'm insulted. Though if you want to forget Drake, be my guest."

He took her mug from her before she could object, walked to the kitchen, and came back out again with the promised refill.

Put some whiskey in it, she thought. But whiskey would be bad for the baby. "So you're a firestarter, Beth is a telepath and Drake is crazy. And the Phoenix Institute is a place to train people with powers so their abilities are under control."

"You've got it, mostly, except as far as I've been able to determine, most of the powers have a psychic source, like moving molecules with the mind, or telepathy."

She held the hot mug in her hands. "What does that have to do with *me*? Why am I involved in this? I'm not anything special."

Alec sighed. "The man who owned this place, Richard Lansing, was the one who trained me to be a weapon. It's all he wanted me to be." Alec looked away. "But he wanted more like me under his command and he got tired of just looking for them. He decided to create them himself. So he founded a genetics lab. He took samples from everyone he knew with special abilities and told the lab to get to work developing viable enhancements." He stared at her. "That's where your baby comes in. We think he's the first successful experiment."

"He's not an experiment. No matter how he got there, he's my son," she snapped.

"I'm sorry. You're right. This is your baby."

"Does this Lansing want him?"

"No, Lansing is dead," Alec said flatly. "I wish I'd found it sooner, but the lab kept working even after he died. I inherited everything but he had a lot of properties owned under shell companies and stuff like that. I didn't find Orion Systems until yesterday. When I went there with Drake, a bomb went off in the middle of our visit. We think Genet planted it."

"Who is Genet, really?"

"We don't know. He knew enough about what was going on with Orion to pretend to be the new owner. Maybe he knew Lansing and was part of the plan and carried it out on his own. Maybe he's working with someone else. We just don't know." Alec stood up and began pacing. "I'm going to find out, though. That's probably where Drake went. He doesn't need much sleep."

Her heart was beating so fast it threatened to jump out of her chest. Yet she had no energy to get out of the chair. She closed her eyes. "Why the hell did they pick me for it? I'm nobody."

"We don't know. I wish we did. Do you have anyone in your family who's got some kind of uncanny sense? Anyone who seems to know what people are going to do before they do it?"

She frowned. "My mother is from a long line of preachers who could whip up a sermon like no one's business. I was little when my grandfather died, but I remember the one time I attended his church. He had the people in the palm of his hand in a half hour, ready to accept Jesus Christ as their lord and savior."

"Huh. I don't know if that qualifies as psychic, at least it doesn't sound like anything anyone could use as a weapon." Alec knelt down in front of her. "I don't want to use your kid, Del. I just want him to grow up happy, with his mother. That's all I want." He cupped a hand in front of her. The air itself turned to flame. "Do you trust me?"

"I'm not sure I trust my own brain at this moment. It's telling me I need to believe impossible stuff."

"Put your fingers in the flames above my hand," Alec whispered. "I won't hurt you."

She swallowed. *I have to know.* She stuck her fingers right into the flames, expecting searing pain.

She felt the heat. The flames danced around her but they didn't hurt her. Alec waved his hand and the fire disappeared.

"Oh."

Alec tilted his head. "You didn't run out of here screaming. I like you."

"Hah." He didn't look like a hallucination. He sure talked like one. "Is my baby a firestarter like you? What kind of special abilities will he have?"

"We don't know that yet, either. Orion Systems was working with three sperm samples. One of them was mine. If your baby is from my genes, he could be dangerous to himself and to you. I couldn't control my fire completely until I was three. I could show your baby." He knelt in front of her. "I don't know how to be a father but I learn fast."

"I bet you do." She smiled. Argh. She liked the madman. If he was the biological father—if *father* was the right word here— he would make a far better father than, say, Hawk's stepfather.

Alec nodded and reached out with his hand. "Could I..." He cleared his throat. "Could I touch him?"

Alec's eyes were wide and open. She took his hand and put it over her swollen abdomen.

"He's not moving," she said. "At least, not that I can tell yet."

Alec looked at her intently. "He's moving. I can feel it with my telekinesis." He drew his hand back. "Thank you. I know you don't know me and that you never asked for this, but if the baby's mine or even if he's not, I want to help."

Before today, her son didn't have a father. Now he might have three. This just kept getting better and better.

"Where did the other two sperm samples come from?"

"A sample from Lansing himself and—"

"Was he a firestarter too?" Would her baby be better off with a dead man as his father?

"No, Lansing had the ability to heal his body of injuries or old age. He basically psychically kept his body from aging. He was effectively immortal and about two hundred years old when he died."

"If he was immortal, how'd he die?"

"He got shot in the op where we shut down the bomb in New York Harbor. He lost blood too fast for him to heal."

"Well, that explains everything then. Okay." She took a deep breath. She had to keep going before she started screaming. "So, who is number three? Does he walk through walls or something?"

"It seems that way sometimes, but, no, Drake is like Lansing. He can heal injuries, though he's more powerful than Lansing because of Beth and her catalyst ability. Drake healed himself from a nasty chest wound not too long ago. It would take more than a bullet to bring him down." Alec stopped abruptly.

"Oh, hey, don't stop with the revelations now."

"Drake's also a black-ops former CIA agent and all-around scary guy. That has nothing to do with his power but I thought you should know."

"I got the all-around scary guy part. Of course, I'm saying that to a man who just made fire fly around the room."

Alec smiled.

"Wait, hold on. Back up." She waved her hands. Secrets were coming out too fast to absorb. Telepaths. Firestarters. Immortals. Catalysts. "*Drake* could be the father of this baby?" Keep her safe. That's what he had said he wanted. *Fuck.* Now she knew why.

"So to speak. The odds are good he's related to your baby. Lansing was his biological father. Lansing used Drake's sperm without his knowledge or consent. But that means your baby could be either Drake's son or his brother."

"Oh." Of course it did. "Does Drake know?"

"I think he probably guessed but we haven't talked about it. I'd say odds are good he knows. He always knows."

That meant Drake had been telling something close to the truth when he claimed to be the baby's father.

"Son of a bitch," she said.

"Yeah," Alec agreed. "He is. But he's on our side."

Chapter Eleven

As the elevator doors closed on Del, Philip clenched his hands into fists. He couldn't hide his anger any longer. He'd barely held onto it until Del was safely aboard the elevator. Yet he had absolutely nowhere to go with it. The object of his hatred was already dead.

Lansing, you fucking bastard.

It had been that last gesture when Del had closed her eyes to smell the room. That was when it had clicked. She'd thought he'd shut down because of some problem with his daughter. He'd let her believe it.

Philip strode down one of the darkened hallways, walked into a bathroom and turned on the lights. He looked at himself in the mirror. He seemed a young man. The image lied. He doubted he'd ever been young.

What had Del seen in him to trust him so quickly?

Not, he hoped, the truth.

He punched the mirror. It shattered. Shards crunched against his knuckles and dug in under the skin. Blood dripped on the sink, on the floor, onto his clothes.

He dropped to his knees and put his head in his hands.

Del Sefton. *Delilah.* He should have realized sooner. If he had, he never would have gone near her. He'd danced with her. Held her in his arms. Had nearly kissed her. He still wanted to do all those things. Just the image in his mind's eye had him thinking of ways to touch her, to kiss her, to—

It was so wrong to want all those things.

Delilah. Lilah.

Lily.

Lily.

That was why she'd seemed so familiar and why he'd liked her from the start. He knew her, possibly better than anyone in his life.

Lily, the little girl who'd been his only friend growing up. Seven years younger, a little wisp of a girl with long hair and big eyes. She'd snuck him snacks when his stepfather locked him in a closet. After one especially bad beating, she had simply curled up next to him, adding warmth while he shivered from shock and cold.

Lily, who somehow had turned out kind and thoughtful despite the many moves, despite how his stepfather had browbeat them all constantly, despite the night the world crashed around them.

The night he'd killed her parents. He thought he was saving her life, but later, he wondered if her parents had merely been pretending to go along with his stepfather's mad plan of murder-suicide that day.

Maybe her parents had been going to save Lily, not kill her.

He would never know.

Philip would be dead too, save that his mother—for the first time in her life—stood up to his stepfather and shot him before he could kill Philip. Then the tear gas came through the windows and the Feds rushed in.

His mother had then claimed to have shot everyone to the Feds. All their tromping around had wrecked any evidence, so they let her confession stand. Philip probably should have told them the truth, but his mother had ordered him to remain silent. He still wondered if he'd done the right thing.

But Lily knew the truth. She had been locked in the bathroom but she heard what had happened. She'd heard her father yell Philip's name and call him "murderer". Oh, yes, Lily knew. His last memory of her was her screaming how much she hated him.

He'd never found her later to tell her the truth of what had happened. Who knew what was really the truth, anyway?

Let Lily hate him. Better than believing that her parents had wanted her dead. And even if Lily got past what he'd done, what kind of friendship could he ever offer? He was nothing any longer, just a shadow of a real person. Beth was his only anchor to reality.

Philip had never even looked for Lily.

Lansing obviously had.

Lansing had handpicked her for this. Philip knew that in his gut. Delilah had had a good life, and Lansing had taken it away from her out of some twisted desire to hurt his estranged son.

That child in Del's womb was likely related to him, either his son or his brother. There was a thirty-three percent chance that Lansing had implanted the child of someone who killed her parents inside Del Sefton, all out of some twisted revenge.

Philip pounded the floor, digging the glass shards in deeper. Pain shot up his arms. Blood pooled onto the floor. He closed his eyes, breathing heavily. Sweat poured down his back. He held up his bloody hands and opened his eyes.

He still imagined holding Del. The lust triggered by the pain spread through his body. He imagined Del in his arms, in the back seat of the Charger. She wasn't a child any longer, she was a beautiful woman, one who'd saved his life, one who—

One whose life had been wrecked so she could carry a child who was either his brother or his son.

Blood slid down his arms, soaking his shirt.

What a mess.

Daydreaming about her wouldn't help. Neither would crippling himself before he caught the men looking for her. Wrecked hands wouldn't help him find Genet, they wouldn't help him interrogate Cheshire.

They wouldn't help him make certain Del and her son could live in peace.

Philip pulled out a pocketknife and flicked the shards out of his knuckles, one by one. Pain slashed at him. He grinned, riding with it, feeling his nerves sizzle with the agony. His erection pushed against his jeans. He ignored it. He'd not give into it, not when thinking about Del. She didn't deserve that.

By the time he was done, both hands were covered in blood and he was shaking but whether it was pain or pleasure, he couldn't tell. To him, it was all the same now.

He closed his eyes and concentrated. Pain mingled with his innate ability, swirling together as one. Philip moaned. Energy enveloped him, invigorated him, honed his anger to a cold edge. He couldn't control his desire any longer. He thought of Del in his arms, her head on his shoulder, and how he'd wished in the car that he dared to be a part of her life.

He sank into the fantasy and he remembered her arm around his waist and the way she felt against him, and how her mouth had been ready for a kiss...

He snapped his eyes open.

I am a sick man.

He'd done enough. He would not come close to her again, no matter how good it felt, no matter the connection he'd felt with Del before knowing who she really was.

He could not see her again. Hell only knew what she'd think if she guessed who he was. It would certainly make her less likely to believe the truth. Let Alec deal with Del. Philip would concentrate on taking out the people who wanted to harm her. He was good at that.

His healing energy vanished, its work done. Philip grasped the sink and pulled himself to his feet. He washed the blood off his hands and splashed his face for good measure.

The bathroom door opened. He turned, knife out, dropping into a fighting stance.

"What the fuck, Drake?"

"Evenin', Gabe."

Gabe. Lieutenant Gabriel, the executive officer of F-Team, Alec's elite assault force. The tall, lanky lieutenant didn't look like much, but he was a soldier and he could fight. His true talent, however, lay in tech and communications equipment. Philip put the knife away without being asked. He rather liked the quietly competent lieutenant. Besides, he would need Gabe's help to track down Genet.

"Are your hands okay?" Gabe finally said.

"Fine."

When Gabe pointed to the blood on the floor and all over his clothes, Philip held up his clean, healed hands.

Gabe looked at the busted mirror.

"Bad day. Had to shoot someone."

Gabe nodded. "That always makes it a bad day."

Philip walked past Gabe and out into the darkened corridor. "Is Dr. Cheshire still here?"

Gabe kept pace with him. "Yep. Alec was able to convince him to come back here after the firefighters talked to them at the scene of the arson. But he's making noises about wanting to go home now. Alec said you'd arrived, so I came to find you and bring you to Cheshire. I figure you might get him to talk."

"Did Cheshire tell Alec anything?"

"He whined a lot about his work being destroyed and how he didn't understand how Genet could be a phony. Alec tried listening, told him he knew it must be hard to lose his assistant like that. It helped Cheshire calm down but it didn't get him talking."

"That's because what Cheshire is really upset about is his missing work, not his dead assistant."

It had been the promise of saving that work that enticed Cheshire to cough up Del's name and address earlier today. Philip judged the same tactic would likely work on him now.

"That fits Cheshire, I guess. Bit of a cold fish."

"That's because he sees himself as God, playing with DNA like the Creator. We're beneath his notice normally, I'd say."

Gabe led them down another corridor. The light blazed bright over their heads. "Alec gave me the thumb drive you recovered from the scene."

"And?"

"It's in code. A scientific code too, or else I'd have been able to crack it. I thought about asking Cheshire what it means but I'm not sure I trust Cheshire to give us a straight answer."

"Smart call. So what will you do?"

"I know some people. I'll get an expert I trust to look over the files." Gabe stopped in front of a door on the right. "Cheshire's inside."

"Good."

"Drake."

Philip glared. "What?"

"Don't kill him, okay?"

Alec had asked the same, earlier, at the scene of the fire. "Kill someone who's been playing God with my DNA? Why would I do that?" Philip growled, then shook his head. "It's only Hollywood spies who need to hurt someone to get information."

"And you think walking in there with blood all over you isn't a form of intimidation?"

"It's subtle." Shit, he'd forgotten all about the blood. His lack of sleep was catching up with him. Still, his appearance might be useful. "I'll be careful with Cheshire." For now. "Are the cameras working? I want a visual record of what he says."

"Yes. I'll be watching as well."

"Good. I want a second pair of eyes." He reached for the doorknob. "This would be easier with Beth." Her telepathy could grab what they wanted to know in minutes. "Any word on when she'll be back?"

"She called Alec when she landed in Charlton City. Daz picked her up on schedule. Daz told me it might take up to two weeks to sort through everything there."

Two weeks. He didn't know if Del had two weeks to wait.

Well, if Beth wasn't around to probe Cheshire's mind for answers, neither was she around to sense the turmoil inside her father's psyche.

He opened the door to the room.

Philip knew the minute he stepped inside that Beth had decorated it, though in an entirely different style than the lobby.

The decor had warmth, from the soft brown of the couch and chairs to the soothing seascapes that dotted the walls, to the natural light streaming in from the windows.

This was Beth all over.

He smiled. His daughter was alive because Philip had saved and protected her. That gave him one on the positive side of the ledger. Protecting Del and her son would be number two. It wouldn't change their past but it would give her back her future, intact.

Cheshire was sitting in one of the chairs, half-asleep.

Philip cleared his throat loudly. "Hello, Doctor."

Cheshire flinched and straightened. "Did you find Delilah Sefton?"

"She's safe," Philip answered.

"Where? Is she here?" Cheshire stared at him. "Dear God, you're a mess. Did you get hurt?"

"Where she is will be a secret until I know I can trust you." He didn't answer the other question. Why should he?

"I see."

Philip grabbed two water bottles from the minifridge in the bar area. Eventually, he might offer Cheshire alcohol to soften him up but water was a much less threatening choice as a start. Philip sank onto the couch. He offered a bottle to Cheshire, and the man took it with a quick nod.

"Thanks. It seems no matter how much I drink, I can't get the taste of smoke out of my mouth."

Good, no more questions about Del. "I've heard that happens with people caught in a fire. It can take a day or two to fade."

Philip opened his water and took a long drink, wishing it was whiskey.

Cheshire sipped his water as if testing it and then took a much longer swallow. When he was done, he rubbed the moisture off his lip with the sleeve of his tattered lab coat. "You look worse than after the fire. You were hurt protecting her?"

"Let's say the day for me didn't get better after the fire."

Cheshire sat straighter. "Was she also hurt?"

Philip wondered if he should lie. But he decided not to tangle lies and truth. Yet.

"No. I found her before Genet's goons had a chance to hurt her."

"You're sure she's not injured?" The doctor's voice cracked with concern.

"I'm certain." There it was. Del was the enticement to get Cheshire to talk. "But if she's to remain safe, we will need your help."

Cheshire waved his hands, animated. "Well, of course! I'll need to examine her and make sure the fetus is growing properly and I'll need blood work and urine samples and—"

Philip looked at Cheshire, who was lost in his own little world, and decided that Del would never meet this man.

The doctor finally wound down and realized Philip hadn't replied. "Is there something wrong?"

"Edward Genet destroyed your lab, killed your assistant and tried to kidnap Del Sefton, and your focus is on your experiment, Doctor?"

"Knowledge is important," the doctor said, but he eyed the bloodstains on Philip's pants. "And Ms. Sefton needs proper medical care."

"Knowledge is essential," Philip agreed. "But to keep Del Sefton and your experimental fetus in good health, I have to find Genet and stop him." He leaned forward and smiled. "I don't need you poking and prodding her. I need you to help me find Genet."

"Are you certain he's a threat? He is arrogant, true, and I didn't much like the man, but he had great enthusiasm for the work, and he was as concerned as I was that Ms. Sefton and her child stay healthy."

"He blew up your lab."

"You don't know that for certain. You're guessing. Maybe someone was after him as well."

Philip wondered if Cheshire was really that obtuse. "Genet was the last person in the area of the lab where the bomb was set. He was also the last person to see your friend and assistant alive."

"I thought it was the explosion that killed Ted Demetrius?" Cheshire leaned forward.

Deliberately obtuse, Philip decided. "No, doctor, Ted was murdered. Half his skull was caved in. The explosion was to cover up the murder and destroy the entire lab, especially all your samples, data and records. That included the knowledge inside the heads of all your employees. None of you were supposed to live. If Alec Farley hadn't been there when the bomb exploded, it would've worked. Everyone would be dead. Including you."

Cheshire's hand shook as he drank more water. A good show, if show it was. Maybe Cheshire was in shock. Murderous intent tended to be something people didn't want to think about. It was too scary knowing someone wanted you dead. Philip didn't understand that. He liked to know when someone was trying to kill him. It made it much easier to find them and kill them first.

"You said it was Mr. Genet who did this."

"Yes."

"How can you be sure, Mr., um, what is your actual name?"

"Philip Drake." Philip caught the widening of Cheshire's eyes. The biologist had heard his name before. "I'm a consultant for the Phoenix Institute. I specialize in protecting people."

"And how do you know Genet's behind all this, Mr. Drake?"

"Because he masqueraded as an adoption attorney. He tried to get Del Sefton to give up her child to him." Drake stared at Cheshire. "This meeting took place today, immediately after he left Orion."

"Oh." Cheshire slumped back in the chair. "How do I know you're not lying to me?"

"How do you know Genet isn't the liar?" Philip sat forward. "If you don't trust either of us, trust logic. Think back on what happened today."

Cheshire closed his eyes. "It's true Genet was the last one to be with Demetrius. No one else could have gotten into the lab after he left. He must have been the one who killed him." He leaned forward and rested his elbows on his legs. "I don't understand. Genet had all the proper ownership paperwork, and he knew all about our work. How?"

"How he got that information is something we're exploring. So far, much of this is murky."

Now he had the man's full attention. "Dr. Cheshire, you're only alive right now because Alec Farley saved you. And we can continue to keep you alive, but you've got to tell me all you know about Orion Systems and its goals. Everything. Even information you don't think is vital could be the clue to finding Genet and shutting him down."

Cheshire nodded. "Well, Alec is the rightful owner of our lab. I don't doubt that. So that makes you my employer. I'll answer what questions you have."

Good, Philip thought. First get agreement on small matters, then larger ones.

"Will I be able to continue my research after? I need to see Ms. Sefton," Cheshire said.

Never. "Perhaps later, if we know we can trust *you.*"

"I simply want to expand science. I've nothing to do with whatever Genet is planning." Cheshire rubbed the back of his neck. "Mr. Lansing made it all sound so wonderful. The work was fascinating. We understood each other." Cheshire looked away, breaking eye contact. "But it all seemed abstract until today, when I saw the firestarter in action. No wonder Mr. Lansing wanted to duplicate his abilities."

It all seemed abstract until today? What about the night you medically raped Delilah Sefton?

Philip nodded. "Alec is unique. Lansing wanted him not to be alone. And his abilities are very useful." He tried to keep the contempt out of his voice. Let Cheshire ramble.

"Mr. Lansing was a visionary," Cheshire said.

If you can call an insane immortal a visionary. "Yes, he certainly was. Alec inherited his dream."

"I suspected that when he came in today."

"Alec and the Phoenix Institute will continue to protect you, but we cannot do it blind."

Cheshire nodded again. "No, of course not. But don't you know everything already if Alec is Lansing's heir?"

The doctor had recognized Philip's current name earlier, and now he had started asking questions. Careful, Philip told himself. Cheshire was scared but still able to think clearly. And perhaps lie easily.

"Mr. Lansing was secretive and he died unexpectedly." All very true. It was always good to convince someone with the truth. "He set up this project under careful concealment to protect Orion. It took some time for Alec to cut through all the bureaucracy and uncover Orion. I would guess that you originally reported directly to Mr. Lansing, yes?"

"Exactly." Cheshire bobbed his head. "He took a special interest in our lab. Did you work with him?"

A trick question, as Cheshire might know the answer. "As you might guess, I used to work for the CIA. I was most often assigned to Alec." Mostly true. "Did Mr. Lansing talk about his personal motivations for funding your work?"

"Oh, yes, he told us about his ward, the firestarter. He was a bit more circumspect about the two other sperm samples, however. I wanted more information, but he said that it was most important that the donors from the other two sperm samples be kept completely anonymous. But he had such plans. It was engrossing work. Mr. Lansing was very supportive."

"A true visionary, as you said."

"Yes." Cheshire smiled and sat back, his hands in a steeple. He was feeling more comfortable by the second. Of course he was. He was getting a chance to show off.

"He gave us the firestarter's sample first, but when we stalled because something in the genetic code resisted tampering, he provided us with the other samples."

"It's good Mr. Lansing was understanding of your difficulties."

"He had such patience with us." He shook his head again. "Such a loss."

"Was he pleased with the results of the new samples?"

"The new samples were helpful, one more than the other." Cheshire frowned. "But there was one part of his orders that baffled me. Mr. Lansing handpicked the woman to be the mother of the child. I objected. I wanted a younger woman, someone in her early twenties to minimize any pregnancy risks, but Mr. Lansing was firm on this matter. He insisted we involve this particular woman. Ms. Sefton. I don't know why. It's not as if her genetic material was unique. I wanted someone whose DNA we had tested and studied."

Philip's mouth went dry. He now had proof that Lansing had deliberately targeted Del, even against the recommendations of the doctor in charge of the experiment. His blood father must have wanted to not only wound but stab a figurative knife into his heart.

Cheshire took a deep breath. "We had gene-gineered sperm ready for implantation so I suggested we hire a woman to carry the child to term, one who would be interested in giving up the child for adoption. That way, we'd be able to monitor her carefully and we would have no trouble about it. Careful records are of the utmost importance." He smiled. "We didn't have an ob-gyn at the lab, so the woman would naturally go to an outside doctor. But we could have chosen that doctor and put him on our payroll. But this...this choice of Ms. Sefton seemed completely random to me. I told Mr. Lansing that."

"And he was adamant about it, yes? Richard could be very stubborn."

"He was absolutely rock-solid that it was essential this particular woman be the mother of the child. I assumed eventually he had information that we did not. Perhaps that she herself had unusual psychic abilities. But Mr. Lansing would not discuss the situation further with me."

"So you still went ahead?"

"I trusted Mr. Lansing."

Idiot. "And you certainly didn't want the work to go to waste," Philip prodded.

"Naturally not."

Naturally. "And it worked."

"It was quite successful. These kinds of things don't always work. So when it did on the first try, I thought, well, Mr. Lansing does know something I don't." Cheshire shook his head mournfully. "But the only problem is that we lacked proper information during her pregnancy. I assumed Mr. Lansing was going to provide that. But when he died, I didn't know what to do. I've been anxious about it. There were some changes made to the sperm's DNA that could cause...problems."

"What kind of changes?" Philip snapped.

"An accelerated growth rate, for one," Cheshire said. "That shouldn't be dangerous but needs to be watched carefully."

"I see how that could be a problem."

Cheshire frowned, perhaps catching the sarcasm. "I thought about contacting Ms. Sefton directly after Lansing died. But I didn't know how she'd react. Mr. Genet said he would take care of that end when he arrived as our new director a few weeks later. He provided us with ultrasound images, at least, and some of her blood work. That helped."

Lovely. So now even Del's doctor or technicians might be in Genet's employ.

"How did you go about the artificial insemination in the first place?"

"Lansing brought the woman to us. She was semiconscious. I made sure she suffered no harm."

Cheshire, the idiot, had convinced himself he'd done the right thing despite it being obvious that Del had been taken against her will. It was either hold to a moral code or continue with his work. Cheshire had picked the work. No wonder Lansing had chosen him for this project.

"She was semiconscious the entire time?" Philip asked.

"Yes. I wanted to talk to her and explain but Mr. Lansing had ordered otherwise. I believe he set up some sort of covert surveillance of her residence to make sure no harm came to her. He also said it was no use explaining it all to her when the procedure might fail."

"But it succeeded."

"Oh, yes!" Cheshire's face lit up.

Philip blanked his expression. "You said you received some of Ms. Sefton's medical records. Did you see anything in the blood work or ultrasound that alarmed you?"

Cheshire shook his head. "No, but we did have serious hints of the accelerated growth rate. She must be carefully monitored—the child could put a strain on her system by growing so quickly. If she's not, I'm quite concerned for both of them." He sighed. "Mr. Lansing should have let me hire a volunteer. Or, better yet, we should have used donated eggs and replaced the entire genetic material. That way, we would have only needed a surrogate mother. It would have been so much less complicated."

How awful to deal with crazy bosses, eh, Cheshire?

"Which one of the two new sperm samples was the source of what was implanted in Delilah Sefton?" Was Del's child his son or his half-brother?

"As I said, we had tried to use the firestarter sample but that effort failed." He sighed. "That was the one Mr. Lansing favored."

"Go on," Philip said, his voice quiet.

"We had two sperm samples with similar healing properties," Cheshire continued. "One we judged from a younger man. We concentrated on that because younger sperm are always the most vital." He smiled. "And that was our success. The result, as you see, is a pregnancy. A healthy fetus!"

A boy, Del had said. A son.

"A healthy fetus now in danger so long as Genet is free," Philip said.

"Oh, you seem well qualified to stop Genet. Get to what you're really interested in, Mr. Drake. Obviously, you want to know if the child is yours." The doctor smiled. "I wasn't entirely sure before but given the amount of blood on your coat and that you survived toxic fumes from the explosion without any ill effects, I'm certain now. You would have to be the origin of the second sample we were given—the younger one. The child was created from your sperm. And excellent sperm it was!"

The cold rage, so familiar for his whole life, descended on Philip. His mind shut down. His body felt numb. Sights and sound came to him as if through a distant tunnel. No hint of anger or any other emotion escaped.

Once, he'd needed this lack of emotion to stay calm while his stepfather beat him because to fight back meant death. Now, it descended when he was ready to kill.

"No one asked my permission for your experiment, Dr. Cheshire," he said in a voice barely above a whisper.

"But you must have—" The doctor cleared his throat. "I didn't know that. But you should be so pleased. Your child is the first of a new generation. We're hoping his healing ability is even more powerful, that instead of being able to heal himself as you do, the child will be able to heal others." He smiled widely. "We called it the Messiah gene. I know, it sounds over the top, but it was more of a joke between us at Orion." He frowned. "I'm going to miss Demetrius."

Philip did not trust his voice enough to speak. Once he vented the fury inside, there would be no caging it.

Cheshire stared at him, his face slowly losing color. "I can see that this is a shock to you. I'm sorry. I assumed, given that the DNA showed you and Mr. Lansing were father and son, that it wasn't an issue."

Philip drank down the last of his water. "The idea takes some...adjustment. I wasn't always on good terms with Lansing." He couldn't say "my father".

"But you must care about the child or you wouldn't have run off to save Delilah Sefton from Genet's people."

"As I said, protecting people is my job with the Phoenix Institute." And Del certainly deserved that. "I didn't know until you spoke that the child was mine."

"That must be a shock. Again, I'm sorry." Cheshire stuffed his hands into his lab coat. "But let me take this chance to say that your healing ability is simply amazing. I know, the firestarting is flashy, but the ability to repair cells at a molecular level is on another plane entirely. It requires such control."

Control, yes. The same control that was keeping him from wrapping his hands around Cheshire's throat.

Philip nodded. "It's useful."

"Your hand and arm were burned when you went to rescue Demetrius, yes? Could I see the healed burns on your arm? I have to see this ability in action."

Philip rolled up his sleeve and held out his arm without a word. Cheshire said nothing as he examined the healed forearm, but he clicked his tongue several times.

While the doctor held his arm, Philip stayed calm by imagining various ways to kill the man. Tossing people off a bridge or cliff was always a good option, as the victim had time to be terrified on the way down and there was no clean-up required. Maybe he should drop the doctor at Del's feet and let her decide. No, he wouldn't let Del get near this man.

"Remarkable. I can see no traces of injury. Were your lungs burned in the fire?"

"I assume they were. It was difficult to breathe until my healing kicked in."

"And yet, you can breathe normally now. Lung samples would tell me so—"

"Not right now. We have more pressing concerns."

"Ms. Sefton, yes." Cheshire sat back down. "I apologize. I do get wrapped up in my work."

He wondered how Cheshire would react if he obtained a lung sample by ramming his hand down the man's throat. All in the interests of science, of course. "We all get wrapped up in our work."

"When can I examine Ms. Sefton? It's crucial that I know how the child is growing."

"As I said, when I trust you. Plus, she's had a shock and she's exhausted. She needs rest."

"How can I earn your trust?"

It'd be a cold day in hell. But this was the lever he needed for Cheshire's cooperation. Cheshire didn't need to know that he was making false promises. "She's also just coming to grips with being involved with firestarters and having men trying to kidnap her. She needs time. A few days, at least, before confronting the man who made her pregnant against her will."

"I suppose that makes sense." Cheshire looked at the floor.

"In the meantime, you can help me."

"I don't know how I could do that."

"We need to find Genet, and we need any of your notes about the altered sperm and any problem you anticipate with the pregnancy. You can help with both."

"I don't see how I could help find Genet."

"You're a genius, doctor. You worked with him for several months. Something you remember might be the clue to finding him."

"That makes sense. I'll answer any questions you have."

Philip nodded. "Good. Now about your research notes—"

"They were destroyed in the fire."

"C'mon, Doctor. You're brilliant and dedicated completely to your work. You must have had those notes or files backed up somewhere off-site."

Cheshire stared at the floor again. "Um..."

"It's safer here than anywhere else. And surely that information will be necessary as you follow Ms. Sefton's pregnancy."

Cheshire nodded. "It is. Mr. Lansing warned me against back-ups. He said someone could steal them, but I had to protect my research."

"Where are your back-ups? Stored on a remote server?"

"No, too many people could potentially steal content online, even on the most secure servers. I stored my notes on a portable hard drive that I kept hidden in my home."

Philip blinked. Idiot. He should have thought to go to Cheshire's home first and search it before confronting the doctor. That was a basic investigative step. The lack of sleep in the past two days had caught up to him.

"I think it's time to make a trip to your home, then, Doctor, before someone else does," Philip said.

The door to the room opened and Gabe walked in with a plate of food. "I thought you might be getting hungry, Dr. Cheshire."

Philip heard Cheshire's stomach rumble. The doctor shrugged, a sheepish look on his face, and took Gabe's offering of pot roast and mashed potatoes.

Philip suppressed his irritation. Gabe had to have a reason for interrupting them beyond feeding Cheshire. As the doctor settled down to eat, the two men excused themselves.

After he shut the door to the room, Philip rounded on Gabe in the hallway. "Why the hell did you interrupt me?"

"Because I'm not dumb and neither is Alec. He ordered me to take a couple of people and check out Cheshire's home already," Gabe said. "But we were too late. Someone had tossed the place before we got there."

Damn. "Did they get Cheshire's back-up hard drive?"

"I have no idea but I thought we'd ask Cheshire that after he finishes eating. Alec's ordered a twenty-four-hour watch on Cheshire. We don't want him outside the facility at all. If Genet didn't find the research, they might try to grab him next."

Philip nodded. "You're right."

"Glad you think so, because my next advice is for you to get some sleep. You look like hell, Drake. You got the woman here safely, Alec's watching over her and I can handle Cheshire. Go get comatose for a while. We'll need you at your best."

"I don't need as much sleep as most people."

"You need some. Look, you were on the verge of strangling Cheshire in there."

"I had reason."

"Yeah, you did, but we need him alive. You got him talking. Now I can go from there by playing good cop. How long has it been since you slept?"

Philip did the calculations in his head. Almost forty-eight hours. "Fine," he growled.

Gabe grabbed his forearm. "Drake? I'm sorry about what he did to you. I'd want to strangle him too if he did that to me."

"I appreciate that." He cleared his throat. "I'll crash in one of the bedrooms the next level down."

"I thought you'd go back to the penthouse and stay near the woman. You two seemed pretty tight when you drove in."

Philip merely stared at Gabe until the younger man backed up a step.

"I'll sleep where I damn well please."

Later, as he settled into a utilitarian bunk in a room on one of the lower levels of the Phoenix Institute, Philip realized he would rather have slept with Del curled up against him. As a child, Lily had always comforted him. It had never been sexual back then, that wasn't even a stray thought all those years ago. It had been all about comfort and love.

Now, however, was another story. Their age gap was insignificant as adults. He thought of her in a completely new way. He kept flashing to how Del had felt with her arm wrapped around his waist, how she'd looked so alive when taking the Charger around corners at such a high speed, and how she'd flirted with him in her bar before she knew why he was there.

He hoped she never guessed he was her Hawk.

It was best if he never saw her again. But that left one problem: the child she carried was also his son.

Lansing had abandoned his biological son. Philip was loath to do the same. But his very presence would anger Del.

He had no answers at all.

So he would kill Genet instead.

Chapter Twelve

Del slept far better than she expected in a strange place. Her mind had been whirling still when she hit the pillow, but the fatigue from her pregnancy must have dragged her down into sleep.

The first thing she did when she woke up was pull her cell phone out of her duffel bag and call Tammy. She wanted normal, she wanted some piece of her old life. She cursed as Tammy's voicemail picked up, took a deep breath and left a quick message saying she was all right but that someone should cover her shifts for a few days and to please make sure to keep an eye out for the beer delivery scheduled for this afternoon.

She put the phone down on the bedside table and looked around. Alec had apologized for giving her a small room and said the guest quarters weren't quite ready yet. Sheepishly, he told her this room was his childhood bedroom and offered her a room in the complex below instead if it was too small. She'd begged off. All she wanted was a bed and quiet.

It was definitely a boy's bedroom, from the lamp with the toy train that went around the base to the glow-in-the-dark stars on the ceiling and the bright blue paint on the walls.

She reached into her duffel to pull out clothes for today. Instead, she found the handgun Drake had given her last night. She pulled it out and ran her fingers along the barrel. A Sig Sauer and probably a nine-millimeter, if she remembered right. A very good handgun from a very strange man.

She settled back on the pillow and stared at the ceiling. Why had Drake seemed so familiar? She reviewed the day's events in her mind's eye, trying to make that maddening connection that seemed just out of her mental reach.

It wasn't until she reviewed their conversation beside the Charger that something clicked. They'd been staring up at a hawk after a lull in the conversation. *I'd rather be a hawk.* That's what Drake had said. Drake. That was also a name connected to birds of prey. Hawk. Drake.

Hawk.

She stood up. Hawk. *Drake was Hawk.*

But, no, he was too young. Hawk would be older than she was. Drake was maybe thirty, tops. That wasn't possible.

Yet when he danced with her, he'd picked *It Had to be You.* She and Hawk had danced to that as innocent children. That was no coincidence.

Wait, Alec had said that Drake could heal his injuries. If he could do that, maybe that included facial wrinkles from age. And she'd pegged Drake as in his mid-twenties until she saw him up close and decided he was older than he looked.

Hawk would be in his early to mid-forties now, if he was alive.

Oh, he was definitely alive.

Hawk, the murdering son of a bitch. Was that why she'd been dragged into this? Hawk had some plan to hurt her? Maybe he'd made up everything and she should get the hell out of here right now.

She had her hand on the doorknob before she stopped. If she left, she wouldn't have a chance to make him pay for what he'd done. She sat back down on the bed and picked up the gun. And not everything Hawk had told her was a lie. Alec's firestarting abilities were absolutely genuine. The men who'd tried to kidnap her were real. How the hell did she sort through all the lies and truth in this?

She put her hand over her swollen abdomen. Oh, shit. If what Alec said was true, Hawk could be the father or brother of this child. The man who murdered her parents had a thirty-three percent chance of being her baby's father. Nauseated, she ran to the bathroom and splashed water on her face. It didn't work. She threw up, chest heaving, her body in agony more than physical.

"Del?"

That was Alec's voice.

"Are you okay?"

She groped for a towel and wiped off her face. She swallowed, her throat raw. "I'm okay," she yelled. "Morning sickness."

"That sucks."

Alec, she judged, was standing just outside the door now. "Anything I can do?"

Not unless he could get her out of this damned nightmare. "No, I'll shower and be fine."

"You up for breakfast?"

The last thing she wanted was food. But she should eat. Otherwise, she'd be lightheaded. "Coffee, at least. Decaf. Maybe some dry toast."

"You got it."

She splashed more water on her face and brushed her teeth. She wanted to like Alec. She wanted to believe him.

But she'd liked Drake yesterday too.

The coffee helped. She begged off on the toast as yet. Alec hovered as she drank. She finally asked if she was keeping him from something important.

"No. You're my priority right now. My team went to investigate a lead last night, and they're doing all they can. If they needed my help, they'd ask." He frowned. "Am I doing this wrong? I don't have much experience being a host."

She smiled, despite her distrust. Alec was such an unusual combination of power and something that was oddly close to innocence. Maybe purity, if his story could be believed.

"You're doing fine." If Hawk had lied to her, maybe he was deceiving Alec as well. This was like being stuck in quicksand. The more she struggled to find out what was going on, the more stuck she became. "You don't sound like Drake is your favorite person, from what you said last night."

"He doesn't like me. Beth says that's because of her."

"He doesn't like you because you're sleeping with his daughter?"

Alec leaned back against the kitchen counter. "That's part of it, but more than that, he thinks what I want for the Phoenix Institute puts Beth in danger. He can't stand the thought of her being hurt. I've seen him do superhuman stuff just to make sure she's safe."

"What do you do here that makes Beth unsafe? I thought Genet was only after me. And Beth isn't part of your assault team. No one's shooting at her."

"I'd never let anyone shoot at her." Alec's face grew solemn. "I was raised in isolation. Beth was raised in a normal life because Drake made sure she was protected from people who wanted to use her telepathy. What I want this place to be is a safe haven where kids with psychic abilities can come and learn about their powers and still have a normal life. The best of both worlds."

"You're talking about something like an after-school program for superpowered kids?" He had to be kidding.

"Exactly!" Alec pointed at her. "Everything open and above-board. Beth had to hide her powers. She's still wary of what they can do. I want these kids to enjoy their abilities, like I do." He waved a hand and his coffee mug floated through the air to him. "Drake thinks being open can only cause trouble. Beth says that's because he's basically been hidden all of his life. He doesn't know how to live in the open."

"My kid isn't even here and someone's already trying to kidnap him," Del said. "So I guess I can see the point there."

"Drake calls it being in the line of fire." Alec sighed. "Beth says he really can't conceive of a hopeful outcome for all of this because of the way his life has been."

"How has his life been? This is because of the CIA work?" How much did Alec know about his sort-of in-law?

"I'm not sure." Alec sat on the kitchen stool in the breakfast nook, right next to her. "Like I said last night, he did CIA black ops and undercover work. I know that means pretending to be someone you're not most of the time. I also know that means he's a trained assassin." Alec turned. "Am I scaring you?"

Del shook her head. "I'm all scared out for now. And I'm curious about the man who saved me yesterday." Damn curious. How had Hawk ended up here?

She wanted to know what his game was. She'd have sworn Drake was being sincere last night, but that was before she'd known he was Hawk. She had to admit their upbringing, where they had to learn to hide from the authorities, would be perfect training for a spy. And maybe joining the CIA, the government agency that terrified his stepfather, had been Hawk's "fuck you" to the man who raised him. She knew one truth about Hawk. He had hated his stepfather.

It didn't explain how she'd been drawn into this. "What do you think of Drake? You can't really think he's crazy."

"I don't know him because he doesn't let anyone know him. He's tightly wound. We talk when we need to work together but otherwise..." Alec shrugged. "I know he's relentless. He'll find out who's trying to hurt you and why. I think you're about to know him a lot better than me."

"Why?"

"I told you we had a lead in this investigation. That's because we talked to someone involved in, um, your baby's creation." Alec held eye contact with her. "Drake's sperm was used in their experiment."

"He's the baby's father," Del whispered.

Alec nodded, almost sheepish.

Well, I did say I wanted to take a hammer upside the head of your father, kid.

She blinked and focused on Alec again. The young man seemed almost disappointed he wasn't about to become a father. "Why didn't Drake come here this morning and tell me this?" Hawk had seemed very protective yesterday.

"He left early this morning to track down Genet. I don't know when he'll be back. I thought you'd want to know right away. I'm sorry if that was the wrong call."

"It's all right." She probably wasn't in the right kind of mood to hear this from Hawk anyway. "You're sure Drake had nothing to do with what happened to me?"

"Never," Alec said. "He's a good father to Beth. She adores him, and I can see why. They connect. When we had to pull her out from Lansing's custody last year, he brought a bag of candy for her. I never would have thought of it, but he knew she'd be scared so he brought her favorite candy."

She looked away from Alec and stared at the wall-size television in the living room. Hawk had always been thoughtful with her as well. That was what had made his betrayal so terrible.

Her stomach growled. Hungry already. Greedy kid.

"You know, Drake didn't tell me much about what happened yesterday, just that an attempt had been made to grab you by Genet's people but you were safe and he was bringing you here. What happened?"

"He showed up at my bar with his Dodge Charger and then told me he needed to speak with me about the baby. I thought he was nuts, but he knew some things that he shouldn't know, like the fact I was attacked." And raped. "And he knew who Genet was. I was following him to a local diner to hear the rest when a van blocked the road." She told Alec how the men had tried to grab her, how Drake had intervened, and the car chase.

"Drake let you *drive his car?*"

She smiled. "I'm an excellent driver."

"I bet. It also sounds like he talked more to you in one day than he ever talked to me or anyone else except Beth."

"He had a lot of explaining to do."

"I guess."

Del went back to the living room with her coffee and sat in the same chair she'd used last night. Alec was pacing. It was exhausting to watch. "What's that supposed to mean?"

"It means you got a glimpse of the real Drake. You asked me if I liked him earlier. Did you like him?"

"I..." Alec, she realized, was no fool. "I did."

"It's a good start."

"With what?"

"You're the kid's parents. You'll need to work together, right?"

"I hadn't gotten that far." *When hell freezes over.* "How did he end up being Beth's father?"

Alec sat across from her, the fireplace between them. "She was raised by a single mother. She was eight when someone grabbed her for her telepathic abilities. Her mother was killed when they kidnapped her. She doesn't talk about her mother a lot." Alec took a breath. "They had her in some facility, studying her telepathy. The CIA heard about this and sent Drake in to get her out. He was supposed to turn her over to Lansing to be raised and trained with me."

"He didn't?"

"Drake hated Lansing and for good reasons. Drake rescued Beth but he faked her death. While the CIA and Lansing thought she was dead, he gave her a new identity, placed her with a foster family and made sure she grew up normally. Drake didn't dare visit her openly or the CIA might track him and know she was alive. But he must have seen her a lot because they know each other really well. She says she couldn't have chosen a better father."

Son of a bitch. That kind of rescue was something Hawk'd pledged to do for *her*. About three months before the Feds got their parents, they had planned an escape. Hawk had said he was old enough to protect her now. She'd gotten cold feet at leaving her parents and told him to go without her. He didn't. He said he'd stay to protect her.

And then he'd killed her parents.

So Hawk had eventually rescued a little girl, if Alec was to be believed.

"I wish this made more sense," she said to Alec. "Besides that Drake is the father, what else did you learn from whoever made me pregnant?"

"We filmed the interview Drake did with Dr. Cheshire." Alec cleared his throat. "Did you want to see it?"

"Yes." She wanted to see this man who'd screwed up her life. She especially wanted to see how he interacted with Hawk.

What she didn't expect was for Alec to pull up the video on the big screen. She was glad she'd begged off on breakfast until after because her stomach felt sick almost immediately while watching.

The Messiah gene. That was the first shock. The second was that Richard Lansing had been Hawk's biological father. Unless she was misreading Hawk badly, he'd hated the man as much as he hated his stepfather.

She wondered if Dr. Cheshire realized he'd been a few seconds from death when he examined Hawk's arm. She knew that look on Hawk's face. Blank, utterly devoid of expression. It hid murderous rage. She'd seen him explode once at some boys they'd run into at the local bowling alley. The boys had been teasing her. One of them had taken her favorite stuffed animal and taunted her with it.

Hawk's stepfather had specialized in noisy, screaming rages. Hawk was the opposite. That day, he'd been so ice cold, it was eerie. He'd made not a sound as he waded into that crowd of boys. Only their numbers had saved someone from being killed. He hadn't learned to be a killer from the CIA. He'd been one when he joined.

"Del, you okay?" Alec asked.

"I could use that dry toast to settle my stomach."

"You got it."

Del kept her gaze glued on the video. When Alec nudged her just a few seconds later, she flinched.

"Sorry." He handed her a plate. Dry wheat toast, just as she'd asked.

She paused the video. "How the hell did you make toast in five seconds?"

Alec held up a hand. "I can hard-boil eggs with my heat too."

She took a bite of the toast. It tasted completely normal. "Thank you."

She munched on the toast, not tasting it, as she watched the end of the video. She leaned back in Alec's comfortable chair and closed her eyes when it was done. She put her hands over her baby, Cheshire's words echoing through her head. Accelerated growth rate, he'd said. *Messiah gene.* A healer, like Hawk and the late Richard Lansing, except her child might be able to heal others.

If her son lived.

Cheshire seemed concerned about her pregnancy. And her doctor had quizzed her already about the date of conception, so that meant her son was growing faster than normal by design. How would that affect her? And his birth? To her eye, her baby bump was visibly bigger than just a few days ago, but that could be fear prodding her imagination.

"Del? Are you hurt?"

Other than her heart bleeding all over the floor, no. "You said you could feel my baby moving last night. Can you still feel him? Can you tell if he's okay?"

Alec knelt as he had last night and put his hand on her stomach. After a few seconds, he nodded. "He's moving around. Seems fine to me, but I'm not a doctor. If Beth were here, she might be able to hear him thinking and we'd know for sure." He sighed. "Do you want to go see your doctor? I'll take you."

"No. Someone leaked my medical records to Cheshire. I don't trust my doctor anymore."

She stared at the floor for a long time. She wanted to go back home and crawl in bed for days. But on the day she'd bought Bar & Grill, she'd stopped running.

Alec started pacing again. "Del?"

"I don't know what to do next," she confessed. "I don't even know how to begin to decide what to do."

"Do you want to keep the baby?" Alec asked quietly.

"He's *my* son." She had already decided that. And even if she hadn't, she wasn't going to walk away and leave him with crazy people. And she'd never leave him with Hawk.

"Then what we're going to do is make sure you're both safe," Alec said.

"And what do I do?"

"No one thinks you should suddenly jump up and do something right now. You're safe here, we're investigating and I'll let you know the minute we find out anything." He waved at the game system. "It's hooked up to a ton of television stations and has instant movie viewing, and there's a computer in the big study. I've got a lot of books too. If there's anything else you want, tell me, and I'll get it for you."

"I want peace and quiet. I want my bar back."

"I'm so sorry you've been pulled into this."

"I know you are." And she believed that. If Alec was some sort of devious mastermind, she'd drink a fifth of vodka. "I wish I knew why Lansing picked me." She pulled her knees close to her chin. Soon, that motion would be impossible as her belly expanded. The easiest explanation for why she'd been picked was that Hawk knew she was Lily and wanted to use her or hurt her for some reason. He'd certainly seemed eager to be in her company yesterday.

But that didn't fit what she'd seen in the interview with Hawk and Cheshire. Hawk had settled into a cold rage the minute he realized he was the father of her son. Cheshire claimed Lansing had specifically picked her, and Hawk had hated Lansing. She didn't think they would've worked together.

She slipped her hand inside her sweater and curled it around the handle of the gun Hawk had given her. He probably never expected her to use it against him.

Or maybe he did.

"I want to talk to H—er, Drake as soon as he's back." If Hawk could be coldly patient, so could she. "We've got a lot to talk about."

Chapter Thirteen

Philip had learned as a child that sleep was a valuable commodity, so he followed Gabe's advice and slept, though fitfully. He'd be no good to Del Sefton and her child if he went about with his mind muddled and his body's reflexes dulled by exhaustion.

As he woke, Philip repeated her name over and over to sear it into his brain. Delilah Sefton. Del Sefton. Del. He had to banish Lily and think of the woman only as Del. Because if he thought of her as Lily, he wouldn't be able to think at all.

He sought out Gabe in the Phoenix Institute's CIC. Combat Information Central. On a ship or submarine, that meant a secure area safe from elements. Here, it meant a panic room whose only entry was a door of double steel, secured by two locks with passcode and handprint identification. This was Lansing's design, and Philip wished Alec had ripped up the entire room and started fresh. Lansing had hidden Orion Systems from Alec. There could be something hidden in this security system that was equally dangerous.

If he'd been Alec, he'd have burned the whole place down and started over.

Inside, the CIC was strictly military design, which made perfect sense given that all the members of Alec's F-Team were veterans. Gray walls, gray floors, gray counters. The chairs were the only comfort in the room, gray-metal chairs with leather padding. It was so utilitarian that Philip was comforted. No sign of Lansing here.

The emphasis was in the gadgets and tech, not interior decorating. Gabe liked his toys. Philip didn't blame him. A wall of computer monitors linked to cameras on the Institute grounds dominated one side of the room. The opposite wall had another set of monitors, these hooked up to various PCs and other devices.

Gabe was already at work when Philip entered, sifting through numerical data on one of the monitors above him. Another screen was covered in symbols that Philip couldn't decipher.

"Is that the flash drive information?" Philip pointed to the symbols.

Gabe twisted in his chair, keeping his feet resting on the metal counter that ran the length of the room. "Yep. What you're seeing right now is the encryption decoder program that a friend at the NSA sent. It's working to put it all into English that we can read but it's slow. There are a lot of obscure scientific words. But at least I got past the fail safes that would have scrubbed the data."

"How long will it take?"

"No telling for certain, but at least a day."

Damn. Philip reminded himself that patience was necessary in investigations. But he wanted Del back in her normal life *now*. "And the other screen?"

"Bank records. I'm tracking the money that flowed into Orion Systems from the dummy company that Lansing created to cover his tracks. Whoever cut the checks for Orion might have known what was going on. That might give us a clue as to how Genet slipped in as the lab's manager."

"Genet had help."

"And money's the best way of finding out who," Gabe said.

Philip wondered if the help had been the mysterious watchers the late Richard Lansing had noted in his personal journal. Lansing had just said "they" were watching and might act. He had feared their interference in his grand schemes. Thus far, Philip had not found any clues beyond Alec and Beth's report of a mental "sponginess" during the container ship assault.

All Philip knew was that someone else was out there with psychic abilities, an unknown agenda and with enough skill to hide their tracks from him. It was possible they were behind Genet. And that their agenda included Del's son.

My son.

"How would you like to do something more direct?" Philip asked.

Gabe swiveled his chair to face Philip. "What did you have in mind?"

"I installed a tracking bug on Genet's car yesterday."

"Shit, why didn't you tell me yesterday, I could've—"

"Genet ditched the car at a commuter lot about two miles from Orion Systems." Philip had checked that yesterday on his smart phone while driving to protect Del.

"Damn."

"It's still a lead, depending on how good you are at accessing systems where you don't belong."

Gabe cracked his knuckles. "Now you have my full attention."

"The commuter lot is right near the entrance to Interstate 80. If I had been Genet, I would've picked that spot to switch cars so I could get somewhere on the highway. Genet was at an office building near Del's home in less than an hour."

"He zipped right down the highway."

"Probably. If we could access state police cameras that monitor the highway or even hack into any local cameras that happened to catch Genet by accident, we could find out what he's driving right now."

"You want me to find a back-door access into the state police?"

"Yes. And any local merchants, like gas stations or convenience stores that have exterior cameras."

"Local merchants usually have closed systems, meaning their cameras feed directly to their computers rather than being on a broadcast signal. I'll have to take over their computers instead of tuning into the right frequency."

Philip crossed his arms over his chest. "Think you can handle that?"

Gabe frowned. "It's hours of work at best, a couple of days' work at most. And I'm already involved in two big projects."

Philip smiled. "You can obviously multitask."

Gabe nodded after a few seconds. "That I can." He turned back to his keyboard.

"Before you get too engrossed, did your team take video on the raid of Cheshire's home?" Philip asked.

"Yeah. It's queued up on computer five." Gabe waved his hands at the PC in the corner.

Philip put on the headphones for computer five, a tricked-up desktop PC that was running what he thought was a Linux system. It could also be of Gabe's own design. He wasn't knowledgeable enough about tech to tell the difference.

He settled back in as the video began running, trying to keep his mind open to all impressions. Gabe's team had likely been through it, but a fresh set of eyes might spot something.

Cheshire lived in a condo development, not unlike the one where Philip lived. Gabe's crew had entered through the front door, presumably using Cheshire's own key. The design was basic as well. There was an entranceway and hallways with a living room to the right. Steps led upstairs, and the kitchen was located at the back of the hallway.

Cheshire had done little to decorate his home. It still had the same dull tan original carpet and white walls. There were no photos or artwork on the wall in the living room. The mantel above the faux fireplace was empty.

The camera moved into the living room first. The television/entertainment area had been obviously searched before F-Team arrived. DVDs littered the carpet and all the contents of all the drawers of the television stand had been dumped on the floor. That was a mistake, Philip thought. He would've confiscated all the DVDs in the theory the back-up discs could be disguised among the movies and television shows. Or perhaps whoever searched the place had found it among the DVDs and simply left the others.

The team moved into the office past the living room. It had obviously been designed as a dining room but Cheshire had packed it with several computers, shelves of books and research materials, three file cabinets and two desks.

This room looked like a tornado had gone through it.

The file cabinets had been pushed over on their sides. Papers, pens and other office materials littered the floor. The side of one cabinet had been peeled back to expose the innards. Someone had hoped to find a hidden compartment in it. He doubted they had because then they would have stopped the search. Instead, desks had been tipped over and walls had been punctured in several places as if someone thought there might be something hidden inside the drywall. Again, impossible to tell if anything had been found, but it didn't look like the sheetrock had hidden anything.

In the kitchen, cabinets and drawers were all open. Cooking utensils and food were scattered on the floor. Someone had opened the fridge but nothing of interest was in there. The fridge itself had been pulled away from the wall.

Upstairs, there was the same chaos. Philip guessed Genet's people had found nothing downstairs and so kept going. The fact the place was in such disorder might mean the original searchers had found nothing or that it took them a long search to find it. How badly did these people want Cheshire's records? Because there was only one place they existed now: Cheshire's head. Philip wondered what would happen if they let the doctor go home to put his condo back together. Would that draw Genet's men out in the open to grab him? They might be even watching the place right now.

If it had been him after the doctor, Philip would have left hidden cameras and audio surveillance in the condo. Just in case anyone came back.

He took off the headphones and swiveled the chair toward Gabe. "Did you look for surveillance left by the searchers?"

Gabe held up a finger to signal Philip to wait a moment. Philip ground his teeth and stared at the monitor with the decoding program running. It still didn't make sense to him.

Gabe finally turned to him. "Yeah, we found bugs. I tried tracking their signal but had no luck, so I shut them down instead."

"They never found what they were looking for."

"I'm guessing not. Neither did we. Our search yielded zip." Gabe sighed. He looked up at the bank records and the decoder program. "I hate slow. Wait. I might have something on a camera at a service station near I-80. They're broadcasting on a common frequency. We got lucky."

Grainy video came up on the sixty-inch screen that dominated one wall. "I've got three vehicles leaving around the time Genet might have had to get on the highway. There's one with the driver as the right height and body build." Gabe zeroed in on a BMW sedan.

"Too grainy for proper ID and the license plate is obscured," Philip said. "But it's close, down to the suit."

"I know."

The video showed the man driving the car getting his tank filled. Not only that, he'd gotten out of the car and purchased a cup of coffee.

"Can your programs run while you're gone?" Philip asked.

Gabe leaned back in his chair. "Yeah, for a few hours. Why?"

"Boots on the ground are still the best for real detective work. Genet's memorable, especially with that imperious air of his. We need to talk to the employees of the convenience store as soon as possible, while their memory of him is fresh."

"What could they tell us other than give us a description, which we already have?"

"Well, that's just it, isn't it? We don't know until we ask."

Philip tossed a vaguely army-like green jacket over his black T-shirt and walked with Gabe into the parking lot. He jingled the keys to the Charger in his pocket, debating whether to take the car.

After a minute of waiting, Gabe spoke. "I thought we were in a hurry."

"I'm deciding how to play it with the store clerks. If I take my car, it'll be remembered. That might be useful, but it also might be foolish, depending on whether Genet finds out someone was asking about him." The Charger had been useful at Del's bar, gaining him instant solidarity with the regulars. This time, though, his instincts said to take a vehicle that wouldn't be noticed.

"We'll take one of the vans. You have keys?"

"Sure," Gabe said. "I'll drive."

Once they were off, Gabe glanced at him. "Do you do that all the time?"

"I don't understand your question."

"I meant do you weigh all the angles and outcomes before you act all the time?" Gabe turned from the Institute entrance onto the road.

"Yes."

"That must get tiring."

"When you start decoding a program or hacking into another system, you investigate all the possible outcomes before you start before deciding how best to approach them. It's the same thing."

"That's tech, though. What you do is a hell of a way to live your life."

Very true. "You were a tech nerd among your fellow officers in the Army. A gay tech nerd. You had to weigh all the angles to survive. That's similar."

"Ah, it wasn't so bad. At first I was the skinny nerd. Once I proved I could handle basic, though, I was the tough skinny nerd. Then when I got assigned to tech in the field, I was the skinny nerd miracle worker. Nobody liked me much—they figured I was gay—but we needed each other. During our first engagement, though, I was able to call in air help. Then I became *their* skinny gay tech miracle worker." He grinned.

"After a year, I had a squad of butch straight guys willing to beat up anyone who made fun of me."

Philip nodded. Combat made the strongest bonds.

"Were you ever with a unit?" Gabe asked.

"No." No band of brothers for him. It seemed like he'd spent his life undercover, blending in by becoming whatever was needed. It had, he mused, included being gay twice.

"If you work by yourself, why ask me to go with you today?" Gabe asked.

"I was nearly blown up, attacked and almost shot yesterday. Not smart to go out alone, even on a job like this, which seems simple. At the least, you'll be a witness if something goes wrong. You're armed, yes?"

"Yes."

Gabe asked no more questions and Philip offered no more conversation. As they pulled into the service station, Philip ran a hand through his hair to muff it up. He hadn't shaved this morning. Good, that would complete the look.

"Follow my lead," Philip ordered.

"If I can tell what it is," Gabe said.

Philip shrugged.

The service station was modern, with a big canopy loaded with blaring fluorescent lights set over the gas pumps. Philip scanned the station workers, looking for the medium-sized African-American woman who'd pumped Genet's gas. For investigative purposes, they were lucky that New Jersey still refused to allow self-serve islands. It meant that Genet had had to interact with someone.

He found the woman working the counter in the station's convenience store. He waited until the crowd thinned out, approached her, and paid for a pack of Marlboro Reds. He pocketed the cigarettes and a pack of matches and took his change.

"So, I'm looking for a man," he said to her.

"Ain't we all, babe," she said.

He smiled. "But I'm thinking you can help me." He pulled out a wad of bills.

She frowned and drew him off to the side. "Hey, I ain't getting involved in anything that requires a payoff. Out." She pointed at the door.

Philip pointed to Gabe. "I'm helping out my cousin. Seems he picked up this hot guy yesterday. They had a good time then this fucker runs out with my aunt's car the morning after."

She looked over at Gabe, who shuffled his feet, hunched his shoulders and looked at the floor.

"Like I care. You could report that to the cops."

"Yeah, then he'd be out of the closet with his mom. She'd fucking kill him." Philip shook his head. "And I'd have to be the one to tell her. Not doing it. Not to mention I'd have to take the bum in to live at my place. Family." He shrugged.

The woman laughed. "I hear that. So what do you want?"

"This guy might've filled up here. I just wanna know if he said anything about where he's going."

She shrugged. "Ain't no guarantee I'm going to remember your guy. Lot of guys come through, lot of them are hot."

"He's really cute," Gabe mumbled. "Blond curls."

"Well, I might remember that," the woman said.

Philip peeled off a hundred-dollar bill. "Help me out. This will be cheaper for me than putting my cousin up." He jabbed his thumb at Gabe. "This guy came in about nine a.m. yesterday driving a BMW. Tall, blond, arrogant. Lots of curls, like he says."

"I like curls," Gabe said.

"Yeah, I like them too." The woman snatched the hundred out of Philip's hand. "I would've liked them on this guy too but they came with a lot of fucking attitude." She nodded. "Your guy tried to get me to bring him a cup of coffee while I was filling him up. I told him get his own damn coffee, it's my job to pump gas, not fetch for some jerk who won't get out of the car. Asshole. He did get his own coffee eventually. After holding up the car behind him."

"Yeah, that's the arrogant son of a bitch," Philip said. "He say anything you remember? Something that might help us find him?"

"Well..." She looked at the wad of money in his hand.

He gave her another hundred. Apparently, she'd get involved if someone pissed her off. "Did he pay with a credit card?"

"Nope, cash, but I got something better than a credit card number." She grinned. "I thought, this guy needs a lesson in manners. I got a cousin too, only mine works for the state cops assigned to I-80. So I took down this asshole's license plate and passed it on to my cousin when I saw the asshole heading out west on the highway."

She had Genet's license plate number? "You got him pulled over? Hah!" Philip smirked.

"I wish." She sighed. "My cousin said he'd try but some idiot in a truck fishtailed and caused a damn mess on the highway and he had to work that instead of patrol."

She gave him Genet's plate number off the top of her head as she rambled about other rude customers. Philip pulled off another hundred as a reward. "Now we can track which way he went. This is really gonna save my cousin's ass. And save me from a whole shitload of trouble." He seized her shoulders and kissed her cheek. "Lady, you're a freakin' genius."

"I know it," she said, nodding and setting her hoop earrings bouncing. "I know it." She looked at Gabe. "Hey, you ever want to play for the other team, I like 'em skinny."

"She probably wouldn't steal your car." Philip nudged Gabe's shoulder.

"Damn straight," she said.

"Shut up, Phil," Gabe said.

"Hey, I'm helping you, ain't I?"

The woman glanced over at the counter and saw a customer waiting. "Good luck with finding the asshole. Give him one for me." She shoved the money into the front pocket of her sweatshirt and went back to work.

Philip took one of the Marlboros out of his pocket and lit it as they walked to the car. He'd quit smoking because it was addictive and sometimes he was in a place where he couldn't get any. It felt good to light up again after so long. It wasn't like smoking would kill him. His lungs would self-repair.

Gabe stuffed his hands into his pockets as they walked back to the van. "I almost bought that act and I knew it was phony. Nice, Drake."

"It's Jersey. Two rules. Money talks and assholes are remembered."

"A license plate number." Gabe shook his head. "I'd never have figured we'd get that."

"Boots on the ground." Philip blew out smoke. "You never know until you get some boots on the ground."

Chapter Fourteen

Philip planned to head out again once he had an address connected with Genet's car registration. This time, he intended to take F-Team with him, just in case.

But Alec greeted him in the parking lot.

Philip lit up another cigarette as he got out of the car. "What?"

"Del is looking for you."

Philip blew out smoke. "So? We've got a lead. She'll have to wait."

"No. She wants to see you, and you're going to talk to her."

No doubt noticing the tension, Gabe walked past them. "I'll run the plate number, Drake. I should have something fast."

Philip nodded and looked back at Alec. "Why is it so damned important to you that I talk to Delilah Sefton?"

"Because you're the father of her kid, she's scared and she said she needed to talk to you." Alec crossed his arms over his chest. "So that's what you're going to do."

Philip took a long drag on the cigarette, tossed the stump to the blacktop and crushed it under his work boot. Alec had appointed himself Del's protector. Interesting. More interesting was that Del was demanding to speak to him. Their tenuous bond from yesterday was too weak, he thought, for her to want his company. She might have been attracted to him but that was in the moment.

No, she either needed to talk to him as the child's father, or Del had realized he was really Hawk.

He'd hoped to never see her again. That was for the best. Alec's stance told him that wasn't possible.

"All right. But before the day gets any busier, I need a promise from you."

Alec hooked his thumbs on the pockets of his jeans, wary. "What?"

"Many things could happen in the next few days. I want you to promise that if anything happens to me, anything at all, that you'll make sure Del Sefton and her son are safe."

"Of course, I'll do that. I'd do that anyway."

"Alec, I want you to swear that if anything happens to me, no matter what it is, that you'll protect Del and her son. *Anything.*"

Alec frowned. "What's going on, Drake?"

"Promise me, Farley."

"You're keeping secrets again."

"Yes. Now, promise. And you make sure Beth keeps it too."

"This makes no sense."

"I know."

Alec glared for a few seconds and finally nodded. "I promise. But you're not planning to get yourself killed, are you, Drake?"

The firestarter was worried on behalf of Beth. "My daughter has you. She doesn't need me." Philip brushed past Alec. "So where's Del Sefton?"

"I gave her one of the meeting rooms, like the one Cheshire was in when you talked to him."

"The cameras in there have to be turned off. This needs to be a private conversation."

"They are. I figured with the baby and all, you two would have a lot to talk about and you'd want to do it in private."

You have no idea, Alec.

Del sat on the couch in the room, her hands curled over the handgun that Drake had given her. Alec had promised to bring him here. Her stomach roiled. She shivered. For many years, she'd blocked out the memory of that day when she was nine years old but now it kept replaying over and over in her head, as if it had happened yesterday. Or even five minutes ago.

Yelling, yelling, so much yelling. She'd pressed her ear to the door of the bathroom. She couldn't make out words, just the voices and the anger behind them. Her mother. Hawk's mother. Hawk, sounding like he was crying. More yelling from far outside, male voices identifying themselves as FBI.

Hawk's mother screamed. A shotgun went off. Del flinched and climbed into the bathtub, trembling. Her mother had stopped yelling. Hawk was still yelling. Her father was screaming and she could hear him say, "You killed my wife, you son of a bitch." Another shotgun blast. Her father didn't speak again. She heard a wail, then the sheer fury of Hawk's stepfather. A third shotgun blast and more crying. She heard Hawk scream.

She'd burst out into the hallway and ran, ran, ran to the living room. Her mother lay crumpled over the coffee table, half her head missing. Her father lay just a few feet away on the floor, facedown, so still. Hawk's stepfather was next to him, lying on his back, looking up at death with a surprised, frozen expression on his face. His chest was covered in blood.

Hawk stood a few steps from the table, his face pale, his cheeks full of tears, his body curled around a shotgun. His mother was on her knees, weeping. Beside her, another shotgun.

Lily stared at Hawk. Her best friend. "I'm sorry, I'm so sorry..." he said.

"You killed her! You killed my mom. You killed my dad. I heard you yell at them! You were my friend and you killed them! I hate you, I hate you, I hate you!"

Tear gas had flooded the room. The front door burst open. She was grabbed by a man wearing a flak jacket and helmet, but she didn't notice him. She squirmed in his arms, her eyes streaming with tears from the gas, shouting over and over, "You killed them, you killed them, I hate you, I hate you, I hate you."

Hawk had never said a word to her after that. She saw him handcuffed outside the isolated home where they'd made their stand against the Feds. He had made eye contact with her as he stood beside a patrol car. His face had been streaked with tears. There had been a new bruise on his cheek.

"I hate you," she'd said one more time. He'd turned away. She was taken in one car, he was taken in another. That was it.

Once she had grown up, she'd tried to understand a little of why he'd betrayed her so badly. He knew she loved her parents. She could only think that he'd been in a rage against his stepfather and her parents had gotten in the way. But why hadn't he shot his stepfather first?

Oh, she'd looked up the court records of his mother's trial. His mother had claimed to have shot her husband and Del's parents, but Del knew that was a lie. Hawk's mother never would have offered violence to anyone. She was too cowed and fearful, too terrified of her husband to even protect Hawk.

No, it had been Hawk arguing with them, it had been Hawk who'd fired, it was Hawk who was responsible. She knew he was capable of it. And she knew once he looked at her that day that he'd done it.

She'd never seen him again. Until yesterday.

The door opened and he walked in. His hair was mussed, he hadn't shaved. She took a deep breath and wrinkled her nose. He'd been smoking.

He closed the door behind him carefully. She stood and stared at him. He stared back. His face had no expression. But she could tell.

He knew.

She drew out the gun and pointed it at him. "Over here. Kneel next to the chair." Her hand was shaking but her voice was steady.

He did as she asked. She stood behind him, gun at his temple. "You know why I'm doing this."

"I know, Lily," he said.

She walked around to face him. "Don't you dare call me that."

"Lily." He stared at her. "You grew up to be so beautiful."

158

Philip saw the blow coming. He made no move to avoid it. He'd goaded her into it. He *wanted* her to hit him. He deserved it.

The gun barrel smashed into his cheek. He fell forward to his knees and felt the blood trickle down his face. Pain exploded across that whole side of his head. She hadn't held back. It was possible she'd even cracked his cheekbone.

"Why didn't you kill me?" he whispered. "You should."

She grabbed his collar to make certain they were face to face. Tears were running down her cheeks. She'd bitten through her lower lip. Blood dripped from her chin.

"You should kill me, Lily. I murdered them."

She hit him again, lower this time. He felt his jawbone crack. He toppled sideways and his shoulder hit the floor with a thud.

"Why? That's what I've wanted to know all these years. Why did you kill them? *Why, Hawk?*"

Philip blinked, trying to clear his vision, trying to focus past the pain to call on the healing power. Oh, God, this was good, the best pain yet. Agony and ecstasy flowed together, became one, became perfect. He curled into himself, every nerve singing, hiding his erection from her.

Half of him wanted her to hit him again, to keep the glorious agony coming. The other half wished she would finish it, end his existence once and for all.

His vision cleared. He felt the tingling of inner warmth as his power kicked in. She stood over him, the gun pointed directly at his forehead. She wanted to lance her anger, lance the pain of the loss of her parents and put it behind her once and for all. He'd give that to her. It was all he had left to give.

"Lily—"

He couldn't speak further. His jaw seemed locked shut. She put the gun under his chin. He offered no resistance.

"Don't call me that. You have no right to call me that," she said again.

"I know."

He closed his eyes, concentrating. He knew a few moves that might disarm her. He had the gun in an ankle holster. A head butt would work and hurt her more than him. He could do a body slam that would knock them both into the wall and loosen her hold on her gun. But she might get hurt with either of those moves. He might hurt the child growing inside her. Her son. *His son.*

He couldn't risk hurting her, not when he'd hurt her so much already.

"Delilah," he whispered. "End it."

She backed up a step, staring at the blood on the floor. She blinked away the tears in her eyes. In the last few months, she'd been medically raped, been the victim of an attempted kidnapping, been involved in a car chase and torn away from her home. And now a nightmare from her past had re-entered her life. People had killed under less stress and for far less reason. At least all this would be over now. He closed his eyes, ready for the bullet.

"*Talk.* Open your damned eyes. I need to know why you killed them," she said.

"It doesn't matter. You should kill me."

"I can't kill you until I have answers."

Hell. He didn't want to look at her. The way she stared at him, with those dark eyes, she seemed the same little girl who'd trusted him. Better, he thought, for her to be angry with him than to believe the people she had loved most in the world had planned to murder her.

"I went crazy. They were in between me and my stepfather."

"No." She knelt next to him, the gun carelessly held in her limp hand. "If you had gone crazy, you'd have killed *him* first."

Him. His stepfather. The leader of their little clan. He'd terrorized them all, but Del's parents had at least protected their little girl from his physical wrath.

"Why, Hawk? I have to know. *I have to know.*"

"No, you don't."

She rubbed tears out of her eyes with the back of her hand.

"Why? You always hated the guns, you were so gentle, you wouldn't even eat meat, and..."

"I use guns now."

"Yeah." Her voice was short and clipped. "Hawk, if you don't tell me, no one ever will." She said the last in the little girl's voice. "I have to know. You owe me that."

"Lily," he whispered. "I wanted...I wanted..." The pain enveloped him. His body felt as if it were a raw bundle of nerves and emotions.

"Wanted what?" She set the gun down on the floor.

Of all the things she could have done, that scared him the most. But she'd made her choice. Hell.

"Please tell me. *Hawk, please.*"

A plea he'd never been able to resist. "You remember that the Feds had closed in on the six of us? Your parents, you, my mother, my stepfather and me."

She nodded. "All trapped in that little one-story house."

"Do you know what our parents were wanted for?"

She nodded. "Yeah. I know. Not then, no, but I checked." She wiped sweat from her forehead with the back of her hand. "They blew up a federal building. So the Feds said. Now tell me something that I don't know."

"Do you believe they did it? That they were terrorists?" he asked.

She stared past him. "I didn't, not for a long while. But I re...I remembered stuff. The one time that my dad hit me, he caught me looking into that chest of his."

He nodded. "The one with the weapons?"

She met his eyes again. "Yeah."

For a second, it felt like the old trust between them clicked into place. "Okay. Well..." Somehow, it didn't seem right, to tell this while lying sideways on the floor. He needed to look her in the eye.

He struggled to a sitting position and leaned against the couch.

"Go on," she said through clenched teeth.

"The Feds had us surrounded." He made sure to keep eye contact. He had to see whether she believed him, he had to know the moment he broke her heart. If all he could do was witness for her, so be it. "Your parents and my parents had never wanted to be taken alive."

She sniffled and nodded.

"Your mother sent you to the bathroom, for safety. They didn't want you hurt when they started shooting at the Feds." He licked his lips, trying to moisten them. "They loaded all the weapons, all the machine guns, all the Uzis. They were going out in a blaze of glory and wanted to take as many of the Feds with them as they could."

"Suicide by cop," Del muttered. She closed her eyes momentarily then opened them again, accusatory. "But that's not what happened."

"No, it's not."

"Are you saying they killed themselves?" She looked over at the gun on the floor between them. "I don't believe you. It doesn't fit. All that yelling and screaming wasn't suicide. You killed them."

"No, they didn't kill themselves. You're right. I killed them."

"Keep going," she whispered. "Why?"

"My mom, for the first time in her life, disagreed with my stepfather and with your father. She worried about what would happen to me and to you. She wanted to send us out to the Feds. There were no warrants on us—she figured they'd let us go. She wanted me to keep going, to have a life. She said that I could take you with me, that at least we'd both be safe and could take care of each other, like we always did."

Lily's face went ghost-white, as if she was on the verge of fainting. Somewhere in her cloudy memory, maybe she did know the truth. Maybe that was why she'd only screamed at him for answers, not killed him. Maybe her subconscious wanted this confirmed.

Maybe she didn't really hate him?

"Your father wouldn't let us go. He said he would never allow the enemy to take us into their hands. Better we all died together, he said. He gave me a shotgun, he said I could die like a good soldier for the revolution. My stepfather agreed. My mom objected, but my stepfather hit her with a rifle butt and knocked her down. That shut her up, like always."

Yet it had been the first time his mother had actually tried to protect him. He'd never known what made her throw off all the years of abuse, of buying in to the bullshit spouted by his stepfather and Lily's parents. But she had. Maybe he did owe her thanks for that one thing. And maybe she owed him a damn apology for exposing him to that in the first place.

"She...your mother...she had a bloody cheek. I remember that," Del said.

"Yeah." God help Lily, she actually did want the truth. He hoped that she could live with it. He sure hadn't done a good job living with it, had he?

"And then your father sent your mother to get you. They wanted..." He closed his eyes. "They thought it would be best for you that way. Quick. Painless."

"They..." A tiny voice. A child's voice. "They were going to kill me?"

"They thought it best. I argued with your mom. That's what you heard, I think. And then your mother turned to go down the hallway, to fetch you as ordered, and I had the gun in my hand and I...I shot her."

"Oh." Del wrapped her knees up to her chin. "Oh."

"Your father turned on me, screaming, and I shot him too." Philip's throat was thick. He felt tears running down his face. Why, he had no idea.

"And then you shot your stepfather," Del whispered.

He took a deep breath and kept going.

"No. I froze after I shot your father. I don't know why." He'd seen his stepfather level the rifle at him. He'd known that he would die as soon as the trigger was pulled.

"It was my mother who shot my stepfather. She grabbed the rifle from...from your father's dead hands and killed her husband."

"She waited until then?" Del choked back a sob. Or a laugh. He couldn't tell. "She should've done that years before."

Philip nodded.

"I heard the shots. I ran out of the bathroom. It was too..." She cleared her throat. "It was too late."

"It all happened in seconds. *Boom, boom, boom.* Maybe twenty seconds, maybe less."

"I still see them dead like that in dreams," she said.

"So do I."

They stared at each other for a long time. He heard the hum of the refrigerator in the far corner, where the little kitchen area was stocked with supplies. Del sniffled and wiped away her tears with her fingers.

His healing was filling him with warmth. Heat lapped at the side of his face. "That's when the Feds broke in, guns drawn. My mother grabbed the shotgun I had and started yelling not to shoot, she dropped the guns and she screamed not to hurt the children. They grabbed her and shoved her down and they grabbed me and did the same."

"I remember the helmeted man who grabbed me," Del said in a small voice. "I could still see the bodies through the smoke, but he wouldn't let me run to them. I screamed at you, I yelled. I'd heard the argument, I thought you'd done it all... I called you a killer and murderer, and I spat on you. I said I hated you."

"I remember." He'd never forget. "You *should* hate me. I killed them."

"They were really going to kill me," she whispered.

"I thought about that later." He'd thought about it so many times. "Maybe your mother hadn't been going to get you. Maybe she wouldn't have killed you. Maybe she'd have turned on my stepfather, like my mother did. Maybe it was just a ploy to save you." He looked away. "I never gave either of them a chance to explain. I just killed them." Like he'd killed so many since.

"Why did your mother take the blame for the shootings?"

"I tried to tell the Feds what happened, but my mother started yelling that I was brainwashed, not to trust me, it was she who'd killed the rest, in a suicide pact but she'd turned on them because she couldn't kill her son."

"She protected you," Del whispered.

"For the first time in her life, yes." He closed his eyes, thought of his mother's face as they'd led her away that day, her hands in chains. Somehow, she had looked freer than she ever had while on the run.

"Live, son. I'm sorry. But now you can live."

Had he lived?

"How could the Feds not know?" Del asked, her voice steadier.

He opened his eyes again. "I don't think they cared. They had what they wanted. Three dead terrorists, one captured."

"And you let the lie stand," Del said flatly.

"Yeah." He stared at Del. "I figured she owed me that."

"Where is she now?"

"In prison, I think." He'd tried hard not to think of her.

"So what do you owe me, Hawk?" Del stood, the tears drying. "You come back into my life, and all of a sudden I'm carrying a baby created from the fucking Messiah gene." She scooped up the gun. "What the hell is your game?"

"I have no game, only truth for the first time in my life." He used the arm of the couch to stand. The room spun. She'd hurt him bone-deep. Getting up had been a mistake. He was too badly injured and only half healed.

"You know, I joined the CIA out of college. I joined my stepfather's enemy. Except they used the same methods as he did." He closed his eyes, trying to shut out most of his life. "So I spent my adult life being deceptive, being a spy, being violent, living a lie. Just like him." He hadn't seen that clearly, not until Lansing had died right in front of him. He was far too much like both his fathers. He'd walked away from the CIA after, but it wasn't until a few days had passed that he realized he had nothing to run to save Beth.

"So I should believe you?" Del's voice trembled.

"I've recently decided to try the truth." He opened his eyes and focused on the gun. Huh. He didn't want to die. No, he didn't want Del to kill him. She'd have to live with it and now he realized he didn't want that for her. "That doesn't seem to be working out too well, either."

She choked back a sob and set the gun on the coffee table. "What the hell am I doing in the middle of this?"

He stared at her, watching the lines of her face. As a child, she'd had a round face. Now, she'd lost weight around her cheekbones, making them razor sharp. And she seemed so sad. She'd been such a happy child. She'd laughed all the time. She'd made him laugh.

"I don't know." He let himself slide to the floor again, unable to stay on his feet. He had no balance. "Maybe Lansing did this to get back at me. He hated me." He cleared his throat and hung his head between his knees. "I haven't had much luck with fathers."

"Oh God." She crumpled to the floor next to him. "Oh God, what have I done? All these years, I blamed you, Hawk, and it wasn't...it wasn't...I'm sorry. Oh God, now I've made a mess of you, I hurt you, I'm sorry...I'm sorry..." She reached out and covered his face with her hands.

He almost moaned, so close to glorious agony from her touch. Come closer, he thought. *Closer.*

"You've nothing to be sorry about, Del."

"I hurt you, look at all this blood..." She pulled off her sweater and wiped the blood away from the side of his face. "This looks bad. I shouldn't have...I...I don't know what's wrong with me... Hell, I think I can see bone..."

"It'll heal." He stroked her face with his fingertips. Yes, she was Lily from years ago. But she was also Del, who'd come back to save his life yesterday. Del, who'd saved them both with her driving, Del who was carrying his son, Del who had flirted and danced with him and who'd been ready to kiss him. Del, who'd heard a crazy story and still trusted him enough to come with him last night.

Del, who had felt so perfect against him.

"We have to get you to a doctor, we have—"

"No." He gripped her shoulders with his hands. "I'll heal."

She dabbed his face with the sweater again, hands shaking. It hurt. It felt *good*.

"I hit you hard. Twice." Her tears started again. "I could have torn your whole face open. How could I do this?"

"Delayed post-traumatic stress from childhood." He pulled her close and put an arm around her shoulders. She curled her head against his chest. He swallowed. His healing was in full force, his face suffused in warmth and his skin sensitive to even the air around him. He closed his eyes and simply held her, letting his power work, wishing he dared do more than hold her.

"What the hell kind of mother will I make if I can do this?"

Her voice was muffled against him. He ran his fingers through her long hair. The strands caressed his palm like the finest silk.

"I could have killed you. I wanted to kill you."

"No. You told me what you wanted. The truth. If you'd wanted to kill me, you would have pulled the trigger, not hit me with the gun butt." He hugged her tighter.

"I hurt you," she whispered.

"I could've stopped you. I let you hit me." He put his fingers under her chin and lifted her head so they were eye to eye. "I wanted you to hurt me."

She lifted her face. Her eyes glistened with moisture. "You *wanted* me to hurt you?"

"I owed you that." He cupped her face in his hands. He felt so alive, so aroused, it was all he could do not to push her to the floor. "Look at my face again."

Her fingers reached out and, gently, ever so gently, touched the broken skin from her blows. "It's...the cut is closing up."

He nodded. "The jaw is already better." He drew her face closer to his. "I taunted you so you'd hit me. It felt good when you hit me."

Her eyebrows furrowed and her mouth went slack as she tried to accept what he'd said. She licked her lips. He focused on the tip of her tongue, imagined it tasting his body...

"Pain felt good to you?" She slid her hands around the back of his neck, putting their faces only an inch apart.

He nodded. "Pain and pleasure. The same. Makes no difference to me any longer."

She kissed the bruise on his jaw, soft, wet lips against his cheek. "Your brain circuits are all miswired. I know why. Oh, Hawk."

"Don't care." He turned his head and their lips met.

Chapter Fifteen

Del thought she'd been lightheaded and dizzy before, overcome with rage, fear, sadness, horror at what she'd done.

She thought there was room for no more.

Until Hawk kissed her.

Her nerve endings exploded, as if she'd jumped out of her skin. She curled a hand into his blood-soaked T-shirt, pulling him tighter against her. When he deepened the kiss, when their tongues touched, warm and wet, her fingers dug into his shoulders. He wrapped his arms around her and they went deeper, until her mind was gone and she was just a quivering lump of raw nerves and lust. Hawk was icy heat and intense darkness, pulling her down with him to the abyss, promising things she'd never heard of...

His hands slid around her waist. She broke the kiss, letting him pull her shirt over her head, closing her eyes as his rough hands brushed against her bare skin. She unhooked her bra and let it fall to the side.

He seized her. Their mouths met again. Her hands tugged at his shirt and covered his chest, absorbing his strong muscles and the hard skin touched by wisps of curly hair. They stopped kissing long enough for him to pull off his shirt. He moaned as the cotton scraped against his cheek.

"Hurt?" she whispered.

"Yes," he hissed, chest heaving.

She straddled him and bent to kiss his injured cheek. It had healed even more, the slice she'd made in his skin only a thin line now. Pain and pleasure all confused. Considering how pain had been so much a part of his growing up, she wasn't surprised. But, this, his healing, it was a miracle, for both of them. She'd wanted to cause him such pain earlier. Now she wanted to make up for it.

His hands cupped her breasts. She bent back and moaned. They grabbed for each other's pants. Hawk's erection was jutting out from his jeans. She exposed it easily and wrapped her fingers around it.

He groaned. She kissed him again as they blindly helped each other out of the rest of their clothes. She straddled him again, naked against his erection, her own body wet and ready to welcome him.

He muttered something. She kissed him before he could say anything else, before he could protest. She wanted this. *Now.* She hurt him, now she wanted to heal him, to feel with him, to be with him. She knew all about pain and pleasure being the same. When it was hard to feel at all, even agony was welcome.

He made her feel. She wasn't going to let that go.

She took him inside. Her spine arched, she threw her head back and felt the place where she'd bitten through her lip with her tongue.

Hawk's hands dug into her hips as she rode. She buried her fingers in his shoulders, heedless of anything except their rhythm as they moved together, moved as one, and came as one.

"Ahhh…" She shivered, out of control. He pulled her close until her face was buried in his shoulder. She smelled the sweat and the blood and remains of the cigarette smoke in his hair. The scents reminded her of the bar she loved.

"Hawk," she whispered.

She wasn't sure how long they stayed there on the floor, Hawk braced against the couch with her in his lap, with him still inside her. She only knew for the first time since she'd woken up on the floor of her bar, something felt completely right.

Hawk stroked her back with his thumb. She made a noise of contentment.

170

"That sounds like a purr," he said.

She lifted her head off his shoulder to face him. "Maybe." She glanced at her fingers. Blood. His shoulders had scratches all over them.

"Damn." She stiffened. "I hurt you again."

"Yes." He seized her hands and kissed them. "Thank you."

She smiled. He smiled.

"We are ridiculous," she said.

"Yes."

"This is insane."

"Welcome to my life."

He slid his hand down her stomach to rest on the baby bump. She swallowed.

"Don't worry about anything. I'm going to keep you safe. I'm going to kill those who want to hurt you," he said.

She blinked, remembering her rage. She'd come so close to killing him. She never wanted to feel that murderous again. It would be going backwards.

"You don't have to kill for me, Hawk. I don't want that."

"But that's all I can do for you."

"It's not. What do you call what just happened between us?" She curled up against him, her heart in pieces. He thought killing was all he had to offer. "We'll figure it out together."

He nodded. "Okay."

"I wanted to kill you for years. Sometimes I'd fall asleep wishing for you to be dead."

He winced. She kissed his lips. "I don't want to feel like that again. But, you, you took all the pain for me. And then I hurt you for it."

"I told you, I wanted you to hurt me."

The pain/pleasure mixture she could understand. Hawk feeling he deserved to be beaten, no. She kissed his neck and brushed her cheek against the rough stubble of his face. "Know what I realized the second time I hit you?"

"That you weren't a killer? You stopped pointing the gun at me."

"Not that." She glanced over at the gun, sick to her stomach at how close it'd been. "Jury's out on that one. No, I realized I was angrier that you'd betrayed me than I was grief-stricken over my parents' deaths." She shook her head. "Talk about your revelations."

Her gut clenched as she spoke, but she knew it was true. Her parents hadn't hit her but they had ignored her. They'd been indifferent. It had been her and Hawk, against the world, always.

"And I remember thinking that day, through all my grief, that at least you'd gotten the bastard at last. At least your stepfather was dead like he deserved."

"I missed you. All the time. I told myself it was stupid, you were just a little girl and I was a teenager and I had better things to do than worry about a little girl who hated me." He sighed. "I never could convince myself of it."

"You were my best friend."

He shook his head. "I'd have killed myself as a child if you hadn't been part of my life. I'd have used that way to escape him."

"I know." They had a bond back then, not sexual, not like siblings, but a friendship that went deeper than anything she'd had since. It had been hard to trust after that night. She'd liked her foster siblings and her friends, but the bonds had never been close to the trust between her and Hawk.

And now it *was* unexpectedly but incredibly sexual, and where that had come from, she didn't know. But it was obviously mutual. Where they went from here, she didn't know and didn't give a damn about right this second.

It was enough they'd stopped hurting and started healing each other.

Hawk wrapped his arms around her. She rested against him, listening to him breathe and hearing his heart beat. She should get up, get dressed, do something but she had no desire but to stay like this with Hawk.

She thought they slept for a while. She knew she must have. When she opened her eyes again, he was stroking her hair. And she was cold.

She moved off his lap. He made no protest. Hawk watched her, naked and unmoving, as she dressed.

"You're so beautiful."

She tossed his shirt at him. "You're just saying that because pregnancy made my boobs big. C'mon, put some clothes on. Sooner or later someone's going to walk in on us."

He blinked and looked around the room, considering her words for a minute before he got to his feet. He swayed. She rushed over to steady him. "Are you okay?"

"I'll be fine. Once the adrenaline wears off, the healing zaps energy. How's the check look?"

"Bloodstained." As was the shirt she'd tossed at him. It was soaked with blood. She found her sweater on the floor and tried to wipe the dried blood off his face again. "The cut's closed up completely."

The sweater wasn't going to work. She led him over to the sink and used paper towels and soap to clean the blood off his face. He said little and kept his eyes closed. "You look better." She ran a fingertip over his healed skin. He had said she was beautiful. But he was goddam gorgeous. "This is a miracle." No wonder Cheshire had called her son—Hawk's son—the Messiah. "But this is nothing new. I bet you could always do this." Hawk's ability to survive his stepfather's rages suddenly made sense.

"What do you mean?"

"I remember the beatings, especially the last one where he kicked you into a closet and slammed the door shut on you. I thought you were dead."

"You stole the key and curled up with me."

"I had to see you. You were barely breathing. You said it hurt to breathe but you healed. You were walking around in a day."

He nodded and pulled on the bloody shirt. If no one looked too closely, the stains might just appear to be sweat against the dark color.

"It was you who kept me alive that day. The healing only works subconsciously if the person really wants to live. With you there, I did."

"Alec said Beth was a catalyst that jacked up your psychic power recently."

He nodded. "I was badly injured, shot and near death. She ordered me telepathically to live. So I did. Since then, I've gained conscious control of the ability."

He looked around the room. Blood had splattered on the carpet. The gun was still on the floor. Hawk walked over and cleaned the gun butt with his shirt. That was his own blood he was cleaning off, she thought.

"Is this new ability to control the healing related to your getting pain and pleasure all mixed up? Or was that always there?"

She asked in a quiet voice, not wanting to anger him. But he needed to talk about it. Hell, she needed to talk about it.

"I'm sure it was always partly there. It got stronger recently. I know it's not normal."

"Well, hell, not much about all of this is normal, Hawk." She ran a hand through her hair to smooth it back. "We can chuck normal out the window for good."

He stared at her for a second and nodded. "Now what, Lily?"

Her real name sounded so perfect in his voice. "People still want me and my kid."

"I'll take care of that."

"Oh, no, *we'll* take care of it." She didn't need to kill them but she needed to find some way to keep them the hell away from her son. "I want these bastards too." She put her hand out, asking for the gun. Hawk handed it to her.

"First thing I want to do is talk to this Dr. Cheshire myself."

"You don't have to expose yourself to him." Hawk frowned.

"I want to make him squirm. I want to make him look me in the eye and say he didn't hurt me. I want him to know what he's done."

Chapter Sixteen

Del was tougher than he would ever be.

All the shocks in the last twenty-four hours and yet Del had pulled herself together and wanted to confront Dr. Cheshire, the man responsible for her rape.

"We'll have to get you a holster for that gun first," Philip said to her. "Tucking it into the waistband of the pants isn't a safe way to carry it."

"I had it in the pocket of this." She picked up her bloody sweater and dropped it again, wrinkling her nose. "I guess you're right."

"I'll get you a new sweater too."

I'll get you whatever you want.

Someone pounded on the door. "Drake! It's been hours. What the hell's happening in there?"

He and Del looked at each other. She smiled. He smiled. If he could have reached up and grabbed the sun for her in that instant, he would have.

Instead, he shrugged and went to open the door.

Alec practically fell into the room.

"Good, you're here. You can get Dr. Cheshire for us," Philip said.

Alec straightened. His eyes widened as he realized that Philip's shirt was soaked with blood. He looked around and saw Del's bloodstained sweater and the rust-colored splatter on the carpet.

"What the fuck, Drake?" Alec grabbed the front of Philip's shirt and slammed him into the wall. Philip made no protest.

"What did you do to her?"

Philip felt the temperature rise in the room, a sure sign of Alec's power. The firestarter was truly angry on Del's behalf. Philip's estimation of him went up another notch.

Del pulled at Alec's arm. "Let him go!"

Alec let him go and backed up, obviously confused. He looked again at the blood splatter. "I don't understand."

"Haw—Philip never hurt me. But we had some stuff to work out."

"So whose blood is that?" Alec asked.

"Mine," Philip said.

"And this happened because...?"

"We had things to work out between us in private," Del said.

Philip was pleased but surprised Del was closing ranks on Alec but he supposed he shouldn't have been. They'd both learned when young to reveal as little as possible. They owed no one an explanation of what had happened between them. Not Alec and, not, he mused, even Beth. Though he would have to think of something to tell her.

"We need to speak to Dr. Cheshire," Philip repeated.

"Uh, not in this room. Damn, what a mess."

"Send me the cleaning bill," Philip said.

Alec shook his head. "I will never get what the hell you're about, Drake, not in a million years."

"It's okay. I do." Del laughed. "It's fine, Alec. Get us another room to talk to Dr. Cheshire, we'll change, and I promise no blood will be spilled this time."

She sounded certain of that. He wasn't. Because he certainly wanted to kill Cheshire. But this was Del's show now, and she'd said she didn't want him to kill anyone. She had the most at stake. He'd follow her lead. Whatever she wanted, whatever she asked, he'd see that it was done.

"I still want an explanation for this." Alec looked at Del. He knew better than to expect answers from Philip.

Del sighed. "It's too raw right now, Alec. Another time. And given that we're all connected now, we'll have plenty of that."

"Drake's not a danger to you?"

"*Never.*"

The conviction in that single word choked Philip's throat. He couldn't have spoken even if he wanted. He didn't know what he'd done to earn Del's trust so completely in the last few hours. His confession shouldn't have been enough. And while he knew why the passion had flared on his end, he could only guess about Del.

It didn't matter.

He'd loved Lily the child as his best friend, his confidante and his glimpse of what people could mean to each other. As an adult, he knew he loved Delilah Sefton in a way that was the same, yet entirely different.

He would not fail her, ever again.

Alec insisted on escorting Del upstairs to change clothes while Philip went to scrounge clothing from the supply closet with T-shirts and jackets that F-Team sometimes used. As Philip was pulling on a new shirt, Gabe arrived to tell him Dr. Cheshire was eager to talk with Del in one of the conference rooms.

Of course Cheshire was eager. It'd been exactly what he'd asked for yesterday. Philip hadn't intended to give it to him but this wasn't his call.

Gabe picked up the discarded bloody shirt from the floor. He frowned. "Drake?"

"Yes?"

"Does this have anything to do with why you smashed the mirror last night?"

"Yes."

Gabe waited, expecting Philip to elaborate. People always seemed to expect him to do that and they were always annoyed when he never did.

"Are you all right?"

Gabe's question wasn't an accusation, as Alec's had been. There was genuine worry in it. Philip had no idea Gabe had taken a liking to him. It certainly wasn't the usual response people had concerning him.

"I'm better than I have been in a long time," he said.

It didn't even matter if what had happened with Del was never repeated, though he was fervently wishing it would be. Her forgiveness had freed something in him.

"Were you watching this on your cameras?" he asked in a quiet voice.

"If I had, I think you'd kill me." Gabe put up his hands. "No, I just...look, there was this guy I was involved with, years back. A gunnery sergeant, wound pretty tight. Of course, he'd have to be, given he had to stay hidden in the Marines for so long. But he'd been injured badly at least twice in the line of duty. That didn't bother him but it changed him. He liked it rough. Very rough." Gabe stuffed his hands in his pockets. "It was hard for him to feel, save for pain. It took me time to get comfortable with that."

Philip nearly snapped that this was none of Gabe's business but instead defaulted to a question. "What happened to him?"

"He took a bullet for someone in his unit just before he rotated out. Got a posthumous award for bravery. It's the way he would've wanted to go, he was near the end of his twenty-five years in. I don't think he had any plan for what he'd do when he got out."

"I'm sorry for your loss." Message received. Would Philip take that bullet under those circumstances? Damn straight.

Gabe nodded. "Thanks. I still miss him. I'd offered to help him after he got out. There was a whole world out there he never knew existed. Tough military vet, still in good shape. God, my friends would have eaten him up. In a good way, I mean." Gabe cleared his throat. "Your Beth worries about you, Drake."

"I know."

"Seems to me that someone who can heal injuries might get numb to pain, like my friend. Might even get off on it."

Philip checked the small caliber handgun nestled in the holster at his ankle. "Is there a point in there?"

"Yeah." Gabe frowned. "I'd kinda miss you if you jumped in front of a bullet."

"That's why I shoot first."

"Good to know." Gabe tapped his phone and looked at the display. "Text says Alec's got Cheshire ready for you. Are you sure it's a good idea for Del Sefton to be in the same room with him?"

"No, but it's what Del wants."

Alec thought Drake had hurt her. For some reason, the assumption angered Del. She dug into her suitcase for a change of clothes. Her jeans wouldn't button. Argh. She pulled out a pair of slacks that were too big. She'd been saving them for later in the pregnancy but had stuffed them into her duffel when she was packing in a hurry yesterday. She put them on. They were still too loose.

She put on a belt, which at least made the slacks wearable, and called out from the bedroom and asked for a sweatshirt. Alec returned with a plain black cotton sweatshirt that was far too big for her. It did, however, hide the gun she stuffed into the back waistband.

Alec frowned. "Let me get you a holster with a reinforced belt for that. It's not safe that way."

"Funny, Philip said the same thing to me."

Alec scowled, which she didn't know how to interpret, and returned quickly. She put on the belt—a thicker material than the one she had—and buckled the holster to it. He helped her fit the gun snugly into place. She closed her eyes and took a deep breath. Keep moving forward, that was the trick. Try not to focus on how she'd almost killed Hawk with the gun. Or on their lovemaking, which had freed something long coiled inside her.

Today, now, protect her son. That meant being calm while talking to Dr. Cheshire.

"Maybe you should rest," Alec said.

"I'm pregnant, not sick." Though there were different kinds of sick. She thought of how she'd dug her nails into Hawk's shoulders. Some might think she was sick. They'd definitely think Hawk was.

She didn't care.

"Alec, why did you scowl when I mentioned Philip a minute ago?"

"He's keeping secrets again. I don't understand why he does that." He hooked his thumbs in the belt loops of his jeans, looking like a male model in a magazine ad. She wondered if he knew how good-looking he was. "Lansing kept secrets from me all the time. I don't like them."

"I can understand that. But in this case, Philip's doing it for me. They're my secrets, Alec, as much as his. So if you're going to be angry with anyone, be angry with me."

"You don't get it. You've only known him two days and you don't know anything about him."

"I've known him since he was a child," she snapped.

That froze Alec. It was a few seconds before he spoke. "You're kidding."

"We grew up together, under lousy circumstances, but for most of that time, we were close."

"Only most of the time? What'd he do?"

"That's enough," she snapped again. "Why do you keep thinking the worst of him? What's he ever done to you?"

Alec backed up. "You're right. Drake's done nothing but help me. But he's made clear he doesn't like me. No, more like he disapproves of the fact I exist. I never did anything to him."

"Except put the only person he loves in danger."

"Yeah, I guess there's that." Alec nodded. "I'm trying to understand him but he doesn't make it easy."

"No, I bet he doesn't, but you're young, you're in love and you're practically oozing with power. You can afford to give Hawk the benefit of the doubt."

Alec nodded. "You called him 'Hawk'. Is that his real name?"

"A nickname from when we were kids but the only one that stuck. Like I said, our childhood was a mess."

"Worse than mine?" Alec led her back out of the penthouse and out to the elevator to go back down to meet Cheshire.

"Did you always have a roof over your head and know where your next meal was coming from? Ever worry if those things didn't happen that someone would beat you senseless?"

Alec slowly shook his head.

"Then, yeah, our childhood was worse than yours."

The elevator doors closed behind them and they started downward. "I'm not sure what to say. You win?"

She snorted. "It's not about winning. Just keep it in mind when you're dealing with Hawk, all right?"

The doors opened and they stepped back into the lobby of bonsai plants and open windows.

"Did your growing up together have anything to do with why Lansing picked you for this, um—"

"Experiment? I don't know. Hawk seems to think so—he thinks his biological father was trying to get back at him. That seems like a stretch, but then, I didn't know Richard Lansing."

"Lansing was capable of that but there might be more to it. He usually had several reasons for doing something." Alec led her down yet another hallway, different from the one that held the room where she and Hawk had gotten, um, reacquainted. *Call it like it was. Where we screwed each other's brains out.*

Hawk and a lanky soldier were waiting for them around the next corner. Hawk's face stayed impassive, but she read the slight widening of his eyes. That was as good as a smile from him.

"Alec got you a waist holster? And the belt's heavy enough to hold it?" he asked.

She nodded.

"I'm coming to talk to Dr. Cheshire with you," Alec announced.

"Why?" Hawk growled.

Of course Alec wanted to be there. Hawk really did give Alec a rough time. No wonder the younger man was resentful.

"Cheshire's here because I brought him here," Alec said. "This is my operation."

"Do you two always do this?" Del asked.

"You mean the dick-measuring contest? Most of the time, they do, yes," the lanky soldier said.

"Who usually wins?" Del asked.

"I do," Alec and Philip said simultaneously.

She smiled. The soldier caught her eye and shrugged.

"Hi, I'm Gabe." He held out his hand and they shook. "I handle a lot of the tech around here."

"You're with Alec's F-Team?"

"Yep."

"Good to meet you, Gabe." He didn't seem the least bit discomfited by Hawk. Good. She wanted to have a talk with him later. It would be nice to get a normal person's perspective on all of this. Though Gabe would have a soldier's perspective, not a civilian one. Close enough.

She glared at Hawk and Alec. "Dr. Cheshire is responsible for screwing around with my life. I'm going to talk to him. In other words, this time, I win. Clear?"

They nodded. They did that in unison too.

Gabe left, saying he was going back to his computer searches. The three of them entered the room together. Unlike the room where she and Hawk had spent half the day, which was more like a mini studio apartment, this was a true conference room, with a central wooden table surrounded by blue-padded chairs. The walls were painted in neutral colors and the window blinds had been closed.

Dr. Cheshire, who had been seated at the table, rose to greet them. "Ms. Sefton!" He walked over to her and offered his hand. "I'm so glad to see you well."

She ignored the proffered handshake and instead turned to open the blinds to let in light. For some reason, she craved light just now.

She sat at the head of the table. Cheshire, flustered, took the seat at her right hand and Alec the one to her left. Hawk sat down at the other end of the table, across from her.

She put her elbows on the table and stared at Cheshire. He looked less haggard than he had in the video she'd watched this morning. In fact, he looked a little pleased with himself. She wanted to wipe that smugness off his face. She didn't want to experience a killing rage again but, hey, that didn't mean she couldn't get angry.

"Am I well, Doctor? What should be wrong? You seemed concerned when you talked to Mr. Drake about my condition."

"Of course, I'm concerned about my patient." Dr. Cheshire tapped his fingertips on the table. "I'm concerned with any patient who I haven't been able to examine properly in some time."

"*Your patient?*" Del said, her hands flat on the table. "Be careful with your words. I'm not *your* anything."

"I don't understand," Cheshire said, though Del was sure he did.

"Wouldn't you more properly refer to me as an experimental subject? Or maybe I'm just the carrier for your experiment? Or, as I prefer to call him, my *son?*"

Cheshire cleared his throat and shrank down in his chair. Clearly, he was displeased with experiments that talked back. "Those are just words, Ms. Sefton. I meant no insult to you, please know that. Quite the opposite, I have the highest respect for you."

"That respect must be why you didn't mind impregnating me while I was unconscious and couldn't possibly consent."

She let one hand drift under the table, to tap the gun. It was more reassurance that Cheshire couldn't hurt her anymore than a desire to shoot him. Pointing the gun at Hawk had felt nauseating and good at the same time. A horrible combination.

What she wanted now were answers. And it seemed like putting Cheshire off-balance was the way to get them. She wanted him to see what he'd actually done. She wanted him to feel what she felt.

"I thought you had consented," Cheshire said in a small voice. "Mr. Lansing said—"

"Lansing lied," Hawk snapped.

Hawk, she decided, carried enough rage for both of them. He burned with it from inside, enough so that it was palpable today, even more so than yesterday. She looked over at him and raised an eyebrow. He leaned back in his chair, receiving her wordless message. They had always understood each other just fine without words.

"Mr. Drake is right. Whatever he said to you, Mr. Lansing lied. I did not give prior consent and, in fact, I had no idea I was even pregnant for a month after you kidnapped me. Clear your mind of your experiments for a second and try to think of how I felt waking up on a cold floor, knowing I'd been violated somehow and with a night-long gap in my memory."

"We thought that was a kindness," Cheshire whispered.

"You thought memory loss was a *kindness*?"

He put up his hands, as if he could ward off her words. "We didn't know for certain if a pregnancy would result. It seemed better to bring you back to your home, where you would be comfortable until it was confirmed. I think that was the correct thing to do, to disrupt your life as little as possible. I suggested you be kept at our facility to be cared for there, but Mr. Lansing said you must be returned because you'd be happier at home. Was he wrong on that?"

"My bar and home always make me happy," Del said, realizing how true that was. She wanted to hear the sound of the lake water lapping at the dock, soak in the open sky and relax in the company of her regulars. Her people.

"You're missing the point. It's not sending me back home that was the problem. Your original decision was flawed. Whatever your intentions, you and your team raped me."

"You weren't—"

"Don't tell me I wasn't medically raped. Do not even try." Del leaned over, glaring at him. "What else would you call it?"

"Oh." Cheshire's face lost all color. He shrank back in his chair. "Oh." He stared down at the table.

"Am I an abstraction to you?" Del asked.

"No. I mean...yes, I suppose...then...I..." He took a deep breath. "You were," he breathed out at last.

"And now?"

The doctor twitched. He stared at his hands. Del remained silent. Let him think of what to say next.

Hawk remained absolutely still, but Del knew that was when he was at his most dangerous. Alec, she guessed, wasn't the most patient person, but all he did was glare at Cheshire. A good guy, Alec. She wondered how often Beth played peacemaker between her father and her boyfriend.

She was going to have to meet Beth soon. She blinked. Hawk's daughter. Oh. How odd was that. Her son would have an older sister.

Cheshire shifted in his chair, gathered himself and sat up straighter. "I never...I tried never to think beyond the work. I get so excited about what might be accomplished that I can't see what's under my nose." He stared down at the table. "I never meant to hurt you."

"It's more accurate to say that the possibility of my being hurt didn't occur to you at all, is that right?"

Cheshire swallowed hard and nodded.

"And now?" Del said.

"I'm sorry. I really wish I'd insisted on my original plan of hiring a volunteer."

He didn't wish he never conducted the experiment or that he'd never been a scientist. He just wished he'd picked a willing victim. She almost laughed. Obsessed people were all similar in their obsessions. Her parents had wished she could grow up in a normal home but they'd blamed the federal government, not themselves, for their crazy life.

"Help me understand why you were so focused. Tell me why you thought my son, the carrier of your so-called Messiah gene, was worth looking at people as lab rats."

Silence reigned for a few minutes. Finally, Cheshire took a deep breath. "Are you sure you want to hear all this? Will it upset you?"

"We're past that point, don't you think, Doc?"

He put his hands flat on the table. "Yes, of course."

He took another deep breath, looking more like a scientist and less like someone expecting a beating.

"We wanted a scientific breakthrough. We wanted to create someone who could heal themselves from hurt as Mr. Drake does." His voice gathered strength. "Wouldn't that be a boon, Ms. Sefton? People who would heal themselves? And if we had a child who could also heal others, who could ensure survival instead of relying on imperfect doctors, well, tell me that wouldn't benefit the human race."

"One baby can only do so much," Del said.

"If this worked, the Messiah gene would have been duplicated and—"

"You wanted to create a passel of Philip Drakes?" Alec said. "Doctor, I'm not so sure that's a boon to humanity."

Hawk snorted. "At the least, they could be counted on to have the bad temper to turn on their creator."

Del laughed.

"I don't understand," Cheshire said.

"Mr. Drake is saying that psychic abilities can sometimes make people unstable," Del said. "Did you account for that in your research?"

"That was a variable. But Mr. Lansing said that proper nurture would have a mitigating effect. I thought perhaps that's why he picked you as the child's mother. A normal person, from a good environment, you could be counted on to be a good mother."

Del shook her head. "Then he didn't know as much about me as he claimed."

"But that's correct, isn't it? You're here now because you want to be close to your child, to protect him from harm?"

He had her there.

"I wanted my research to change the world for the better. I wanted to provide hope for the next generation. I realize part of that is ego, but I had the best of intentions. Please understand that." He focused on Del. "You didn't have the abortion, Ms. Sefton. You must want the child, yes?"

"How the hell did you know that?" Del stood.

Cheshire shrank back in his chair. "I, well, Mr. Lansing reported that he was concerned about the child. He said he had reports that you might not be a, um, as cooperative a subject as he'd hoped. But he said he'd take care of it, that we'd bring you in and explain what was going on. That I would get what I wanted, a chance to monitor you and the child, to ensure all was going well." Cheshire frowned.

"And yet, he didn't bring me in." Now, she did feel the rage building. "What happened?"

"Mr. Lansing said the next day that keeping you at the facility wouldn't be necessary. I was disappointed and concerned."

"Disappointed you didn't have your research subject under your thumb?"

"No! That wasn't it at all. I wanted to make certain the child was healthy and growing. I was worried. You have to believe that your health and the health of the child is of utmost importance to me."

Del remembered Cheshire had been concerned about her when talking to Hawk as well. He might even be more concerned now that he saw her as a person. Or, maybe not. He could be saying what she wanted to hear.

"Why are you so worried about the baby?" she asked.

"The Mes—your son," he corrected, "was designed to grow at a slightly accelerated rate. We hoped his brain function would be more advanced at his birth. But there was only so far we could push neural and brain development. The child still needed time to develop proper lungs and other organs. If all goes as planned, the baby will be at full growth a month early but you may still carry him the full nine months. You're twenty weeks from conception, yes?"

"You would know." Del sat back down. She felt faint and vaguely sick. She'd gotten used to being viewed as an experiment. But talking about her son's neural development was another matter.

Hawk moved behind her and put his hand on her shoulder. She put her hand over his. She had no doubt he was also glaring at Dr. Cheshire.

Cheshire squirmed in his chair and shook his head. "I'm truly sorry, Ms. Sefton. I should've thought further about the woman Mr. Lansing brought to me. I should've done so many things differently."

"Yes," Hawk said.

And, Del thought, Dr. Cheshire might have more cause to regret what he'd done to her. Hawk clearly wasn't going to forgive him. She wondered if she could stop Hawk from hurting him. She didn't like how his first instinct now seemed to be to kill to solve the problem. He'd not been like that growing up.

"Dr. Cheshire, how did Mr. Lansing know I'd planned to have an abortion and changed my mind?" she asked.

"I can answer that," Hawk said. "I'm certain they planted bugs and perhaps hidden cameras in your home and bar when they returned you that first night. So they knew you'd made the appointment."

"I'd have kept it too." Maybe. "Except for the accident at the Ledgewood Circle."

"No accident," Hawk said. "Dr. Cheshire just said Lansing planned to grab you. I would guess that's what the accident at the circle was about."

"But they only stole my purse and medical forms." She turned to look up at him.

"That wasn't the plan, I believe. Operations are tricky and those involving variables like traffic inevitably have problems. I'd guess they wanted to cause a minor accident to stop your car in traffic and then covertly lead you into the van at gunpoint."

Del wondered how many times Hawk had led "operations" over the years. No, no need to go down that road.

"They didn't expect the minivan to flip over and create such a serious accident," Hawk continued. "That caused you to rush to the aid of those in the minivan, which means they couldn't grab you quietly. So they took your purse and medical forms as a stop-gap measure."

Cheshire sank lower in his chair.

"Your heroism saved you from a disappearance. And you canceled your appointment after, so they canceled the operation altogether. And then Lansing died." Hawk walked over and slapped a hand on the table in front of Cheshire. "Isn't that right?"

"After he died, I had no further information about you or the—your son, Ms. Sefton." Cheshire pushed his chair back.

Well, she'd at least gotten Cheshire to think of his experiment as a person. Del gestured to Hawk. "Let him finish."

Hawk walked back to his previous place at her shoulder.

"I was worried sick about you and the child. But then Mr. Genet arrived and I started receiving reports again."

Reports from the doctors or technicians that she'd trusted. She put her hand over her baby bump. She'd been worried about sliding into paranoia, like her parents. She hadn't been nearly paranoid enough.

"And when I turned down an adoption, Genet came after me."

"I wasn't part of that as you well know from the fact Genet tried to kill me," Cheshire said firmly. "I only wished to speak to you and to treat you and your son so you are both healthy. I know you value your son. So do I. As I said, the possibilities for a psychic healer are endless." He sat up straight. "And all of them beneficial, with no harm to your son."

Del rubbed the bridge of her nose, suddenly exhausted. She didn't want to look at the situation from Dr. Cheshire's point of view. She didn't want to see any of his points. She didn't want to think of the baby growing inside her as some Messiah.

She just wanted home.

Except home wasn't safe any longer.

Sensing her shift in mood, Hawk took over.

"Dr. Cheshire, even if I choose to believe that the ends you wanted were good, the means were deplorable. I can also guarantee what Lansing wanted from your research wasn't a world full of healers to help the unfortunate."

"But we shared a dream!"

"He trained me to be a soldier," Alec said quietly. "I can do a lot of things with my power, but he trained me to be a weapon instead."

"A powerful healer can also be a powerful weapon. Alec's power is visible and tangible. Lansing wanted a different sort of weapon. A healer could cause a heart attack with a look," Hawk said.

"No! That's not what I wanted!" Cheshire said. "I can't answer for what Richard Lansing wanted. What I wanted was to make advances in treating disease. It's not just about healing one person at a time. A healer could potentially teach cells to replicate in a laboratory. Nerve cells, especially brain cells, are lost forever when damaged. What if a healer could force them to replicate? Imagine the advances we could make in treating brain and spinal injuries. People could walk again. They could regain lost brain function." He put his head in his hands.

"If Mr. Lansing wanted a soldier, that is news to me. You have no idea how much this research could have benefitted people *peacefully.*"

"Oh, I have some idea," Hawk snapped.

"Um, yes, you would, Mr. Drake, with your abilities. I stand corrected."

Del almost laughed. Cheshire was accepting Hawk's words as a correction of fact, not as an insult.

Cheshire pushed his glasses up and rubbed his eyes. "If your child is safe and grows up healthy, Ms. Sefton, he will be a wonder of the world. Can you say you truly don't want that?"

"A good result doesn't excuse rape," she snapped. "And there's a lot to be said for normal versus world savior. My parents were big on their need to save the world from evil, Dr. Cheshire. Turns out they weren't chasing destiny. They were the evil they feared."

Cheshire stared down at the table again. "I was very wrong. I'm so sorry." He looked at her. "What can I do to atone?"

Del's hand slipped to pat the gun again. She didn't trust Cheshire's turnaround. He'd do anything to stay close to her son, his precious Messiah, his world savior.

"I don't know, Doctor, you tell me, what can you do to make it up to me?"

"I would love to examine you and check on the child's progress."

Fuck you.

"You're not putting a finger on her," Hawk snapped.

Del put up a hand, and Hawk subsided. "You're not an ob-gyn, Dr. Cheshire. What do you mean when you say 'examine me'?"

"An ultrasound would gather the information I need for growth," Cheshire said. "The last one I saw was over a month ago. Another look at how your son is growing is essential and it needs to be done soon." He paused. "I would only need to see the result, not perform the test."

"I'll think about it," Del muttered.

"Please, even if you won't let me see the ultrasound results, find a qualified doctor and have it done. It's important."

"So was my consent to carry this child." She stood. She was not going to sit here and listen to pleas from him, even if he was truly repentant. She might not want to kill him but she was nowhere near being ready to accept him as her son's doctor. And she sure as hell wasn't going to let him see her worry about whether her son was healthy.

"There is a way you can help." Hawk grabbed a legal pad and a pencil from the cabinet on the side of the room. He slapped them in front of Cheshire. "Write down every conversation you ever had with Edward Genet. Any little detail, anything that can help us find him."

"And the ultrasound?"

Hawk curled his hand into a fist.

"This isn't a negotiation," Del said. "If you want to atone, if you truly feel badly for what you've done, you'll help us find these people out to take my baby from me."

Cheshire nodded. "I understand."

"Anything you remember might contain a clue," Alec said. "You should want Genet too, Doctor. He blew up your lab, killed your assistant and trashed your home."

"I will do my best." Cheshire bent to the legal pad.

"You damn well better, because my son deserves it. I grew up with parents who dragged me all over the country to 'protect' me. I won't have my son live the same life."

Chapter Seventeen

Philip insisted to Del that she get some rest after they left the room. She agreed so readily that he knew he'd guessed right about her exhaustion. With the baby growing at an accelerated rate, that was no surprise.

Alec agreed to stay with Dr. Cheshire and get what he could about Genet from him.

"Alec, one last thing," Del asked before he went back inside. "It's a little thing and it's going to sound dumb, but could you ask Cheshire if he ever saw Genet wear a tie with lions on it?"

"Doesn't sound dumb, especially if the tie was distinctive," Philip said.

"It was. The lions reminded me of those symbols you see on the shields of knights in the movies. There were three golden lions, facing outward, on a red tie."

"I'll ask Cheshire."

"And we can do a Google search as well," Philip noted. "After you get some rest."

Alec ducked back into the conference room, and Philip was alone in the hallway with Del. He slipped an arm around her waist. Instead of objecting, as he'd feared, she leaned her head on his shoulder for support. He drew her into his arms. He closed his eyes, trying to sear the moment into his memory. How long since he had felt as human as this? He couldn't remember. Maybe he never had.

"How close are you to finding Genet?" Her voice was muffled against his shirt.

"We're tracking how he managed to infiltrate Orion Systems, and we have a lead on his vehicle from this morning. I'll check on it as soon as I see you safely resting."

She shook her head. "No. I want to go with you to check on that."

It would be quick enough to take her to the CIC where Gabe was likely still working. "All right."

He led her to the entrance door to the lower level, the one that looked like wood but was steel underneath the paint.

"You take no chances here," she said as he opened the door and ushered her through.

"I'd feel better if we weren't still working off Lansing's security system."

Gabe had said he planned to upload another program to run the various locks, cameras and other devices that kept the Phoenix Institute safe. But writing the program took time, and it also took finding people they could trust to do it.

Now that Del was here, Philip wondered how paranoid he should be. He'd rather take Del to one of his safe houses, havens known only to him. But Genet and his people surely knew where Del was at the Institute. They might pounce the minute she left the facility. With planning, he could work around that and find a hidden way to get her out. But not today.

Del stopped at the top of the metal steps that led to the lower level and looked from side to side. "Holy crap."

He grunted. "Lansing intended Alec to be the beginning of an army. He built a facility to support one."

"And no one in the government noticed this?"

"They knew about it, at least, most of it. Alec's F-Team has a contract with the CIA for special missions."

"Yes, he told me. But seeing this is another thing altogether. So the government really does sanction these secret military teams." She smiled, and it was wistful. "I can hear my father saying, 'I told you so,' inside my head."

He stuffed his hands in his pockets.

She started down the steps, holding the handrail tight. "So, are you really retired from the CIA, Hawk?"

"Yes."

"And you look so young because...?"

"I was testing my new conscious control of my healing power. This is the result." He sighed. "I liked my gray hair better."

"Well, the young look has its benefits. You looked damn good when you walked into my bar. So what have you been doing since the retirement?"

"Rebuilding the Charger. Watching over Beth." Being aimless. "Discovering old friends."

"That last one nearly killed you."

"That's not the part of our reunion I remember."

He followed on her heels and steered her to the CIC, pausing to get through security at the door as he had that morning.

"Did you know I had a crush on you when we were kids?" she asked.

He froze. "No."

"Easy, Hawk, I had no idea what it meant at the time. I just knew you were the most important person in my life."

As she'd been for him. "We created our own world. We had to."

She nodded as they stepped inside the CIC. Gabe, as he had been earlier that day, was hard at work over a keyboard. Del whistled as she took in the room.

Gabe raised his head. "Hey, Drake. Look, we're deciphering that thumb drive. Finally got my friend's program working."

"Excellent."

Del walked over to the collection of numbers scrolling on the top view screen. "These are payroll records."

Gabe nodded. "It's a way to track anyone who ever worked for Orion Systems and their holding company. I'll find the money trail. How'd you know they were payroll?"

"It's similar to a program I use for the bar."

She turned to Hawk. "What did he mean, deciphering the thumb drive?"

"Cheshire's assistant, the man who died in the fire, was clutching it in his hand. I assume it's research information. What we've deciphered thus far indicates that."

"You didn't tell Cheshire about this."

"No."

She shook her head. "I wonder if he really wanted to use volunteers as mothers. He'd probably have found some. There are a lot of desperate people in the world who would've turned over their baby for cash. Such a smart man, and yet he didn't see through Lansing or Genet. Of course, Genet oozes charm."

"So did Lansing, when he wanted to," Gabe said. "When he recruited me for the Resource, Lansing talked about a chance to save the world and an opportunity to work with the most extraordinary person we'd ever meet. His pitch to me to join F-Team had me stoked to do this. He was right that Alec is fucking unique. Lansing just didn't mention how Alec had been raised and that this place was essentially Alec's prison."

"Wait, you worked for *Lansing*?"

Philip smiled. Trust Del to cut to the core of what Gabe had said.

"We quit when it became clear what he was doing to Alec," Gabe said, face reddening.

Philip cleared his throat to forestall more interrogation from Del. Gabe had tried to help him earlier. This was the least he could do in return.

"Did you trace the license plate the gas station employee gave us, Gabe?"

"Yes. And it was registered to the same dummy company that owned Orion."

Philip swore. "A dead end?"

"Not completely. They had to give a different address to the DMV and that may be an excellent lead. But accessing DMV files has gotten a lot harder than it used to be since Homeland Security cracked down. I'll find the address but it will take an hour or two instead of instantly. But it's in New Jersey."

"Somewhere not far away," Philip mused. "Genet planned it that way, to stay close to Del."

"So you can go and get him when you have the address?" Del said, her voice rising with eagerness.

"We'll have to conduct surveillance and plan an assault. That will take time. Plus, we should get government sanction on this," Gabe said.

Philip scowled.

"Legalities must be observed in some form, otherwise we're no better than the bad guys," Gabe said.

"Legalities are the fiction made by those in power to stay in power."

"Still don't trust the government, Hawk?" she asked with a smile.

"Even more so since I've seen how it works from behind the scenes."

"I'm still not much for rules, either." She nodded. "All I want now is to go home. I don't care how you find Genet. Just find him."

"Soon," Philip promised. "Soon."

Hawk settled her in a suite on the first floor of the underground level. It was very utilitarian compared to Alec's place, but it had a living room, kitchen, bathroom and bedroom all her own.

They took time to Google the image on Genet's tie. There were a ton of lion symbols. Del frowned and finally pointed to one on the monitor.

"That's it," she said.

"English royal crest from the time of Richard the Lionheart, I think."

"Well, Genet sure expected to be worshiped and obeyed like a king."

"It's probably some sort of symbol of his ambitions. Lansing thought he could control the world, or at least part of it. If

Genet is connected to him, somehow, then maybe he had the same idea."

She sighed. "It won't help us find him."

"You never know. And it's good to know what we're dealing with."

She rubbed the bridge of her nose. "Argh."

"Here, you need bed."

Like the rest of the suite, the bedroom was barren of decoration. But that was secondary to the beckoning bed. She collapsed facedown on the mattress and closed her eyes. She'd be too huge in the belly to lie down this way much longer. She'd get big fast, if Cheshire was to be believed. Accelerated growth rate, he'd said.

She shuddered.

After what Cheshire had said in that conference room, she'd have panicked if Alec hadn't done his own version of an ultrasound this morning. Her baby was moving and active. She held on to that.

Hawk was hovering near the doorway to the room. Wondering if he was welcome? Wanting sex? "How long until you go after Genet?" How long was she stuck here?

"If it were up to me, once we have a location, I'd go in and clear it out."

"Meaning you'd kill Genet and everyone who was with him."

Hawk nodded curtly. "Yes. Would you want me to do differently?"

He was stone-faced. He was worried that she'd be appalled at the way he talked about murder. She supposed she should be scared of that, but she was more bothered that he was so familiar with killing. She suspected that had done horrible things to his psyche. Not that he'd ever admit it.

"I've been wanting to take a hammer to their skulls," she said, choosing her words carefully so as not to hurt him. "So clearing them out sounds okay to me. I just wish you didn't have to kill."

His shoulders sagged and his face relaxed. Was he so desperate for her approval? "Whatever you want," he'd said to her earlier.

"Will you be careful when you do this?"

"Sure."

"You won't run into bullets to get off or anything? Because if you want more pain, I've got some fingernails I didn't break earlier."

He smiled. Oh, good, she could still tease him after all these years.

"Your offer's definitely incentive to stay out of the path of bullets." He sat down on the bed and rubbed the small of her back. Perfect. That might help her sleep. She could use sleep. Then her mind would stop whirling. *I want to go home.*

"Ahhhh..." She exhaled. "I wish I could go with you and see Genet myself. What the hell does he really want?"

"Probably nothing sane."

He began kneading her shoulders. She moaned. Okay, maybe she didn't want to go home right this second.

"What I wish is that you'd never been pulled into this mess," he said.

"Yeah, well, while you're wishing that, wish for both our parents to have been good people. It'll do as much good."

He halted the massage. "Don't stop," she said.

His hands began working up and down her spine. "That's great."

This was doing a lot for her. As his hands massaged the knots in her back, as his fingers caressed her, her body heated. She'd barely come down from their lovemaking session earlier but apparently her body wasn't satisfied. She wanted him to flip her over and screw her until she couldn't see straight again.

But would that be enough for him without the violence?

She rolled over and laced their fingers together. He waited for her to speak.

"Hawk, did you need me to hurt you to get off?"

She watched his face go blank. Incredible, how he could do that, go from sexy and charming as he had at her bar, to this person who closed up and faded into the background. That's why she'd made sure to hold onto his hand. She was afraid he'd leave.

"Yes. That or some sort of adrenaline rush, like during the car chase." He looked down at the bed. Anywhere but at her.

"But you got hurt then, too. You were riding the pain."

"Yes."

"So you're probably not enjoying this massage the same way I am?"

That perked him up. He smiled. "I'm glad you're enjoying it."

"That's not the point." She sat up, to put them at eye level. "We both need to enjoy it."

"I enjoy making you happy."

"But it doesn't get you off." She rested her forehead against his.

"No," he answered in a whisper.

"I can't beat on you like that again."

"That's all right." He started to pull back.

She pressed her lips against him, nipped his tongue and kissed him until he responded. God, even her nipples were aching for him. They had to find a way to make this work.

"I don't think what you want is wrong," she said. "That's not it. I just can't...I mean, it made me sick after my anger was gone. I'd done to you what I'd seen your stepfather do, maybe hundreds of times. You could tell me over and over it's what you want but I'm not going to be able to get that out of my head."

Still holding her hand, he lay back on the bed. She set her head on his shoulder. At least they knew how to comfort each other.

"I understand," he said.

"Are you sure? Because I get it. The pain/pleasure stuff is all swirled together in your head. The problem I have is I don't know how to do that for you."

"There's no reason for you to try."

She raised her head. "Oh, stop the bullshit, Mr. Martyr. You fucked me silly earlier and I loved it. We both loved it. You touched me just now and I was ready to go again. I'd like for it not to be one-sided if we're—"

"To have a future? Are you certain that's what you want?"

"When Alec told me you were the father, I swore hell would freeze over before you'd have anything to do with this baby. I hated you. But you've melted that down."

"And now?"

"I don't know. But it seems to me, since a simple massage from you can get me going, that we ought to try and figure this out."

"I'm not trying to put you off. I'm telling you, honestly: whatever you want, I'll do it for you. Whatever you want."

She sensed the depth of that statement from him this time. He meant that literally. If she told him to stay away, he would. He might watch her from a distance to ensure her safety, but he'd fade from her life.

No.

"Oh, God, Hawk, what happened to us?" She rested her head on his chest, so she could look him in the eye.

He shook his head. "That's a multipart question."

She laughed. "It is, isn't it? Let's start from the beginning. Tell me what happened after that night."

No need to elaborate on "that night". The night their first life had ended and the second one had begun.

Hawk looked up at the ceiling as he began to speak. His voice was without emotion as he described the group foster care home that he'd landed in after being taken into state custody. He'd been just sixteen. She'd been nine. She'd ended up with a family. He'd ended up with guardians.

Their experiences after that night sure had been different.

Hawk talked of his foster home as a quiet though barren place and described having to get along with other kids for the first time.

"I did better with the younger kids," he said. "There were a couple that had just turned ten, only a little older than you. They were brats. I think the state classified them as incorrigible. But I liked them. They weren't that way with me."

"You had practice because of me."

He nodded and started talking again. She closed her eyes, concentrating only on his voice. It'd grown deeper over the years, and she wouldn't have recognized him by it. It had been his manners and his way of moving that had tipped her off, along with his choice of song for their dance. Her subconscious had known exactly who he was from the second he walked into her bar.

She was glad to have the truth about her parents. She must have always suspected what had really happened but had turned her rage at them on Hawk instead. Now, maybe, she could let it go completely. With a clear eye, she could see that it'd been Hawk she loved back then, far more than her distant parents.

And now?

"High school was a true shock," he said after talking about the suburban community where he'd landed.

"Oh, yeah," she said.

Hawk in high school? What a mismatch. She remembered her first day of real school. Uniforms. Everyone in uniforms. Her father would've been appalled at all the conformity. Her foster parents were not. They'd been completely unworried, telling her that it would be all right. They'd been so nice, so kind, that she'd wanted to please them. But all those new faces, all those new people when her number one lesson in life had been not to trust anyone. It had taken days for her to speak and that had been in answer to a teacher's question.

"Crowds are hard. And school kids are worse."

He grunted in agreement.

She'd coped by watching and then imitating the other kids. And then there'd been drama club. Pretending was easy. It was reality that had been hard. Had he had the same problem?

"So what did you do in high school?" She'd had time to learn to fit in. Her foster parents had been right, it had gotten a lot better. And she'd grown close to her youngest foster sister.

She didn't think that had happened to Hawk.

"I tried to be a ghost and float in the background to stay away from everyone. I liked class. History was especially interesting. My stepfather's revisionist tales forgot a great deal of the truth. He was always yelling about constitutional rights. But I don't think he ever read the Constitution." He put his hands behind his head, more relaxed now. "I went out for baseball."

"Remember all the times you made me play catch with you? And chase your fly balls?" The long summer nights, the cool breezes off the lake, the white ball smacking her hand. They hadn't had any gloves. He'd been so upset the time that he'd missed his throw and given her a black eye.

He smiled. "I remember. You were a good sport."

"Were you good at baseball?"

"I was an excellent outfielder but an average hitter. All that playing catch helped but I never really had the chance to face any good pitchers. And, yes, every time I caught a fly ball, I thought of you." He closed his eyes.

He'd thought of her and probably how she'd screamed that she hated him. Ouch.

"Still, I had teammates for the first time ever. It gave me a sort of identity."

"And so you fit in."

"For a while, yes. What about you?"

"I played soccer."

"How'd that go?"

"Pretty well. I had a growth spurt and that helped. Between soccer and the drama club, it worked. Some days the past seemed a dream and far behind me."

"And others, the past was a nightmare that lurked a hair's breadth away."

Never more than a hair's breadth away for him, she guessed. "Yes."

"I never forgot you. I hoped all the time that you were doing well."

"I was. I am." She'd never forgotten him either, but when she'd thought of him, she'd cursed his name. Better not mention that. "So what did you do after high school?"

"College. I majored in history and languages. History, because I want to know as many versions of the truth as possible. And language because I seemed to have a gift for picking them up."

"And for accents." She grinned. Hawk had been the best actor among them. Give him a week in a strange place and he'd speak the dialect as well as the locals. "You must have done well at college."

He'd always wanted to learn more. He'd hid so many books from his parents. They both had.

"I did well enough to attract a CIA recruiter. I think he liked the language skills. I often wonder what would've happened to me if I'd turned him down. My life might have taken a truly different path." He rolled to face her. "Add that to the list of my bad choices."

"Saving my life that night wasn't a bad choice. I'm grateful for that, Hawk."

"I'm...grateful that you forgive me." He paused. "So, no college for you?"

"A community college, and some paralegal courses. But...I hated being in an office. It felt confining."

"I understand."

He would, she thought. "I got a job as a bartender to pay the bills for my community college courses and found out I liked it. I was good at it."

"You can multitask."

"Not just that. If you work in a crowded bar, you have to recognize the mood of the crowd and how to keep it fun. I was good at spotting ways to do that, good at keeping things lively without getting behind on the drink orders. And I was good with deflecting troublemakers."

"You were always good at that. You knew how to avoid my stepfather, or when you couldn't, you were the best of us at deflecting his rage. So that's what led you to own Bar & Grill?"

"Eventually. I worked in some great clubs in Manhattan and saved a ton of money. Like I said, I knew how to work the crowds for tips. I thought I'd open up my own place there. But I found Bar & Grill while just driving around one day. I started by going there once a month. Then it was once a week. When it came up for sale, it seemed like fate. I've owned it five years now. I'll never get rich that way but..."

"It's home."

"Yeah. Now you've got to tell me something."

"What?"

"How did you end up with a daughter? Alec said you rescued her?"

He smiled—no, it was more of a grin. Alec had said that Hawk adored Beth. That was easy to see.

"My work with the CIA went well for a while. I started with information gathering, watching people and trying to guess what they'd do next. Like you, I was good at that. And then I was promoted to undercover work. I was excellent at pretending to be someone else."

"Is that how you ended up as Philip Drake?"

"The CIA gave me a new identity when I first went undercover. They needed a default 'real' one. So I went with that name."

"It suits you."

"Any identity apparently suits me. And when I was pretending to be someone else, it was easier to go over the line to stay in character." He sighed. "Sometimes there was no line.

It turned out my handlers cared as little about how they got things done as my stepfather. So long as it got done."

She put her hand on his chest. He pushed a strand of hair out of her face and his fingertips brushed her cheek. She blushed.

"I was already sorting this out when the job came up to rescue Beth. She'd been identified as a telepath and her mother was contacted by the CIA about helping to train her." He scowled. "She was only eight years old and already people wanted to use her. But then another group grabbed her and killed her mother in the process. My job was to get Beth out and turn her over to CIA handlers, which meant, in the end, turning her over to Richard Lansing. He had a contract with them to raise her."

"Alec says you hated Lansing."

"Alec certainly talked a lot about me," he snapped.

"He's trying to get to know you better. You confuse him."

Hawk grunted. "Getting Beth out of that facility took weeks. I was able to go undercover as one of her guards but getting in is always easier than getting out. Plus, I had to gain her trust or else she would've been as scared of me as she was of them."

He rolled to his back again. Del put her head on his shoulder. He let his arm rest around her waist.

"Beth was so little and so brave," he said, his voice far more animated than before. "We had to work as a team to get her out. I needed her telepathic ability to read minds to get the alarm codes. But we did it."

She raised her head to look at his face. He was grinning.

"And Alec said that you faked her death so you didn't have to turn her over to Lansing as ordered?"

His grin grew wider. "She needed a home and a family, not to be turned over to him, not to be trained as a weapon." He frowned. "I didn't know he had Alec at the time. In any case, faking Beth's death worked, though Lansing always suspected I'd hidden her. But he had no proof. I should've faded away from Beth's life, as it was dangerous for me to visit her. Contact between us might have led to her discovery. But she made me promise to come back each time I visited. I couldn't refuse her."

"She loves you."

"Yes." His voice softened. "She's the one completely good thing I've ever done."

"You saved my life. So that's two."

He said nothing.

"So how did Alec enter the picture?"

"When I found out Lansing had Alec, I knew I had to tell Beth because she'd want to help him."

"You gave her the freedom to choose that we didn't get." Maybe Hawk hadn't had a good example to use as a parent but he'd certainly learned what *not* to do.

"I tried. And then she chose all this, to walk into this world that I never wanted her in. For Alec."

Thinking of Alec, Del could hardly blame Beth. The young man was smart, charismatic and kind. She knew plenty of people who only pretended to be kind. You couldn't fake that, at least no one could fake that to her. She'd doubted her instincts when she found out Philip was Hawk. Now she knew they'd been right all along.

"Beth's still your daughter whether she's with Alec or not."

She felt a vibration from Hawk's waist. He shifted. "Phone," he explained. He pulled it from his pocket and checked the display. "Speak of the devil." He answered. "Yes?"

"Dad, what the hell is going on with you?"

Del nearly laughed.

"What do you mean?" Hawk said.

"I want to know why your blood ended up all over that room. Alec says it soaked the carpet."

Del flushed. She wondered if she should move away and give Hawk some privacy. But he grasped her hand tight.

"That's not strictly true," he said to his daughter. "Much of the blood ended up soaked into my shirt."

A pause. "That's not funny."

"But true." He took a breath. "Delilah Sefton and I had things to work out from years ago. So we did."

"Alec said that you and she grew up together."

"Yes."

A pause. "It wouldn't kill you to actually tell me stuff instead of evading the question."

"I'm not evading. I'm refusing to elaborate. There's a difference. What I had to work out with Del is private."

"Alec said she was a danger to you. He said he didn't know what was going on when you made him promise to take care of Delilah Sefton and her child, no matter what happened to you. He didn't realize you made him promise because you thought she might kill you. He only put that together after all the blood. Dad, she *hurt* you."

Alec, Del thought, was no dummy. And Hawk had made him promise to take care of her? He really had thought she might kill him. Her fist clenched as she recalled what it had been like to hold the gun on him. The waist holster dug into her hips. Hawk had walked into that room thinking she would kill him, and he had planned to let her.

Oh, Hawk.

"I'm in no danger from Delilah Sefton," he said into the phone.

No, not any longer, Del thought.

"You're sure?" Beth asked.

"Certain."

"Dad, you make this hard sometimes."

"Only sometimes? Tell you what, we can talk it out when you get back."

"And you'll really talk to me?"

"I'll try."

Del closed her eyes. Beth loved him. They obviously had a good relationship. Hawk could be a good father. Was it even possible, that they'd have even a semblance of a real family after all these years?

"How is it going in Charlton City with your client?" he asked.

Del closed her eyes and settled back to cuddling Hawk. She heard Beth say something about her client not trusting anyone and being skittish, especially about a telepath.

"You have to let her decide that she wants help. Back off and work the case instead. Let her see you do that, let her see who you are. She'll come around."

"It's damn frustrating. She makes me feel like a freak."

"If that wasn't such a sensitive issue for you, Beth, you'd realize that she's projecting. From what you've said, she's the one who feels like a freak."

A pause. "Oh. Right."

"There you go. I'll talk to you when you get back."

"I want to meet Delilah Sefton first thing when I get back."

Hawk stroked her shoulder. "If she wants."

"I don't care what she wants. I need to talk to her," Beth said.

"I'll let her know."

"And try not to bleed all over the carpets again, okay?"

"No promises."

She heard Beth laugh on the other end. Hawk cut off the call.

"She's pissed at me on your behalf," Del said.

"I'd no idea that would happen. She wants to meet you to read your mind and make sure you're not going to hurt me."

Del sat up. "She could do that?"

"She can, but normally she doesn't without permission. I didn't know she'd be so worried. You don't have to meet her if you don't want to."

"I want to." Beth. The older sister of her son. Had that part occurred to Beth yet or was she too busy worrying about her father?

"How do you feel about trying fatherhood again?"

His face blanked. "Do you want me to?"

Answer a question with a question. He feared rejection that much. "I asked first."

"I told you, whatever you want."

"Then tell me what you want, Hawk. No futzing around. Flat-out tell me what you want."

"You kept referring to the child as your son in the conference room. Unconsciously or not, it's clear how you think of him."

"I didn't—" Yes, she did. "Today's been a hell of a day. I'm having a hard time adjusting to all these changes."

"Then don't decide anything now. There's no reason to rush or to have this discussion. We have months. Whatever you want, Lily, that's what I'll give to you, for you and the child. I failed once to protect you. I won't do that again."

"You didn't fail me, you saved my life." She kissed him lightly on the lips. "I'm pregnant from a medical rape, I've been thrown in with a bunch of would-be superheroes, been chased by minions of some villain, and we've just had a hell of a reintroduction. I know very little of what I want." She laid her head on his shoulder.

"But please don't vanish, Hawk. Please don't vanish. I don't think I could stand to say goodbye to you again."

Chapter Eighteen

It took some time but Del fell asleep. Philip waited until she was breathing peacefully before slipping out of the bed. He couldn't sleep. He was far too restless for that.

The door to the apartment opened. Philip drew his gun.

Alec stopped in his tracks. "That's the third time you've pulled a gun on me. It could make a person paranoid."

"Next time, knock."

"There's no one here who'd hurt you or Del, Drake."

"No one that I know of." Philip holstered his weapon. "What do you want?"

"We found something."

Good. He nodded.

"The address Genet gave to the DMV looks good as a target location. It's a small office building out in an industrial park in Elizabeth. Looks like a perfect headquarters."

"What's the plan?"

"I want to go in, now, today. The sooner we get to these people, the sooner Del and her child are safe."

Philip nodded again. "Not going alone, are you?" Though Alec was certainly capable of taking on an army.

"I called in F-Team, but I'm hoping they won't be needed. We surround and ask for surrender. I'm just waiting on our Homeland Security contact to get the clearance to go in."

"Going through these channels could tip them off, if Genet and his people are as well-connected as they seem to be."

Alec frowned. "So what would you do?"

Reduce the building to rubble? No, that would be a bad idea—there could be records inside that could help them track whoever was backing Genet. And it was always possible there were innocents inside the building. Del wasn't bloodthirsty. In fact, after realizing how close she'd come to killing him, she seemed to have decided against it as a way of solving problems. What she didn't know wouldn't hurt her.

"I'd slip in and take them out, one by one," he told Alec.

"You mean, you'd go in and murder anyone who might be a threat to her."

"Yes."

"And sneaking up on people and murdering them doesn't bother you?"

He shrugged. What was more blood on his hands? At least these kills would be for a tangible reason. What had Del said? She wished he didn't have to kill any longer. But that was preferable to letting anyone harm her or the child.

"What you've done never bothers you?" Alec asked.

"What do you know about my life, boy?" Philip growled.

"Nothing. I know nothing about your life except that you're CIA black ops, that you protected Beth and you've got some sort of connection to Del that left you bleeding and bloody in one of my rooms. It adds up to a damn cipher. I want to help, but I can't begin to figure out how."

"I don't need your help."

Philip felt the heat rise in the room.

"You want a fight, Farley?" he said in a low voice.

"If that's what's needed. Del's under my protection. I felt that baby with my TK. I'm not about to trust her welfare with a..."

"Murderer?" Philip said, voice very low. "Sociopath? Insane killer? C'mon, Farley, surely you can think of the words for it." He felt the quiet stillness descend over him, as it did whenever he faced a mortal threat.

"How the hell do I know what you'd do with her?" Alec raised his arm, as he did when marshalling his TK and his fire.

"You don't." Philip idly wondered if Alec could kill him. The firestarter had the raw power, but he had a tendency to pull his punches one on one. It'd likely be a draw or they'd kill each other. "Either trust me or get rid of me, if you can. But stop wasting my time."

"Why the fuck is telling me what's going on so hard for you?" Alec backed up, putting space between them. "You got beat on as a kid, Del said."

"So what?"

"That's all you have to say?"

"There's nothing else to say. Now tell me about the Genet operation."

"Not before you give me answers."

"You'll get none."

Alec took a deep breath. "You don't have to make this so damn difficult. I'd like to help you and I promised to protect Del. You want me to trust you? Then trust me. Tell me what's going on."

"You owe your life to me," Philip snapped. "I'm the one who sent Beth in to get you away from Lansing. I'm the one who helped you break free from Lansing. I'm the one who stepped aside when you dragged my daughter into this damned idea of helping people like yourselves." He rolled his shoulders and drew himself up straight. "Words are *nothing*. It's actions that count."

"I see your point. Maybe." Alec paced the room, something he did when he was frustrated. "And the actions that resulted in blood being shed earlier?"

"My blood, not Del's. That should tell you all you need to know."

The heat in the room ebbed. Alec was powering down. "I didn't...I don't understand you."

"So you've said. Well, you don't need to. Now back to Genet. What's your estimated time of departure?"

They glared at each other for a long moment until Alec finally spoke. "Our ETA is about two hours. I assume you're coming with us?"

He'd like nothing better than to confront those who'd wrecked Del's life. But...

"What arrangements have you made for Del?"

"She can't come on the op, obviously. She'll be perfectly safe and secure here while we're gone."

Philip blinked. Triggered by Alec's words, *she'll be perfectly safe*, a long-ago scene played out in his mind.

Lily clung to him, screaming. "No, let me stay with Hawk! I wanna stay with Hawk."

"I want you out of the line of fire!" Lily's father insisted. "There are men with guns surrounding us. You'll be perfectly safe in the bathroom. C'mon, Lily."

She still clung to him. He couldn't stand to let her go. But he knew they were surrounded. They all might be killed. This was it, this was the end, he knew.

"Hawk, it'll be better for her in there," Lily's mother said softly. "She'll be perfectly safe."

He nodded, unable to speak. He peeled Lily's arms away from his waist. She started crying. "I wanna be with you, Hawk."

"It'll be safer there," he whispered. "Trust me, Lily."

She blinked away the tears and followed her mother to the bathroom.

If he'd kept Lily with him that day, he could've protected them both. He could've grabbed her and run out to surrender to the Feds. He could have spared her the sight of him standing over her murdered parents. He could've started a new life without being a killer.

Please don't vanish, Hawk.

His place was here, with her, now and for as long as Delilah Sefton wanted him to be with her.

"I'll stay here with Del."

The firestarter's eyes widened. "You're kidding."

"I won't leave Lily alone."

"Lily?"

"Del, I mean."

"You called her Lily when you were kids together?"

Philip nodded. "I promised to help her then. I didn't do it right. I will now."

"But there's the regular guards, and she's on the secure level, and—" Alec stared at him for a long moment. "You don't want to leave her side."

"No."

"Okay." Alec turned to leave then hesitated. "Beth called me after she spoke to you."

"Of course she did." No secrets between him and his daughter any longer, were there?

"She says you gave her good advice with her new client."

"Good."

"If Del's hurt, I'm going to hold you responsible."

Philip took a deep breath, too curious not to ask. He cocked his head. He wanted to know how far Alec would go to protect Del.

"Would you really attack me to protect Del and the child? Even knowing how Beth would react?"

"I could take you out without killing you. Beth would be pissed, but I'd do it."

Philip nodded. "Good. Then you're not entirely useless."

Chapter Nineteen

Del drifted as she slept, sometimes slipping into disjointed memories of her childhood with Hawk.

A hot summer day, a long climb up a cliff somewhere in rural Tennessee. Just them, the two of them, the adults left far behind, arguing about where to go next. The sun beat down. He gave her water from an old soda bottle several times, drinking only a little for himself.

"How much longer?" she said.

Six, she'd been six. He'd been thirteen.

"Not much. C'mon, Lily, wait till you see the view."

He held her hand for the last few yards. The cliff summit was every bit as spectacular as he'd said, though he wouldn't let her get too close to the edge.

"Here." He found a flat rock about six feet from the edge. "Lie down on your back and look up."

She did, trusting him. They lay shoulder to shoulder, staring up at the sun, holding their hands up to shade their faces. A hawk, high above, crossed in front of the sun.

"That's what I want to be," he said.

"You want to be a bird?"

"No. I want to fly high and free."

"Then you're a hawk," she said. "You're Hawk."

"Wish it were that easy."

"It is. You're Hawk and that's it. I'm never calling you Rod or Nathan or whatever they name you next time. You're Hawk. You're my Hawk."

He offered her the water bottle again. "Okay."

She'd kept her promise.

"I'll help you fly, Hawk."

She stirred in the bed, half awake. Being exhausted was one thing, but now her head felt fuzzy. Panicky with worry about the baby, she yelled for Hawk.

He stumbled into the room, barely able to keep to his feet. She tried to get up but her body wouldn't obey her.

"Some sort of gas," Hawk whispered. He turned to stand in the doorway, drawing his gun. He fumbled for the doorframe to help himself stand but fell to his knees.

He cursed. She cursed.

"What's happening?"

She thought she yelled that, but her voice was now a whisper as well.

"Under attack. Gas. Dammit, should have disabled that. Lansing, you bastard." Hawk didn't bother to try to stand any longer. It seemed to take all his energy to keep his gun out, protecting her.

She heard the door open and people rushing into the outer room.

Fuck. She cursed Lansing too, that Hawk had blamed him was good enough for her. She rolled to her side, able to move that much, but it only made her dizzier. Her vision wavered. Voices sounded like they were far away. Her head fell against the pillow.

She stirred. Now it felt as if she was flying, like the Hawk in her memory from earlier. It was as if her bed had been lifted into air and she was being carried. No, that couldn't possibly be right.

She was going away from Hawk. She struggled to wake up and to open her eyes. Her vision was blurry but she could see a small sliver through the haze. She wasn't on a bed. She was on some sort of gurney. She flexed her hands and felt straps holding them down but lacked the strength to even pull on them.

People were taking her away from Hawk.

"Lily!"

Hawk's scream was anguished, but it ended abruptly. She opened her mouth to yell back but couldn't. "Hawk," she whispered, and could hardly hear herself.

"She's not fully out," said a voice behind her.

"That's okay, she's not going anywhere but with us." The gurney gained speed. Her vision blurred again, and she couldn't hold on to thought any longer.

Hawk.

Philip saw the blow coming but he was helpless to stop it. He couldn't even lift his gun with his body lethargic and filled with what must be some type of drug released into the air.

The butt of the rifle hit his cheek and split it open for the second time today. All he could do was try to cover his face by curling into a fetal position. He couldn't move after that, and he barely held on to coherent thought.

But he could hold on to the pain. He felt the surge through his system as the healing kicked in, grinned as the agony triggered the now-familiar thrill. Consciousness returned, full force.

C'mon, hit me again.

"How the hell is he still awake?" said the man standing over him.

"Genet said the gas might not be distributed evenly in the room. He probably got a low dose."

"We should kill him if he's not completely out. He's fucking dangerous."

"Genet won't pay if he's dead."

"Fuck, then help me get him into the car."

Philip went limp. Fine, let them get him out of this gas-filled room and where he could recover. Let them even hurt him again. It was all to the good. It made him stronger.

But would it be in time to get Del back?

They rolled him to the side, handcuffed him and began dragging him. He felt the blood drip down his face from the cut made by the last blow. Alec was going to have blood all over one of his rooms again.

He heard the hum of the elevator and then felt the warmth of the sun on his back as they half-dragged, half-carried him outside. His left leg felt abnormally light. They'd stripped him of the ankle gun while he'd been semiconscious. Damn, the escape would take longer.

He was shoved into the backseat of a car. Though he gave no sign of consciousness, it apparently didn't satisfy one of his captors, who bashed his head with the rifle butt again.

Philip moaned and rode the agony, felt it blossom inside his skull and grow until he was near drowning in pain and pleasure. He moaned again when the car started up and his injured cheek was slammed against the seat.

Lapped by a sea of pain, he went to work on dislocating his thumb to pull his hand out of the cuffs. Each pull caused the metal to rip into his skin and peel it off, sending new waves of searing ecstasy through him. He clenched his teeth but let a groan escape. Let them think he was weak and defeated.

They'd taken Del away. They were dead men. They just didn't know it yet.

A heavy blanket landed over him. They probably wanted to hide him from anyone who looked into the car. Good, that provided even more cover for slipping out of the cuffs.

"He's barely moving. You shouldn't have smashed his head."

"Drake's practically indestructible, that's what they said. He'll live, long enough to do whatever they want."

"Do you know why we couldn't just kill him?"

"Genet didn't say. He never tells us hired help much of anything. Pays well, though."

His captors weren't psychics, only normal men. And he didn't have to worry about keeping one of the goons alive for questioning. They'd just admitted they were useless on that front.

He couldn't feel his right thumb but he'd dislocated it and almost had the hand out. Blood from torn skin flowed into his palm, making his wrist slick. It provided lubrication as he finally pulled the hand free from the cuffs.

He ached to move. His body was bursting with energy. But if they were taking him to the same place Del was going, he might as well let them. Otherwise, he might never find her.

"What'll we do if he wakes up before Genet comes to meet us?"

"Hit him again. Genet said they wanted to get the girl secure first before coming to get delivery of him."

That sounded as if Del had been brought to an entirely different location. Fuck. The sooner he got out of this car, the better. He listened for the sounds of the two men moving so he knew exactly where they were before he attacked. The one in the passenger seat began tapping on the window. Good.

He sprang up, threw the blanket over the passenger, wrapped his hands around the man's covered face and twisted.

His neck snapped audibly.

One down.

The driver screamed, slammed on the brakes and reached for the gun at his waist. The car's sudden swerve threw Philip against the back driver's side door. Pain blossomed in his shoulder. He grinned. If the driver had intended for the swerve to toss him to the other side of the car and out of the way, he'd miscalculated.

Philip jammed his arm around the driver's neck and squeezed.

"Control the car or I'll kill you. Both hands on the wheel."

"Fuck you." The driver abruptly veered left. Philip lost hold and was tossed across the seat and onto the back floor. The tires squealed, and he smelled burning rubber. The car jumped from pavement and started sliding sideways on wet grass. Stones crunched under the wheels as the car plunged down an embankment. The driver swore. Philip's stomach lurched. He covered his head. Best he could do now. They were due to slam into something.

The car sped down the hill. Branches scraped along the passenger side. A huge splash as the car hit water hard. Philip was thrown against the front seat as the car finally came to a stop.

Water gurgled and started spilling in from the smashed front windshield. Philip edged between the front bucket seats. Airbags engulfed the driver and the dead man on the passenger side. From the green tint of the water and the rotting plant smell, Philip guessed they'd landed in a swamp or pond.

One deep enough to sink the car.

The front end was almost entirely under water now. Philip grabbed the gun at the driver's waist, yanked the GPS off the dashboard, twisted to the back and smashed open the rear window with the gun butt. He rolled out and over the back of the trunk and landed shoulder-deep in water. He held the weapon and GPS over his head to keep them dry.

The car disappeared into the greenish muck of the swamp they'd landed in.

Two down.

The handcuffs still dangling from his wrist, Philip backed out of the water, gun pointed at the spot where the car had gone under. Always possible the driver could regain consciousness and try to swim out. He wiped dirty water out of his eyes and blinked. Where in the hell was he?

He had no idea how far they'd driven from the Phoenix Institute. He'd been too focused on getting free without being noticed to track the time. Even if he had kept track, he couldn't trust his perceptions because he'd been drugged.

If he could hook the GPS back up, he might find out where his captors had come from. They had started this trip somewhere. If he was lucky, that place was where Del had been taken and he could find it by back-tracking the last trip. If Del was somewhere else, the location might still have clues to where she was.

He damned not having a cell phone to contact Alec or anyone else.

Breathing heavily, he put his back against a tree and shoved the gun into his wet and dripping pants. He gritted his teeth as he popped the dislocated thumb back into place. The snap of pain caused his vision to blur. He grimaced and tried hard not to fall to his knees. He would not pass out.

Odd the injured thumb caused more agony than the blow to his head. Heat sprouted in his hand as the healing went to work, chasing away the pain. Or perhaps turning it to pleasure. He grabbed a large rock and smashed it down on the cuffs until they gave way. He slipped and hit his wrist several times. That didn't matter. It just added to the pain and fueled him. He tossed the broken cuffs into the swamp.

He took several long, deep breaths.

He had to get Lily. Del. He had to go get her *now*.

He shoved the GPS into his front pocket and drew the gun, just in case. He stepped away from the tree. It took a few seconds for the world to stop spinning. When it did, he could finally take a good look at where he was.

This wasn't a swamp or a pond. It was one of the fingers of Lake Hopatcong. He could tell by looking past this small section and out into the open water. It could be another lake, he supposed, but it made sense Genet had put himself near where Del lived.

Hopatcong or not, if he followed the shore of the lake, he'd find help, a phone to call Alec, or transportation. Something.

Without glancing back at the watery grave of the men who'd kidnapped him, Philip started out. He walked the swampy edge, stumbling through cattails and mud. His throat grew dry. Sweat rolled down his back. Gnats, probably attracted by the dried blood, swarmed to his face and hand. He waved them away.

He stopped. He heard music. He backed away from the lake edge to more solid ground, following the sound. He climbed a rise covered with pine needles and ferns.

On the other side he saw the greater lake spread out before him. About a hundred yards offshore sat a man in a rowboat. He had a boom box in the boat with him, the source of the sound.

There was a battered Ford truck parked on solid ground near the shore.

Perfect.

Philip scrambled down the rise, straight to the truck. Not only were the windows down, but the keys were still in the ignition.

And they said people didn't trust each other in New Jersey.

He looked over at the rowboat. The man had barely moved. Probably he came out to this spot often, trusted that it was isolated enough to protect his truck and provide him with quiet.

Philip almost felt guilty about stealing his truck.

He opened the door quietly, fumbled around in the glove box and found a piece of paper and a pen. He used the dashboard as a brace to write a note. Blood dripped onto the paper as he wrote.

I owe you one truck. Hawk.

He put the note on the ground and put a rock on top to hold it down. If he lived, he'd follow through. If he died, well, it didn't matter, did it?

He slid behind the steering wheel and plugged in the GPS, praying it hadn't been damaged in the crash. It lit up immediately. Philip pushed the buttons for last trip. An address and route popped up on the screen.

It wasn't the address Gabe had found in Elizabeth. It was about twenty miles away, in rural Sussex County. Likely, Genet's true location.

Del, I'm coming.

He peeled out, the tires spewing dirt behind him.

Chapter Twenty

Del woke slowly, too mired in fatigue to even open her eyes. She felt something soft under her, like a bed, and a pillow under her head. Her clothes remained, and at her waist she wore the heavy belt that Alec had given her, but the weight of the handgun was gone.

She wanted to scream in terror and frustration, but her mouth didn't seem to work. Ever since she'd discovered she was pregnant, her life had been spiraling into chaos. She'd grabbed at Hawk as if he were a lifeline. But now he was gone, she was alone and she couldn't even open her eyes.

She was paralyzed and powerless.

Was Hawk even alive?

"You're certain the gas caused no harm to the child?"

"I am *now*. You should've consulted me before you used it."

Del recognized the first voice as Genet by the cultured, imperious tone. He must have found a way into the Institute, despite Alec's reassurances. The second man was Dr. Cheshire, sounding snippier than he had just a few hours ago. Well, of course he was pissed. Someone had possibly injured his precious Messiah. She wanted to reach up and strangle both of them, but her limbs were like dead weights. She doubted she could even flutter her eyelids.

She'd sworn to protect her son. Her stomach tightened, and she could almost taste the bile in her mouth. She was in no position to protect anyone.

"How long will she remain unconscious?" Genet asked.

"At least another two hours," Cheshire replied.

He thought she shouldn't be even conscious. Huh. She was suddenly glad she hadn't moved or even moaned.

"The dosage was high enough to render Drake helpless, and he has the natural immunity. For a normal person like Ms. Sefton, it will keep her asleep and inert easily. It also could have easily harmed the child," Cheshire chided.

"A risk that had to be taken."

Oh, fuck you, she thought. They thought she was no threat. She had an edge. If she could get her body to move.

"Good, if she's stable that means we can move soon," Genet said.

Not going anywhere with you, asshole. First, though, she had to find out what had happened to Hawk.

"You're assuming I'm coming with you, Genet."

Was he working with Genet or not?

"Of course you're coming with me," Genet snapped.

"You tried to kill me."

"If I wanted you dead, I'd have killed you like I killed your assistant. Instead, I specifically told you not to open the door to the inner lab before I left that day, didn't I? The bomb was set on a timer to explode in the middle of the night, when the lab was empty. It's not my fault you opened the door against my orders."

"Mr. Farley insisted. He's my ultimate boss."

Would they stop sniping and say something about Hawk?

"I'm your ultimate employer. Farley's only a part owner and a minority one, at that. How do you think I could pass as your boss? It's because I actually am. Lansing never brought Farley in fully, and even Lansing didn't know the extent of our involvement. Farley has no idea what's going on behind his back."

"Apparently, neither do I," mumbled Cheshire.

"You know what you need to know." Genet's tone assumed that imperious air again. "You're the one who called us while you were at Farley's compound. You're the one who tricked the guard there into allowing us enough access to trigger the gas still hooked into Lansing's security system. You made your choice. You're with us now."

"I'm here for her and the child. She shouldn't be harmed."

Del guessed Cheshire had pointed at her.

"Feeling guilty because you finally had a conversation with your test subject?"

"Yes, I am. She didn't ask for this. We should've used a volunteer, as I insisted. Instead, Lansing apparently picked her as part of some personal vendetta against Philip Drake. Look where that got us. The man wants to kill me. And you. Hell, probably the whole world. I'm only on your side, Genet, because Drake will kill me the first chance he gets. The man has no conscience whatsoever. I hope to God that's not an inherited trait."

As if *Cheshire* was in a position to judge. Hawk had a conscience or he wouldn't have been so haunted by killing her parents, and he wouldn't have been willing to let her kill him for it, either.

Though Cheshire was right on one thing. She'd no doubt Hawk planned to kill him at some point. Right now, given that Cheshire had betrayed her to Genet, she'd volunteer to help Hawk hide the body.

"Drake's not in a position to hurt you any longer, thanks to me," Genet said.

"For now. You should've killed him."

Hawk, where are you?

"Besides, Drake's egocentric. He's far too obsessed with his hatred of Lansing to see the truth behind Sefton's involvement."

Egocentric? Oh, go look in the mirror, you pompous asshole, Del thought.

"What truth? I need to know *all* the information to deliver this child healthy."

"I thought you knew, Doctor. Apparently, Lansing was more tightlipped about this than I thought. Delilah Sefton was chosen as the child's biological mother because she comes from a long line of what we call 'charismatics'. Her people have used the persuasive talent mostly to preach religion, which is a waste, if you ask me, but they were tremendously effective."

What?

Sure, her people were preachers, and her grandfather had been charming as all hell, but...

None of this made sense. She concentrated on listening again.

"Those preachers didn't realize their success was the result of psychic abilities, preferring to believe they were God-touched. Still, the talent's been passed down reliably over five generations. This one's grandfather was loaded with it. Lansing deliberately got close to Drake's mother because she was best friends with Sefton's mother, but Lansing gave that up as a false lead when he couldn't find evidence of the charismatic in Sefton's mother. Still, he had hopes that the talent would eventually show up.

"He checked Sefton's DNA several years back from a hair sample obtained secretly and found she'd inherited the gene. Since then, he's kept an eye on her, and your work gave him the perfect opportunity to bring in her valuable genes. Lansing imagined a charismatic healer, Dr. Cheshire. Now, that would be a real Messiah, in every sense of the word."

The bottom dropped out of Del's stomach. *I've just fallen deeper down the rabbit hole.* If being charismatic meant having good instincts for people, she'd claim that. She had answers now. She just didn't know what to do with them.

She had time. She might be Alice in Wonderland, but she had a few months' reprieve before this arrogant king lopped off her head. They wanted her baby. That meant they had to keep her in good health. For now. That meant they were limited in what they could do to control her. It'd give her a chance.

She had to get out. Her limbs began to tingle, the same feeling of being stuck with a million small needles as when circulation returned after being asleep. Please let that mean she'd be able to move soon.

"Still think we should've used a different test subject, Doctor?" Genet asked.

Del sure as hell did. More, she wished she could do anything but sit here and listen to this. Any more talk along these lines, and she'd believe she was as nuts as the Mad Hatter.

"I knew nothing of this. I thought Lansing favored artificial insemination because he worried about the viability of the altered sperm, and this was simpler than an in-vitro."

"Lansing was worried about viability, yes, but he also wanted this woman's full genetic heritage. Once the child is born, think of what you could do with the afterbirth cells. You'll have even more material to create your Messiah."

"Again, you're assuming I'm coming with you, Genet."

"You've nowhere else to go and no other choice to make if you want to continue your work."

Her shirt was pushed down from her neck. Del felt a round, cold metal on her chest, probably a stethoscope. "And her? Del Sefton's an innocent in all this. She shouldn't be harmed."

It was a little late for the doctor to worry about her. But she gave him partial credit for arguing with Genet.

"Her welfare and the child's welfare are hardly a separate matter at this point. After the child's born, well, that's up to her and whether she wants to cooperate, as you are. She might, once I explain what's really going on."

"Just what the hell am I cooperating with? Was Farley right? Did I create a weapon for you?"

"No, you created a boon to me and my kind. For that, we will thank you. You'll have our patronage and support."

His kind? Patronage? Del tried to not react but it was hard not to gasp or take a deep breath in reaction to all this.

The tingling feeling spread to her arms and legs. She thought she could move them.

"How will 'your kind' thank me? Just what are they? Firestarters like Farley?"

"I'll tell you two things. If you had examined my DNA, you'd have found me possessed of the same quirk that allowed Lansing to survive for twice his natural lifespan."

"Oh! You're also a self-healer, and immortal like Lansing and Drake?" Cheshire's voice went higher as his interest was piqued. "You wanted a child who could take the healing to the next level. Well, that makes sense. But why not use your own sperm?"

Del could almost hear the wheels click in Cheshire's head. Now, he had a firm grasp of his subject and his work. Now, he sounded satisfied. So much for Dr. Cheshire, her protector.

"As you found with Lansing, the sperm degrades somewhat over time on the microscopic level. Our samples would be no better. Remember, you went with Drake's because it was the most viable. We think that's partly his relative youth and partly the fact his healing seems to be more powerful."

"I see."

"We're very appreciative of those who serve at our court. You'll be honored and given all you need to continue your work."

"And the healer? I'll have access to the child to see what he can do as he grows?"

"Naturally, though under my supervision."

Never, Genet.

"Well, all right, then," Cheshire said.

All right, then? She wouldn't forget that easy dismissal.

"You said you're even older than Lansing. Just how old are you, sir?"

"Far older than Lansing. Here's a hint. My real name is not Genet. It is Plantagenet."

That meant nothing to her, save Genet's statement about a court probably related back to the royal symbols on his tie.

Del felt a hand against her cheek, cutting off her musings. Fingers stroked her lips. She wanted to bite them off. "She's beautiful, in her raw way. My queen would approve. If she's intelligent, she'll make the right choice for her and her son. Take good care of her and the child for us. I'll be back to check on you just before we move. I've work to do before then."

"Drake?" Cheshire asked.

"Not your business any longer."

The hand left Del's face. She heard footsteps headed away and a door shut quietly. She and Cheshire were alone.

The doctor was on her left. She carefully flexed her right fingers, hoping he wouldn't see. They moved! She wanted to wrap them around Cheshire's throat. But not until she knew she had the strength. That meant waiting until she was fully recovered.

Something metal crashed against wood. She flinched despite her vow to remain silent. Her eyes flickered open.

Cheshire had his back to her. One arm was braced against the wall, his head was down and he was muttering curses. She chanced a glance around the room. She'd expected a medical facility, but this looked like a normal suburban bedroom. It was exactly the kind of neat, clean room she'd longed for in her crazy childhood.

Back then, all she'd wanted was normal. When she'd grown up, she'd learned that normal was an illusion. Bar & Grill, with its eclectic customers, was her family, odd as it was. Look at the way Tammy had been worried about her, even trying to protect her from Hawk. That was where she needed to be with her son, and God damn their plans for him as a Messiah.

"You think that I don't know you'll get rid of me at your leisure, Genet?" Cheshire muttered to himself. "I'm not an idiot."

So Cheshire had been play-acting with Genet. That was smarter than she'd expected. Or maybe he had a better-developed sense of self-preservation than she'd guessed. He'd had enough to lie to her and get away with it. And he'd guessed Hawk meant to kill him, and Genet was a proven murderer. She supposed to Cheshire, all the choices looked bad.

His fault. He'd volunteered for this. Unlike her.

He started to turn to her. She closed her eyes and heard him walk to the bed. He stopped right next to her.

"A doctor's first oath, do no harm, and look what I've done to you. You were right, it was medical rape. I was so blind I talked myself into it because Lansing said it was fine. No, I let him blind me because I was so excited about the possibilities

231

inherent in the child. I should've confessed everything to you. If it'd been just you and not Drake..." He sighed.

This, she realized, was the clearest picture she'd gotten of Cheshire. She wondered if he'd apologize to her if he knew she could hear it.

"I'd get you out of here if I could. I'd get us both out. I never should've called Genet." He swore again. "I thought he'd rescue me from Drake. Turns out I'm as much a pawn and in as much danger here as there. And you're in far more, given how protective Drake was of you. Strange that you have such hold on a man like that." He lightly brushed fingers over her baby bump. "I was so proud I'd helped create a new life, child. And now I might've killed your parents." He was silent for a time. "I'm sorry," he whispered.

Were those just words, or would he live up to them? She opened her eyes. "Want to really apologize, Doctor? Get me out of here."

He drew back in shock. He reached into his pocket and pulled out a handgun.

So much for apologies. "I thought a doctor's first responsibility was to do no harm."

The gun trembled in his hand. He braced it with both hands.

He was losing it, being overwhelmed by fear. "Did you mean what you said?" She sat up.

"I meant it." He glanced at her legs. "How are you moving and conscious?"

"Beats the hell out of me."

"The child. It has to be! Your son must be conveying a kind of healing to you." He swallowed hard. "He's a healer, as I'd hoped."

"I guess you do good work." She slid off the bed, hoping her unsteady legs would hold her. Success! She only swayed a little. "Let's blow this pop stand. Live up to your words. Fix your mistake."

"And go where?"

"I don't know about you but I want to go home."

He still had the gun in his hands. Sweat ran down the side of his face. She didn't know him at all, she'd no idea what he was capable of when protecting himself, and, if she was any judge, he was starting to go a little crazy. People were always dangerous when that happened. She'd seen it a few times when working as a bartender. People snapped.

But she carried Cheshire's precious Messiah. She bet he wouldn't hurt her. "So are you with me?"

"You want home?" He choked out the word. "I can't go home. My home is wrecked. And you might be safe on the outside but Drake will kill me first chance he gets. If he's alive, that is." He wiped sweat off his forehead with the back of his hand.

"He was alive when they captured him. I'm betting he's alive now." Sweat was running down her back too. So close, she just had to say the right words. "Philip Drake won't kill you. I won't let him."

"Let him?" Cheshire barked. "I'm supposed to believe he'll do exactly as you say? No. The aura of violence surrounding the man is almost palpable."

"He'll listen to me."

"And what kind of hold do you have over Drake that he's at your command? I mean, other than the obvious?"

Cheshire still held the gun, but he'd lowered it.

"Hawk is..." How could she explain him to this man? Cheshire wanted logic and facts. She had none of that. Whatever she wanted, Hawk had offered. She knew he meant it. "Hawk's mine. He has been since we were children. You saw us in the conference room together. You saw how he listened to me. He'll do what I say."

Cheshire slowly lowered the gun. "Genet's a liar. Drake's a killer. You, I think, might be telling the truth."

"Philip Drake's more than just a killer." She knew that. She wondered if Hawk did.

"I hope you're correct." Cheshire put the gun back in his jacket pocket, closed his eyes and took a deep breath. "All right, I'm listening, Ms. Sefton. How do we get out of here?"

"Give me the gun first." She stepped toward him and put out her hand.

With trembling fingers, he drew it out of his pocket and gave it to her.

"I'm trusting you with my life," he whispered.

"I understand." She wanted to hate him, she wanted to hit him, she wanted to betray him as he'd done to her, but she couldn't find it in her. All the violence had flowed out of her after she'd beaten Hawk near to death.

She never wanted to be that person again. She never wanted to hate that much again.

"My parents wanted to kill me as part of some cause, and, hell, I still love the assholes. I'll never know if they would've realized their mistake and made it up to me. They never had a second chance. You do."

Cheshire nodded, steadier now. "But what's the plan to get out?"

"The safest thing is to make it look like I have you hostage."

"They'll shoot you."

She grinned. "No, they won't. They want my son. And, as Genet said, the two of us are hardly a separate proposition right now."

Cheshire smiled back, tentatively. "And if I'm not armed, they won't shoot me either."

"Exactly. So tell me, how many of these minions of Genet's are out there? And can you get one or two to come in here?"

"You're going to kill them?"

"Not my first choice. Do you have a better option?"

He pointed to the dresser table, which was covered in medical supplies. He picked up a needle and filled it with a liquid. "These will knock them out."

"Cheshire, keep this up, and you might even meet my kid when he's born."

Chapter Twenty-One

A mile from the destination on the GPS, Philip pulled off to the side of the road. He checked the magazine on the Glock he'd taken from the driver. It was full, which meant over thirty shots, but that might not be enough, depending on how much resistance he'd encounter.

He jumped into the bed of the pickup and unlocked the storage chest there with a key from the key ring. There should be something he could use in there. Crowbars, chains, rope, something...

He grinned at the sight of a shotgun, neatly packed in a padded scabbard, and several boxes of shells. Who said rednecks only lived in the South?

He loaded the shotgun, pleased it didn't have a plug and could hold five rounds. He grinned. He felt invincible, as if he could accomplish anything. Even the thumb, either broken or dislocated, wasn't a problem now. Every time he moved it, the pain morphed into pleasure.

This, he knew, was why people were scared of him. When he was like this, people could tell he was a killer.

He set the shotgun on the seat beside him and stuffed a bunch of shells into his pockets. He couldn't reach Alec and he'd no idea how long Genet would keep Del in the same place. Frontal assault, it was.

If it took his last breath, he'd see them both safe and whoever stood in his way be damned.

The GPS ordered him to turn right, onto a dirt road. The device indicated his destination was only one tenth of a mile ahead. He had two choices. One, park, get out and evaluate what was up ahead and slowly pick them off one by one. The second was to charge in like a maniac.

He pushed the gas pedal to the floor. The truck responded with a roar and a burst of speed. In a few seconds, he saw the closed metal gate and the old farmhouse beyond. He reached for the crowbar on the seat beside him.

A gunshot pinged off the grate of the pickup. Philip ducked, braced the crowbar between the gas pedal and the seat, and rolled to the passenger side. The speedometer was stuck on a hundred miles per hour.

More bullets pinged against metal. The windshield above him shattered. The truck hit the gate with a force that tossed him against the passenger side door. He heard a tremendous clang and men shouting. He grabbed the shotgun, opened the passenger door and rolled to the ground.

The combination of the truck's speed and his own momentum tossed him hard against the ground. He rolled, trying to get as far away from the vehicle as possible.

The muffled thuds and spurts of dirt as the bullets hit the ground around the truck signaled that they'd bought his deception. He rolled behind a tree, apparently unseen, as he'd planned. The truck plowed forward, metal gate stuck under one wheel, and hit the side of the house with tremendous force. The bumper was sliced in two, the hood crinkled to cover the broken windshield. Wood shingles rained down from the roof of the house onto the cab.

Men swarmed out to the truck, guns drawn.

Prone, Philip braced the gun with his elbow, took aim and fired three quick shots. Three men were down before it even registered to the remaining two that they were being picked off. They shouted and vanished into the hole made by the truck. Now he had a clear path to the front porch and the beckoning door.

He rushed from his hiding place, leapt up onto the front porch and blew the lock off the door with a shotgun blast. The door banged open inward. Philip entered low. A bullet screamed over his head. He took out the man firing from the entranceway with the Glock. He heard the thump as the man hit the floor.

Just how many men did Genet have, anyway?

"Dell!" No sense hiding. They knew he was here. Let them come.

No answer. Damn. Stairs to his left, the rest of the house laid out to his right. He saw movement in the kitchen at the back of the house. Stairs it was. He'd have the advantage of high ground.

The handgun in his right hand, the shotgun in his left, Philip pounded up the stairs. The railing that overlooked the downstairs was to his left. There was a doorway at the end of that. To his right were two rooms, both with closed doors.

Damn. A lot of rooms to clear.

"Dell!" he yelled again.

"Hawk!"

Her answering bellow, nearly as loud as his own, came from the right. He backed toward her voice, keeping an eye on all the doors to his side and the one at the end of the hallway.

Out of the corner of his eye, he saw her rush out of the door closest to the end of this side of the hallway. He sidestepped to her, keeping his body in front of her. She put her hand on his shoulder.

"I'm okay," she whispered into his ear. "You look like hell."

He grunted. He heard movement behind and spun to encounter Dr. Cheshire. She put her hand on his wrist. "He's with me. He gave me a gun."

He had no bullets to waste, so he didn't kill Cheshire. Boots pounded up the steps. The door at the other end of the hallway opened. Genet appeared, holding an Uzi. Philip fired first, driving Genet back into the room.

He shoved the handgun into his pants and leveled the shotgun. Genet leaned out the other doorway, seeking a clear shot. Philip pulled the trigger. The blast destroyed the doorframe and drove Genet back again. Another guard appeared at the top of the steps. Philip pumped and fired again. The guard fell backwards down the steps.

"Cover!" Philip didn't wait for Lily to grasp what he wanted; he pumped the shotgun again and charged the room where Genet was hiding. He had to get that Uzi away from the man. A few feet before the door, he slid, feet first. People tended to fire waist- or head-high.

He fired the shotgun again as he hit the door. The wood splintered, and he was into the room. He grabbed the handgun and shot blindly, hoping to find Genet before he was cut down.

He heard a muffled cry of pain to his right. Damn, he'd gotten lucky. He whirled. Genet stood in the corner of the room, between windows, the Uzi dangling from the fingers of a bloody right arm.

Philip pumped the shotgun and pulled the trigger. It jammed. Genet's expression changed from fear to triumph. Philip tossed the shotgun at him. Genet instinctively ducked, Philip fired the handgun, but this time he heard the bullet break the window. No more lucky shots. A shard of glass sliced through the back of his hand, the same one with the damaged thumb.

The thumb jerked, Philip lost his hold on the handgun and had no choice but to bull-rush Genet.

He went in shoulder-first, his right side taking Genet square in the chest. He chopped downward with this forearm, slamming the Uzi out of Genet's hand.

Genet hit him hard on the side of the head with a closed fist. Dizziness hit, and Philip damned his previous head injury for not being fully healed. He lost his grip on Genet and stumbled back. Genet leapt past him, and Philip realized he was going for the Uzi.

Philip felt the weapon against his back heel and kicked hard. He turned and saw the Uzi slide all the way out into the hallway. Genet kept going after it. Philip ran and followed him. As Genet closed his hands around the stock of the machine gun, Philip tackled him. Genet rolled hard, Philip felt wood crack and give way against his back, and suddenly they were falling.

The force of Genet's roll had broken the railing and sent them over the edge.

Fuck.

Chapter Twenty-Two

Philip twisted in midair, trying to get Genet on the bottom so he'd hit first, but it only worked halfway. They both hit hard on their sides. Philip felt something snap. A rib, he thought. He rolled to his feet. He'd landed in the living room, near the front door. Genet had hit near the fireplace.

He couldn't see the Uzi. Genet swore in a language that sounded like French but oddly off. He rushed to the fireplace and grabbed something off the mantel.

Light flashed. Something metal moved. A sword! Philip swore and spit blood out of his mouth to clear his head. Genet rushed him. Philip went low and grabbed the leg of an end table and held it up as a shield.

The edge of the blade sliced into the end table, near splitting it in two but deflecting it just enough to prevent Philip from being spitted.

Genet laughed.

Philip backed away and put the couch between them, expecting Genet's guards to rush in at any moment. But he didn't hear anyone else.

He focused on his opponent. Genet had a two-handed grip on what seemed like a damned broadsword. "You always have a sword over the fireplace?" Philip asked to distract him. Why was Genet not more injured from the fall? He'd hit as hard as Philip had. And he'd been shot.

"It's poetic justice that I defeat you with the sword. I never did like modern weapons." Genet leapt over the couch, showcasing impressive agility.

But the move also left the man open. Philip went low, got under Genet's guard and grabbed the sword hilt with both hands, trying to wrench it away.

They were locked together, seemingly evenly matched.

"I heard you were insane, Drake, but I have to say, I never expected you to smash a truck into a house. You could've killed your lady with that tactic."

"Never." His entire right side was in agony, on fire from the smashed ribs. Warmth overwhelmed him, energy surged through him, and he laughed.

Pain only gave him strength.

He grinned. Genet's eyes widened.

"I'll spit you like the bastard you are, Drake. You were a mistake Lansing should've fixed a long time ago."

He wrenched left to tear the sword from Philip's grip. Philip hung on. "Lansing's dead, and you will be soon."

"God's eyes, you're an arrogant son of a bitch. I can't die, certainly not at your hands."

"That's what they all say." This was going on too damn long. All Genet had to do was hold him here until one of his armed minions had a clear shot, assuming any were still alive. Philip took a deep breath and released the pressure on the sword, just slightly.

Genet felt it and seized the chance, as Philip hoped. Genet swung left, wildly. Philip ducked, the blade missing him by the smallest of margins, and grabbed Genet's elbow with one hand. He pushed at Genet's arm, forcing the sword to continue its arc.

Before Genet even realized it, his own sword was buried deep in his side. He fell, shock on his handsome face. Philip grabbed the sword from his flailing hands and ran him through.

Blood gushed from Genet's mouth. He looked at Philip, incredulous.

"I can't die," he whispered.

"Everyone dies."

"Not me. This will be my kingdom," Genet whispered, the color leaching from his face as the blood left his body. "They'll kill you for this."

"That won't do you any good." Philip twisted the sword. Genet's eyes rolled back in his head. His body went limp. It was only then that Philip noted Genet was wearing the tie with the three yellow lions against a red background that Del had mentioned.

Whatever that meant to Genet, it hadn't helped him.

Philip heard a whimper behind him. Sword out, he spun toward the noise.

"Hawk." Del stood on the stairs, feeling far too euphoric that Genet was dead. "I found a phone in the room Genet was in."

"Get it, and let's go."

"It's a land line."

Damn.

He rushed up the stairs after her.

She watched his back. She didn't see anyone else downstairs. Maybe Hawk had killed them all. But he looked terrible—one whole side of his face was bruised, blood dripped down one arm, and he was holding his side. One of his hands was bloody too. She didn't know how much his healing could do at once but it had to be at its limit.

She wished she'd been a good enough shot to hit Genet, but they'd been moving too fast. She'd been scared of hitting Hawk.

They rushed into the bedroom that Genet had come from. Cheshire had the receiver of the phone in his hand already. She grabbed it from him. "Help Hawk barricade the door," she ordered.

As they pushed the bed against the damaged door, she asked Hawk for Alec's number. Hawk went to his knees as she was dialing. He gestured to her to give him the phone. Ringing. Thank God, it was ringing. She put the phone to his ear, listening. Someone must have picked up because he spoke. "Get here now, Alec. It's a damned mess. Yes, we're alive." He took a deep breath and hissed in pain.

She knelt next to him, keeping the phone steady. "Yes, I'm hurt. Del's fine. Remaining combatants unknown. I'll keep this line open but I need to watch, not talk." He rattled off an address. Del set the receiver on the floor.

Only then did he turn to her. "Del?"

She hugged him, lightly, because his side seemed to hurt. Not satisfied, he pulled her so close that she had to push him away to breathe.

"Easy, I'm real." She took his face in her hands. "I knew you'd come."

Now that she was closer, she could see the fierce bruises all over his face. Blood covered his hand from a slash across the back of it. God knew what was wrong with his side. He'd hit hard when he fell.

But he smiled. *Hawk.* She traced his jaw. "I thought messing you up was *my* job."

He kissed her, a light touch of his lips. Now was not the time, and he knew it. Finally, she allowed herself to be afraid and relieved all at the same time. He struggled to his feet, looking around the room again. "Help's coming, we just need to hold them off until then. Stay away from the windows." The phone squawked. He plucked the receiver off the floor and asked Alec for an ETA. She overheard Alec say, "Fifteen minutes" and something about a chopper.

Hawk dropped the receiver. It dangled on its cord.

He glared at Cheshire, really looking at the doctor for the first time since they'd entered the room. Cheshire hugged the wall, face scrunched up in horror.

Hawk advanced on the doctor. Del curled her hand over his forearm. "Don't."

"He's as responsible for this as anyone. He knows who you are, where you live, what your child will be capable of. He's too dangerous to survive."

"He helped me escape. He was as much Genet's pawn as I was."

Hawk turned on her. "Oh, so he was forced to impregnate you without your consent."

"I promised to protect him."

Hawk growled. She'd been wrong. He hadn't come down from combat yet. He was still a little berserk.

"Lansing sold him a bill of goods about helping humanity. Genet threatened him. He's sorry. He's salvageable."

"He's a threat to you and the child," Hawk said.

"You never intended to let me live from the moment you found out I was involved, did you, Drake?" Cheshire asked, his voice bitter.

Dammit, Cheshire, shut up.

"All I wanted to do was create a new life. All I needed was funding. Lansing was the only one who believed. After that, all the choices were bad."

Del stepped between the men. "I promised to protect him."

Hawk took a deep breath. "Get out of the way. Now's the time."

"Do you remember what you said to me earlier today, Hawk? That maybe you'd been wrong to kill my parents, that maybe they'd been going to rescue me, not kill me."

He stepped back, as if she'd physically hit him. No, the blow was worse than striking him. He knew how to deal with that pain. This pain was his worst nightmare.

But this was where she was going to draw the line for their new life. For them and for their son.

"You saved my life that night, and I'm grateful. You couldn't have picked differently, you couldn't have risked my life on a guess." She reached out and stroked Hawk's bruised cheek. "But that's not the case here. Cheshire's not armed, he's not threatening me at this moment, and he wants a chance to atone. I'm giving it to him. So are you."

"I've found it's best to remove danger before someone is hurt," he whispered.

"He's not all evil, any more than my parents were," Del said. "Until that last night, they tried to be good parents, at least as much as they were able. Listen, he tried to protect me from Genet. He's changed. He gets another chance."

Hawk's shoulders slumped. "Is this what you want?"

She nodded, very slowly, holding his gaze. Time seemed to stop, and no one existed save the two of them.

"You don't have to live this way any longer."

"I don't know any other, Lily."

She blinked away tears, realizing he'd swapped back to calling her Lily. "I'll show you. We could always do anything together."

He blinked. His own eyes were wet. "I'll try." He looked at Cheshire. "You live."

"Remind me to be ever so grateful," Cheshire said. "Lansing lied, you kept me prisoner, Genet claimed I'd be honored at some court and now you vote, and I get to still live. Son of a bitch. I'm so tired of this."

"Now is not a good time to rant," she snapped.

"Why not now? He'll try? And leave me twisting in the wind until he gets pissed off again? And will there be another vote when Farley gets here? Will he just twitch his hand and cremate me?" He shook his head. "All I wanted was to study DNA and help save people's lives. But, no, that's not good enough for anyone. So far as I know, Drake, you're just obeying her now and planning to kill me later."

Hawk put up his hands. "No, we're done."

"You bet we are."

That didn't sound right. Del reached for the handgun that she'd shoved into her pants and put her hand around the grip. Cheshire sounded unhinged. She'd worked bars with drunks for years. She knew unhinged. Edgy, logic circling back on itself, eyes wide and rambling. He sounded, she thought, like Hawk's mother on that last night, her voice cracking, claiming she'd killed them all to the Feds. Taking blame for all that bloodshed.

Hawk's mother had snapped that night. All those years, she'd been a victim until something had finally broken loose. Cheshire's manner gave her the same vibe. He was going to attack.

"Anger is good, it shows you're not broken. It's a new beginning. We'll sort it all out," she said to him.

"One side wants to use my work to benefit some court of immortals. The other side wanted a weapon. And the child's father wants to kill me. I know too much, you resent me and what I did. I see it all clearly now. I'm just a pawn tossed in the wind."

His words were slurred together and spit dribbled out of his mouth. Del tightened her grip on the gun.

"If you've had a normal life until now, that makes you lucky. People find a way to hurt each other all the time, without benefit of psychic abilities. You need medical care and counseling for trauma. I'll help, once you're better. You'll be able to go back to work."

Yes, she'd save him, like she hadn't saved her parents. She could look her son in the eye and tell him his life wasn't bought with blood. So could Hawk.

"Work for you, you mean," Cheshire said, using the wall as support. "A minion. Fuck it, I'm a goddamned minion. I've had enough of being told what to do! I'm not going to look over my shoulder the rest of my life. It ends now."

His arm snapped forward, revealing a gun. He fired before she or Hawk could react. Hawk crumpled to the floor, clutching his shoulder.

Anger surged through her. The world narrowed to her finger on the trigger of the gun. Time seemed to stop as she pulled the trigger. This, she thought, must be what Hawk feels when he attacks.

Her aim was true. Cheshire was thrown into the wall by the force of the bullet. His blood splattered all over the wallpaper, and he slid to the floor, lifeless.

Now she knew what killing felt like.

"You fucking idiot! I wanted to save you!" she yelled at the dead man, waving the gun. "Where the hell did he get that gun?" she muttered as she fell to her knees at Hawk's side.

"Must have been mine. I dropped it in here when Genet attacked," whispered Hawk.

"Don't talk. Just hold on." Blood covered his chest. Oh, God, this was not happening, this was not happening. She couldn't lose him now. *This is my fault!* Tears stung her eyes, near blinding her. She dropped the gun, pulled off her sweatshirt and pushed it against the hole in his upper chest, trying to staunch the blood flow.

"Heal, dammit, Hawk, heal yourself."

His eyes flickered. There was life in them yet. "Blood loss bad," he whispered. "At my limit. Can't fix it."

"Yes, you *can.*"

"Safe. You're safe. Alec's coming." He closed his eyes.

"Goddammit, I am not safe, not without you. Jesus, Hawk, stop being a fucking martyr." She slapped his face. "Don't you give up on me. Heal."

His eyes opened again. He licked his lips. "Better off without me, Lily."

"I don't care about your stupid fucking self-pity. Heal."

His forehead furrowed. "Will...try."

But his eyes began to roll back in his head. No, she'd not lose him, she couldn't, she needed him, their baby needed him. His eyes flickered again. At least he was trying to stay with her now. He was fighting. Where the hell was Alec? They needed help, they needed a hospital, he needed to live. She could hardly see through all her tears.

She yelled Alec's name, remembering that Hawk had left the line open, yelling for an ambulance, yelling at the phone for help. She hoped he heard but didn't want to fumble for the phone to check.

She pushed down harder on Hawk's chest, trying to remember if this pressure stuff really worked. "How can I help?" she whispered out loud.

Hawk's hand brushed her abdomen. "Your son is safe," he whispered so low that her heart broke into a thousand pieces. He shuddered. She was losing him.

"The boy's *our* son, Hawk."

"'S'good."

His voice was so low now she barely heard that. No, no, no. He was supposed to be invulnerable, indestructible, immortal. He would never leave her again. She held his hand to her face, kissed it and put his palm over their baby. "Hawk. Stay with me. Stay with our son. *Heal.*"

Warmth rose from inside her, beginning from her stomach and bursting all the way to her fingers and toes, like some internal fireball. Her head snapped back and she bit her tongue, tasting blood. *What the hell?*

Hawk's hand twitched, but she didn't let go of it. Maybe she was getting some sort of healing overflow from him. She hoped so. This had to be from him and it had to be a good thing. It meant he was getting better. She gripped his hand tighter. His hand over their baby, her hand over his.

"That's right, that's right, heal, get better. Fight."

Her hands throbbed with each breath she took. Her body seemed to be pulsing molten fire, as energy of some sort flowed from her into Hawk's hand and then into the rest of his body. She squinted. The energy seemed almost visible between them, a faint glowing red haze.

His eyes flicked open, meeting her gaze. They stayed locked together, breathing as one.

Vaguely, as if from far away, she heard someone yelling her name. That voice on the phone sounded awfully loud.

The door crashed open. The dresser Hawk had used to block it smashed against the far wall. Alec stood revealed in the doorway.

That explained why his voice sounded so loud.

Alec dropped to his knees across from her. "Help's here, Drake. You'll heal, because Beth will kill me if something happens to you."

"I...Lily." Hawk's eyes shifted focus to his hand, the one connecting them together over their child. "I'm healing but...not all by myself. Not all from me. Our son's helping."

"The baby's helping to heal him?" Alec asked her.

"Must be. I'll be damned if I know." Her son could do that? Already? Thank God. No, she decided. Thank the late Dr. Cheshire and his accelerated development.

"Listen!" Hawk insisted.

She leaned over so her ear was just above his mouth.

"Del...Lily...healing is draining. You have to stop this, you have to break the contact between us. He could die...the baby could use himself...up."

"Die?" Her panicked voice broke the word into two syllables.

"Yes," Hawk said, his voice stronger. "I can't move. I can't break the connection. You have to...you know what to do."

"But then you might die!"

"You know...what to do."

He closed his eyes. She closed hers. Yes, she knew what to do. She gritted her teeth and carefully peeled Hawk's hand away from her, away from their baby.

His hand fell limply to the floor.

The molten heat flooding her body receded. Cold spread through her. The world spun.

"Help him!" She reached across Hawk and grabbed Alec's arm. "Save him!"

Someone caught her from behind as she began to fall sideways. Spots appeared before her eyes. Her stomach flopped, as if she was about to be sick.

Inside, she screamed in grief, fearing she'd lost them both.

Chapter Twenty-Three

Del flitted in and out of consciousness, not sure when and where she was for what seemed like a long while. When things finally came into focus, Alec was at her bedside.

"Hawk?" she whispered.

"Critical," he said in a low voice. "We transported him to the ER fast, in our helicopter."

"Is that where I am?"

"In a hospital, yes."

She put her hands over her stomach.

"The baby's okay," Alec said, anticipating her question. "They ran a boatload of tests while you were unconscious. They finally concluded that you were mostly suffering from exhaustion. The baby seems to be unaffected by it all. I told the hospital we were family, that I was the baby's uncle, so they let me watch the ultrasound. Damn, he's a kicker."

"Hey, you are family, right?" Del looked at her stomach. A round device was strapped around her baby bump. There was a regular beeping sound in the room that finally registered on her hearing.

"That's a monitor for the baby's heartbeat. They wanted to take no chances."

"Oh. So you've been watching over me all this time?"

"I promised Drake I would protect you. And I promised you too. I meant it." He looked away. "I've just done a lousy job of it."

He was feeling guilty. *Join the club, Alec.* "It's not your fault. Cheshire tipped off Genet's people. That's how they got into your place and released the gas."

"Gabe's beating himself up over that. There was a backdoor in the old security program that he didn't find." Alec sighed.

"Genet claimed he knew Lansing, that he was the true owner of Orion, where Cheshire worked. I don't know if he was conning Cheshire or not, but if that's true, that explains why Genet knew about the Institute's alarms, right?"

"Yeah, I guess. I should've found out more about Lansing's businesses."

"Oh, puh-leeze. We've all got enough guilt to go around."

She'd ordered Hawk to spare Cheshire. She'd forced him out of his learned way of thinking into something new. Now he was fighting to live. She'd been wrong about Cheshire, and he'd been right. She'd been stupid enough to believe that the scene would somehow play out better than the night her parents had died. That was on her.

And she'd let Hawk choose their son's life over his own. She didn't feel guilty about that. That one was on him. She couldn't do anything but follow his wishes.

It would've been very wrong not to do what he wanted. Not because she valued the baby over him—how could she pick one over the other?—but because Hawk would've never recovered, emotionally, if the baby died for him. He'd live maybe another few months, enough to ensure she was back in her home, with her friends and safe, and then he'd disappear so he'd die alone.

She didn't need telepathy like his daughter, Beth, to know that. She knew Hawk.

Oh, God. His daughter. "What did you tell your girlfriend?"

Alec dropped his head. "I didn't call her yet. I was hoping for better news. But none of the doctors will say anything except he's critical, the blood loss was bad, the injury's severe... I held the artery together as best I could with my TK but it was in tatters, I couldn't repair it. He needed surgery to repair it. I didn't get all the details but he's still in surgery and it's been hours."

She closed her eyes. All those years, she'd spitefully wished Hawk dead to pay for her parents' murders. If she prayed for him now, would that make up for it?

"Is Genet really dead?" she asked.

"You saw him run through with the sword, right? What makes you ask that question?"

"He claimed to be an immortal, like Lansing, except a lot older."

Alec's eyes widened. "That explains a lot, especially about how he was connected to Lansing. But he's really dead. The CIA grabbed his body for cold storage when they helped us clean up the op. Not that Drake left us much to clean up except bodies. And he damn near took down that house with the truck."

"Hawk never did anything halfway."

"You're telling me. We traced the registration on the truck and found out someone had reported it stolen. Drake had left him a note that he owed him one truck. Gabe talked the guy out of pressing charges if we paid for a brand-new truck." Alec shook his head. "The guy's got no problem shooting down a nest of bad guys but when he steals a truck, he leaves a polite note."

"He probably figured the truck owner hadn't done anything to him." She smiled.

"Did Genet give any clue as to why he did all this, other than wanting control of your child?"

"You don't know?"

"We found some records about Orion and Cheshire's research in the warehouse we raided but nothing conclusive. Gabe's still going over them. Makes him feel less guilty. What did Genet tell you?"

"He told me nothing—he thought I was unconscious. But he said a lot. He claimed that his name was really 'Plantagenet'. He offered Cheshire patronage and talked about a court with a queen. There are definitely more immortals out there. He seemed to think Cheshire should know what that meant. I think it just freaked Cheshire out. And when he was fighting with Hawk, he claimed he should never die. He said others would avenge him."

"Holy shit," Alec said.

"You know what he meant?"

Alec leaned back in his chair, arms crossed over his chest. "Yeah, I think. It has to do with that damned tie too. It's a long story, though."

"Tell me."

"First off, Plantagenet is the name of a dynasty that ruled England in the Middle Ages."

She listened intently as Alec spoke, glad for the distraction as they waited on Hawk's fate. Edward V, a boy king, had supposedly been murdered in the Tower of London by his evil uncle, Richard III. That rang a bell. She'd studied Shakespeare's Richard III in high school.

"Edward V and his younger brother were imprisoned in the Tower and never seen again," Alec said. "But a lot of people think Richard III didn't kill them. The contemporary records don't claim he's their killer until a generation afterward. Some people think that the king who defeated Richard III in his last battle killed them."

"Wait, I know this. This is Shakespeare. Richard III is the guy who yelled 'my kingdom for a horse'?"

"That's him." Alec smiled. "No traces of the boys were ever found, at least not conclusively, though some bones that are thought to be them are buried in Westminster Abbey." He frowned. "Lansing loved telling me that story. He was nearly obsessed with it. He also had a real fondness for Richard III, said he'd been maligned by history."

"So you're saying Edward P. Genet the Fifth was this Edward V Plantagenet who disappeared? Oh, c'mon, Alec! He'd have to be over five hundred years old."

"More like seven hundred. You know firestarters and healers are real, don't you? Lansing was about two hundred years old. Older immortals are possible, even likely."

"Genet's not a few hundred years old any longer. He's dead."

Alec looked solemn. "And he mentioned a court and someone coming to avenge him. There's sure to be others. And Lansing knew. They must be the watchers he talked about. Fuck." He stood up and began pacing. The room suddenly felt warmer.

"Guess there are more psychics than you ever thought, huh?" She drew in a deep breath, wincing, remembering what else Genet had said. Her family was apparently among those psychics.

Alec was at her side in the blink of an eye, misinterpreting her wince.

"Are you hurt?"

"Not in the way you mean." She explained what Genet had said about her preacher grandfather being a "charismatic", whatever that was.

"Huh, well, that makes sense. Beth once said most people have a touch of psychic ability, they just don't call it that. They call it intuition."

"You wouldn't find this so easy to accept if you'd just learned about your family being from a line of mind-altering preachers." Of course, it wasn't as bad as her parents being crazy terrorists, so there was that.

"Hey, I've been hit with that before. I didn't know Lansing was two hundred years old or so until after he died. But I guess it was dumb of me to think that he was the only immortal. Drake was right that I'd no idea what I was getting into."

"If you'd known, would it have made a difference?"

He grinned. "Nah. But it'd be nice to know what we're facing."

"You do now."

"Thanks to you. And Drake. I misjudged him."

"He's well aware of his shortcomings, trust me." Far too aware. The humor disappeared as she remembered that he could well be dead. There was silence for a few moments while she stared at the walls and listened to the beeping that reassured her that her son was alive.

"Hawk never had a chance, you know. His stepfather used to beat him senseless. It's a miracle he ever survived to grow up, though I guess maybe that was his innate healing ability saving him."

"He said to me once that killing my father figure was no way to start a new life. Is that what he did?"

She nodded and told him about their childhood. She poured it all out, everything she could remember. Secrets would do them no good now, and it felt right not to hold it inside. She trusted this young man. Hawk did too, or he'd not have trusted Alec with her safety.

As she spoke, Alec's expression dissolved into shock, then sadness.

"I shouldn't have been so pissy about what happened between you at the Institute. You really did have things to work out."

She nodded and glanced at the door.

Alec answered her unspoken question. "They said they'd come for me as soon as they knew."

"Okay."

"What happened to Drake's mother?"

"She never protected Hawk, if that's what you mean."

"No, I meant what happened to her after the arrest? Is she still alive?"

Del blinked. "I think she's in prison still. That's what Hawk said. Why?"

"It's just that she finally stood up for him. Then she made sure Drake didn't go to prison. I wonder what she's like now, after all these years."

"Should I care? Should Hawk care?"

"I don't know. Maybe. Lansing was a son of a bitch, but he died protecting me. I wish I'd had a chance to see what he might've been like after making a decision like that. Do you think it's possible for people to change?"

"I don't know. My parents never had the chance." She'd given Cheshire a chance, but he too had been a lost cause. It had felt so good to try but that feeling wasn't worth Hawk's life. "I'm sorry, that's not much of an answer."

"No, I'm the one who's sorry. For all of it. I've done a lousy job of protecting you and cleaning up after Lansing, I know, but I'm going to get better at it." He paced to the door. "I'm tired of waiting. I'm going to find out what's going on."

Del stared at the ultrasound photo, so much clearer than the original one she'd kept on the fridge in her home.

"Del, c'mon, the cupcake will do you good." Tammy offered the tray again.

More to please Tammy than out of any desire for food, Del took one. Chocolate with chocolate frosting, of course. Out of habit, she ate the frosting first.

"Thanks for visiting me," Del said.

"Are you kidding? We've all been worried sick."

"Everything's fine with the baby, as you can see." Del handed over the photo.

"But not fine with you?"

Del shook her head. Not with Hawk still unconscious. The surgery had repaired what the doctors wanted, but he was in a coma. The doctors weren't sure why. They talked about shock and blood loss.

She wanted to see him. She'd pleaded with Alec for it. But he'd said if Hawk said it was dangerous to the baby, she had to stay away. She knew he was right. But she'd given him a copy of the ultrasound photograph to show Hawk. Maybe it would make a difference, though she didn't know how. Alec said Beth being here would help. He said Beth could reach Hawk telepathically.

She was due in this morning.

"You're not giving me the whole story," Tammy said.

"I can't, it's all classified by Homeland Security." And that was the truth. "All I can say is that Philip Drake is the baby's father and they came after me because of him." Also pretty damn close to the truth.

Tammy shook her head. "I found you unconscious on the floor of the bar that morning, Del. What was that? Rough sex?"

Del shook her head. "No, Drake had been to visit me and left before they arrived. The men after him drugged me to see if I could tell them where he was. That's why I couldn't remember."

It was a good lie because it was almost true. She closed her eyes, realizing she'd been taught to lie like this at a young age. This was for a better cause, at least.

Like Alec, she wanted a better world for the next generation. But it'd have a hole in it without Hawk.

"Dad?"

"Tired. Go away."

"Dad, I'm not going anywhere. Wake up. I need your help."

"You have Alec."

"Well, yes, but neither of us has any idea how to deal with a baby brother."

"A brother?"

"Your son, Dad."

"He's alive? Lily's alive?"

"Of course he's alive, and she's sick with worry and guilt about you being so injured, so you'd better wake up and talk to her."

"If she's alive, why didn't she come to me?"

"You told her to stay away. You told her it'd be bad for the baby, remember?"

Philip opened his eyes to find Beth standing over him, tears in her eyes. He was alive. Huh.

"Figures." Beth wiped the tears off her cheek with the back of her hand. "I've been trying to prod you awake telepathically for an hour by talking about stuff we did together, but one mention of Del Sefton, and you're back."

"You have Alec now." His voice sounded raspy and unclear. "You don't need me."

"Oh, bullshit." She smiled. "Besides, if I ever have kids, who's going to scare them into good behavior if not you? Alec will just spoil them."

He smiled back, his disordered thoughts finally coalescing into some sort of order. "Del and the baby are both fine? Is that what you just said?"

She nodded. "She's due to be discharged today. The doctors ran a lot of tests. She was very dehydrated and there was concern about the baby's heartbeat being unsteady but it all looks normal now, except the child's as big as a six-month fetus, not a four-month one."

He nodded. He knew why.

"Want to see a photo of your son?"

He frowned. Beth held up the ultrasound photo. He stared at it for a long time.

"Dad? Going catatonic on me?"

"I'm not sure I believe it."

She held his hand, smiling. Her face took on that faraway look, the one that signaled she was talking telepathically. To Alec, he guessed.

He tried to speak again but his voice was scratchy. She gave him a glass of water. He drank, feeling the cool of the water as it went down his throat. He asked her about her client in Charlton City. She filled him in, mind to mind. It was a unique experience, as she provided not just a narrative but images and emotions that went with it.

She thought he'd like Al, but he suspected he'd find more in common with Noir, the damaged one.

"You did good work there," he said out loud.

"I hope so. They did more for each other than I did for them."

The curtain next to his bed was pushed aside and Del stood there.

He blinked to make sure she was real.

She smiled, and the words that he'd been planning to say vanished. She sat down next to him and took his hand. She brushed something wet from his cheek.

"I'm sorry, Hawk. I nearly got you killed."

He frowned. "Genet kidnapped you."

"I meant with Cheshire."

"Ah."

She leaned over and kissed his lips.

"You tried to save him. It was worth a try."

"Not if this is the result," she whispered.

Behind her, Beth moved toward the door, giving them some privacy.

"It was the right thing." That Cheshire had shot him didn't matter. That he'd reached the point where he could give Cheshire a second chance, *that* mattered. That meant he could change. He didn't have to be a killer.

"How is the baby? Is he growing normally?"

"Our son is fine. Alec told me they finally found Cheshire's back-ups in his home, buried inside his stereo equipment. Once we find a doctor we can trust, they'll have the right information in case of any complications."

"Good." A long pause. "Stay with me."

She lay down beside him. He sighed happily. "Now what?" he asked.

"Whatever you want, Hawk," she answered. "Whatever you want."

Gabe drove her home the next day. She liked his company. His quiet was soothing rather than painful. But as they turned off Interstate 80, he finally spoke.

"So Drake's coming to stay with you once he's cleared to leave the hospital?"

She nodded. "Absolutely."

"You love him."

"Absolutely." She didn't even need to think on it. If Lily had loved Hawk like a friend, Del, her adult self, loved him an entirely different way. Now if they could just manage to live together.

"Um, do you know about his problem?" Gabe asked.

"The problem where he kills people who even look funny at me?"

Gabe snorted. "Nah, not that one. I'm talking about his thing for pain. I figure you must know, given all that blood in the room when you two, uh, talked."

"You're very polite, Gabe. Yeah, I know." Hawk had been open with her about it just before Genet's goons had grabbed them. They hadn't had a chance since then to sort it out, with the whole almost-dying thing, but it worried her. How could their relationship be a two-way street if he couldn't get going without pain? Because she was done beating on him.

"So how do you know? I doubt he told you." What was between Hawk and this guy?

"I caught him smashing up mirrors the night he brought you in. It wasn't too hard to figure out." They stopped at a red light.

Del noted he'd taken the long way around, the route that avoided the Ledgewood Circle. "Ah."

"I recognized the signs. I used to go with a guy like that." He sighed. "Not the easiest thing in the world, but we found ways to make it work. Thought you might need some tips or something."

She looked out the window, glad for the familiar sights, even of the local strip mall. "Like Hawk, I'm not good at asking for advice, but you're right, I've never had to deal with anything like this. He'll do whatever I need but..."

"But you don't like hitting him."

"Damn straight. Since you brought it up, does this mean you have a solution?"

"Depends. How open are you?"

Del sat back, her hands over her baby bump. They'd gone past the strip malls and were firmly in a residential area now. Soon, they'd hit one of the roads that snaked around Lake Hopatcong. Overhead, the leaves were turning brilliant oranges and red. She could tell Gabe she'd figure it out on her own, but he seemed to want to help. He was reaching out.

Trust her instincts. Now that she knew she was a little bit psychic, there was even more reason to do that.

"I worked clubs in New York City for years. I'm not innocent. I'm open to a point. No other partners, though. I can't handle that, even if it's just a dominatrix. Besides, Hawk likes pain, but I'm damn sure he doesn't like being bound or tied up. So what does that leave?"

"More than you think," Gabe replied. "There are what's called passive restraints. Wrist cuffs or collars with spikes or even just uncomfortable materials sewn on the inside, so they cut, scrape or bruise. They cause pain or discomfort without the partner having to do anything."

"Oh."

"And there are brushes with harsh bristles, too. Even cock rings, if you want to try those. All that means no hitting, so you don't feel like you're beating on someone. Because that's the tough part, like you said."

"Gabe?"

"Yeah?"

"You're kinda disproving the whole tech-nerds-are-socially-maladjusted myth."

He laughed as they made the turn onto the road that led to Bar & Grill.

"So how does one get this stuff?"

"I can get you some. I know a guy."

"Everyone knows a guy in New Jersey." They turned onto the driveway to Bar & Grill. Home. *Home.* "It's what I love about it."

Philip pulled the Charger into Bar & Grill, debating with himself, as he had the entire drive, if he should have agreed to move in with Del. Protect her, yes. Watch over the child and help her get through the pregnancy, of course. Live with her? He'd never lived with anyone, not really. Only as a cover.

He left his headlights on. They cut through the darkness and over the water. He'd timed his arrival until after closing time, so he could talk to Del alone. He'd had offers to drive him out. His makeshift family still seemed to think he was too frail. But physically, he was fine.

He turned off the headlights and got out of the car. The front door to Bar & Grill opened and Del stood silhouetted in the light from the bar.

So beautiful. And yet, he knew that might not be enough in the bedroom. It didn't matter. As long as he could satisfy her, it should be all right.

"Hawk?"

"Here."

He walked to her.

"I was afraid you wouldn't come," she said.

"I'll always come if you ask."

"Somehow, I think it's more complicated than that."

She closed and locked the bar door while he sorted out if that was a double entendre or not. It reminded him that no matter how well he knew Lily, he barely knew Del at all. The locks, at least, were comforting. The Phoenix Institute team had installed some very sophisticated security in and around Bar & Grill. Just in case.

Del slid her arms around his waist and kissed him. He sighed, and peace descended.

"I've got a surprise for you."

"I'm not here to cause you extra effort."

She punched his shoulder. "Just shut up, Martyr Boy, and follow me."

He stared at her ass as they walked up the narrow steps to her apartment. Idly, he wondered if her breasts would swell further from the pregnancy. They were already a nice shape. He concentrated on that. Maybe he could get truly aroused without pain, if it was Del.

They went inside. It was his first glimpse of her home. He approved. Neat, clean but lived-in. It felt permanent, even to the slightly tattered couch.

"Couch looks comfortable enough," he said.

"Did you even bring a suitcase with you?"

"I have toiletries and essentials in the trunk of the Charger."

"But you left them there in case this didn't work out beyond tonight."

Lily had always been blunt. Del apparently was too. "Yes."

She disappeared to her bedroom and returned with a cardboard box. "I want you to know two things. One, you're not sleeping on the couch."

"I see." He opened the box. He'd thought maybe she'd bought him clothes. He certainly didn't expect—

"Where the hell did you get these, uh, toys?"

"I know a guy." She hugged him from behind. "And here's the second thing you need to know. Pregnancy has this nice side effect. And I don't intend to do something about it all by myself."

He pulled out a black leather wrist cuff with sharp spikes on the inside. Between Del holding him and the thought of how those spikes would dig into his skin, he was already hard. "This could get messy."

She laughed, grabbed the cuff from him and started to buckle it around his wrist. "Hell, when have we not been messy?"

Epilogue

Hawk didn't want to take the last few steps up those rickety stairs to the rusted-out trailer. In the background, he heard guards pacing the prison yard and the vague sounds of laughter and squeaks coming from the other trailers used for family visits at the prison.

"If you don't start walking again, I'm going to push you through the door. Either that or I'm so round now that I'll lose hold of this railing and roll back down the steps."

"I'm scared," he admitted.

"You came this far to see her and pulled so many strings to get permission. You're not walking out of it now, Hawk. You have to try."

"I don't want to."

"Yes, you do. That's the fear talking. When have you been afraid of anything?"

"I'm afraid of everything to do with my family. What's my mother going to think, after all these years?" She might very well hate him. She might be filled with bitterness at a life spent in prison because she'd taken responsibility for what he'd done. She might be so angry that she'd never heard from him over the years that she wouldn't talk to him at all.

"Who knows?" Del said with a deep sigh. "But you'll have honesty and truth for once. If she hates you, well, that's some sort of closure too. Time we faced it all."

He grunted. Truth and honesty. He still wasn't sure what those were. But Del seemed sure.

"I love you," he said.

"Love you too."

He put his hand on the doorknob, turned it, and stepped inside the open door.

The woman inside was so small she was almost wizened. She sat, all pulled into herself, on the stained couch, wary, as if she'd been afraid of who might be coming through this door. As afraid, he guessed, as he was. He probably should've made sure she'd been told who was coming, but he'd worried that he'd not follow through at the last minute.

Her hair had gone completely gray. Her arms were thin, but he saw stringy muscles through her sleeves. Her face had more wrinkles but her high cheekbones, courtesy of her Native American mother, were more pronounced than ever. She had a scar on her lower cheek from where his stepfather had smashed her on the night all their lives had been shattered.

His mother stood to face them, frowning, her shoulders set. She stood straight and she didn't flinch from eye contact. He realized that whatever changes had been wrought in all the years since that night, somehow, she wasn't broken.

In fact, she seemed stronger than when he'd been a child. She'd been afraid of her own shadow, then.

"I don't..."

Her voice was soft, quiet, confused but not angry. She didn't recognize them, which made some sense, as he should look older than he appeared. And he'd not recognized Del when they met again. She'd grown into something different than her child-self, so why shouldn't his mother be confused?

His mother blinked, twice. He wanted to speak but his lips seemed glued together and his throat closed up. Even if he could talk, what should he say?

Her gaze shifted from him to Del and to her obviously pregnant belly. Any day now, the doctors said.

His mother's eyes widened and her face transformed. Her wrinkles seemed less prominent, her eyes more awake, and her body somehow radiated energy.

"Lily?" She shook her head and blinked again. "Hawk?" She covered her mouth with trembling hands. "Oh, God," she muttered. "My God."

"Hello, Mom," he whispered in a voice barely audible. "How are you?"

Tears burst from her eyes, along with a cry of joy from her throat. It broke his paralysis and opened the dam of memories he'd kept long shuttered away. When it was just his mom, he'd felt loved.

He rushed forward and hugged her. She hugged him back so tight that it felt like a vise grip, her hands digging bony fingers in his shoulders. "Hawk, Hawk, Hawk..." She said his name over and over again, and the tears kept flowing. It wasn't until she raised her blotchy face from his chest that he realized his own face was tearstained too.

She put her hands on either side of his face. "You came to see me." She sniffled. "You *wanted* to see me. Dear God, I prayed for this day. I never thought I'd see it."

"I should have come before. I owed you that."

"You owe me nothing. You would have been perfectly right to never forgive me."

She tried to pull out of the hug, but he wouldn't let her. He wasn't sure he'd believe this was real unless he kept hold of her.

"I'm so glad you're here. I'm so glad you're alive. I never knew what happened to you, I couldn't find out anything about you, ever."

"I changed my name," he said.

"Good." She pulled away from him, wary again. "What brings you here now?"

"I wanted..." He looked away. "I wanted to see how you were. To see if you'd changed." Or if he had.

"Change? I don't know. I like to think so, but I'm not the best judge of that. And even if I had, I would never expect you to forget or forgive what I was and what I did to you."

"I haven't forgotten," he said, voice thick. "But maybe I'm old enough now to move forward."

She nodded and sat back down. He sat beside her. Lily handed her a wad of tissues, her own eyes wet with tears.

"It is you, isn't it, Lily? Dear God, you of all people shouldn't forgive me."

"I won't carry hate, not anymore. I spent too many years letting it tear me up. Bad for the baby. Bad for the future," Del said.

"Is it...are you ..are you together?"

He took a deep breath. "Just recently, but yes."

"Praise God." She put her head in her hands again, hyperventilating. Del sat down next to her and held her. His mother kept murmuring something over and over, but he couldn't tell what it was. A prayer, he thought. Her prison records said she'd found religion. But records sometimes lied. He tried to speak, but his tongue was too thick, his chest so tight that even breathing was an effort.

"God is good." His mother laid her head back against the couch pillows. "I should die now." She took another tissue from Del. She blew her nose. "Because I'll never have a better moment."

"You will," he said.

Del nodded, giving permission, anticipating what he'd say. "We thought we might come visit again, after the baby's born. The three of us. If you want," he said.

Her spine stiffened and she straightened. "Oh, that's something to live for, Hawk. Something to hope for." Her voice dropped to a whisper. "Thank you. I don't deserve it."

"We all need to get past who deserves what. I found my biological father. That rearranged my ideas somewhat on who should have done what and when. It takes two to screw up. You at least stayed around for me."

"That wasn't the right thing. I ended up exposing you to someone far worse. I was a terrible parent. I know it. I ask God's forgiveness every day for it." She looked at the floorboards. "I still lived in foolishness when I first came here. I told myself that I'd done the best I could for my son and for my little goddaughter. I told myself that I'd just been caught in a bad situation, that I had to stay in it for a lot of reasons. I told myself a lot of tales so I wouldn't have to face the truth, which is that I'd been a selfish, horrible mother who failed her son."

That was all true, he supposed. He'd just never expected her to say it. "When my stepfather wasn't around, we did stuff together." He'd forgotten that in his anger and pain. He'd forgotten the hikes, the swimming lessons in the creek, sitting on the couch, reading together. He had them back now.

She smiled. "Key point there. When your stepfather wasn't around. Whatever good I did, he piled on more bad. I was afraid of him. You see, you were my one ray of light in that whole existence. I told myself that I couldn't run, that he'd find me if I did, hurt us both, especially since I also had to hide from the authorities after that first bombing. And maybe that's true. But after a lot of therapy—they offer therapy here, did you know that?—I realized that what I was afraid of was that they'd take you from me, Hawk. That I'd be all alone. So I kept you close by, knowing how you were suffering because I was selfish."

"I...appreciate you telling me that."

She nodded. "I was a known fugitive, on the run. If I took you to them to protect you, they would have made sure you were safe by taking you away from me. And they would've been right too. But I couldn't bear to lose you. I needed you with me to stay alive. I kept you for me, not for your best interest."

"I wouldn't have necessarily been better off in foster care," he said.

"Oh, sweetheart, you couldn't have been much worse off, could you, considering how it ended? But I wanted you, because it was the only piece of my life that gave me joy. I should have gotten both you and Lily out of there, no matter the cost. Don't tell me I'm wrong. I'm right now and I was wrong, wrong, wrong then. Let me at least take responsibility for it."

Del was silent. His mother was silent. It fell to him to say something but he'd no idea what was appropriate. He was tired of feeling nothing deeply but pain and anger.

"All right." He nodded to his mother.

She brought a cross that she was wearing around her neck to her lips and kissed it. "Thank you, Hawk, for letting me bear the burden. And thank God for the strength to acknowledge my sins."

His world tilted again. He'd had an image of his mother from all those years ago. But she was no more the same than Del had been. Or himself.

"I don't understand religion, but I understand that you're different and that you regret what you've done."

What would've happened if she'd given him up?

He'd done the opposite with Beth. After her rescue, he'd placed her with a good family and watched from afar with only scattershot visits. He'd told himself that Beth was better off that way, but he'd wondered if he was simply too selfish to take care of her fulltime.

Hard to know the true reason.

Which was part of why he'd come to visit his mother. If he was going to be a father to the boy inside Lily's womb, he had to put the past in the past. He had to be himself, whoever that was.

That was the way Beth had put it, anyway. She'd been so pleased he'd asked her advice. To him, asking her for help seemed backwards. Beth, however, was touched by his trust.

He took Del's hand.

He didn't know himself still. He knew that he loved Del. Maybe that was the way to build who he was—define himself by those who loved him, against all reason. First there'd been Beth, now Del, and soon, their son. And maybe even Alec Farley, who was trying so hard to do the right thing.

His family.

There were worse ways to measure a man.

About the Author

Corrina Lawson is a writer, mom, geek and superhero. She is a former newspaper reporter with a degree in journalism from Boston University. She turned to writing fiction after her twins were born (they were kids three and four) to save her sanity.

Corrina is currently senior editor of GeekMom and a core contributor to its brother site, Geek Dad, both on Wired.com. She is the cowriter of *GeekMom: Projects, Tips & Adventures for Moms and Their 21st Century Families*, published in October 2012.

Often you can find her hanging out on comic book writer Gail Simone's forum on Jinxworld.

She is the author of three stories in the alternate history Seneca series, *Freya's Gift, Dinah of Seneca* and *Eagle of Seneca*, and three stories in her superhero romance stories, *Phoenix Rising, Luminous* and *Phoenix Legacy*. You can find her at www.corrina-lawson.com, on Facebook as Corrina Lawson and Twitter under @CorrinaLawson.

He was born to be a weapon. For her, he must learn to be a hero.

Phoenix Rising
© *2011 Corrina Lawson*
The Phoenix Institute, Book 1

Since birth, Alec Farley has been trained to be a living weapon. His firestarter and telekinetic abilities have been honed to deadly perfection by the Resource, a shadowy anti-terrorist organization—the only family he has ever known. What the Resource didn't teach him, though, is how to play well with others.

When psychologist Beth Nakamora meets Alec to help him work on his people skills, she's hit with a double-barreled first impression. He's hot in more ways than one. And her first instinct is to rescue him from his insular existence.

Her plan to kidnap and deprogram him goes awry when her latent telepathic ability flares, turning Alec's powers off. Hoping close proximity will reignite his flame, she leads him by the hand through a world he's never known. And something else flares: Alec's anger over everything he's been denied. Especially the passion that melds his mind and body with hers.

The Resource, however, isn't going to let anything—or anyone—steal its prime investment. Alec needs to be reminded where his loyalties lie...starting with breaking his trust in the woman he's come to love.

Available now in ebook and print from Samhain Publishing.

SAMHAIN
PUBLISHING

It's all about the story...

Romance

HORROR

www.samhainpublishing.com

CPSIA information can be obtained at www.ICGtesting.com
Printed in the USA
LVOW12s1404121213

365035LV00002B/191/P